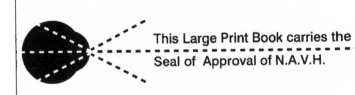

This Large Print Book carries the
Seal of Approval of N.A.V.H.

Pipsqueak

Brian M. Wiprud

WHEELER
PUBLISHING

Published in 2005 by arrangement with The Bantam Dell Publishing Group, a division of Random House, Inc.

Wheeler Large Print Softcover.

The text of this Large Print edition is unabridged.
Other aspects of the book may vary from the original edition.

Set in 16 pt. Plantin by Ramona Watson.

Printed in the United States on permanent paper.

Library of Congress Cataloging-in-Publication Data

Wiprud, Brian M.
    Pipsqueak / by Brian M. Wiprud.
       p. cm.
     ISBN 1-59722-036-1 (lg. print : sc : alk. paper)
     1. Collectors and collecting — Fiction.   2. Taxidermy — Fiction.   3. New York (N.Y.) — Fiction.   4. Large type books.   I. Title.
PS3623.I73P57 2005
813'.6—dc22   2005009663

Dedicated to friends, authors, and reviewers who helped champion my first novel, *Sleep with the Fishes*, and who continue to support my work, especially Lee Child, Sarah Lovett, and the friends who enthusiastically authored the fine blurbs for the covers of this book.

As the Founder/CEO of NAVH, the only national health agency solely devoted to those who, although not totally blind, have an eye disease which could lead to serious visual impairment, I am pleased to recognize Thorndike Press* as one of the leading publishers in the large print field.

Founded in 1954 in San Francisco to prepare large print textbooks for partially seeing children, NAVH became the pioneer and standard setting agency in the preparation of large type.

Today, those publishers who meet our standards carry the prestigious "Seal of Approval" indicating high quality large print. We are delighted that Thorndike Press is one of the publishers whose titles meet these standards. We are also pleased to recognize the significant contribution Thorndike Press is making in this important and growing field.

Lorraine H. Marchi, L.H.D.
Founder/CEO
NAVH

* Thorndike Press encompasses the following imprints: Thorndike, Wheeler, Walker and Large Print Press.

This story is due in part to the
inspiration derived from
Ranger Howell and Oswald the Rabbit;
Commander Retro and Dr. Strangedog;
and Cap'n Tugg and Fantail the Parrot.
Gentlemen and animal sidekicks,
I salute you!

Chapter 1

It didn't matter that I was cruising the higher, supposedly cooler elevations of northern New Jersey. August's ambient blast furnace was running full-throttle and not doing the car's upholstery any good. If hyperbole serves me correctly, the black Naugahyde seats were hovering about two degrees below magma. I drive a '66 Lincoln convertible and depend on the kind of old-fashioned kinetic air-conditioning that went out of style with two-stick Popsicles. Though, admittedly, with all the windows open, the airflow is about the same as when the top is down. So my practical side was thinking of pulling over and putting the top up, while my aesthetic side was thinking otherwise. Canvas up, you just don't have that invigorating hemispherical perspective vital to the convertible driving experience. When you drive with the top down, tin-top motorists are Mr. Magoo to your James Bond.

Cresting a hill, I saw a checkerboard valley of farmland and shopping centers spread out below, New York City's carbon monoxide smudge beckoning on the horizon. Factoring in the tunnel traffic, I estimated home and the embrace of my gal, Angie, were about two hours away.

I'm one of those people who has a hard time making up his mind about where to pull over for gas, food, or even just to turn around. "That would have been a good place. And that too." What can I say? I don't like pulling into strangers' driveways or *did-ding*ing a gas-station bell for naught.

Odd but true, I even had a hard time making up my mind about pulling into the parking lot of the dusty antiques store that approached on my right. I'm a collector by trade, and I was returning from canvassing little rural junk shops across northern Pennsylvania for bargains. TINY TIMELESS TREASURES, the sign read, and my resolve waffled. I'd noticed the place before. Having visited literally thousands of antiques stores, knickknack huts, and junktique boutiques across this great land, I've learned to size them up quite accurately from their outward appearance. Personally, I go for the type of rustic log shack that has all manner of woodsy stuff hauled out onto the porch, the proprietor your basic ill-shaven blue-eyed coot. Tiny

Timeless Treasures had all the makings of a doily shop with crafts posing as antiques. And so I drove by.

And so I applied the brakes. In passing, I had, of course, scanned the contents of the shop window, and I spied what looked like a penguin. Throwing my arm over the seat, I whirred and wiggled the Lincoln in reverse into the dirt parking lot, a feat made all the more difficult by the little cargo-loaded flatbed trailer I was towing. The dust cleared, and I saw that it wasn't a penguin in the window. It was a loon. Which is not to say I was disappointed.

Maybe not such a big deal to most people, but to me a good loon — or a penguin, for that matter — is a thing of rare beauty. And value. My business card reads: *Carson's Critters — TAXIDERMY — Renter, Procurer, Broker, and Vendor.* This bird was a *find*. I pulled around back and parked the Lincoln in the shade to let the upholstery cool, right across from another vintage car. By the hood ornament, I guessed it to be a Chrysler Saratoga, one of those chubby-cheeked chariots from the early fifties. The dark green paint was badly faded.

As you would expect of a place like Tiny Timeless Treasures, a wee bell tinkled when I entered, the smell of cookies and potpourri all over the place. Not two beats passed before a strapping woman popped out from behind a rear curtain. I don't mean to suggest she was fat, just that she was full-figured and had a very forthright deportment. She was dressed in cuffed denim dungarees, red and white checked shirt, tomato-red lipstick, and beauty-parlor copper hair. Her every move seemed initiated by her broad shoulders. This woman was straight out of a Coca-Cola ad from a musty *LOOK* magazine, or out of a 1956 TV spot driving the latest Ford wood-paneled station wagon, or even possibly out of a billboard picnic with one of them newfangled tartan galvanized Thermos coolers. What I found odd was that she didn't seem to be much over twenty-five, but her eyebrows were turning white. Not exactly the fashion wave that makes me hang ten, but I'll take it over grunge Sunday through Saturday.

"Welcome to Tiny Treasures," she said, striding behind the register. Her voice was loud, but reedy, like an accordion. "Let me know if there's anything I can help you with." I was favored with a quick toothy smile, her upper teeth smudged with lipstick.

"Okay," I smiled, pretending to be some chump searching for a set of cork coasters for Granny. "I'm just looking." I like to fancy I can cut a pretty nonchalant, neutral figure, although I'm often worried that my unruly blond hair has a habit of tipping my mitt. Garth Carson is one of those dull types who opts for the same variety of clothes every day of his life. Drab sport jacket, white oxford shirt, baggy cuffed chinos, running shoes. It's eminently comfortable, affordable, respectable, and decision-free. I deny categorically that I dress like a high-school drama coach, no matter what some people say.

"Just let me know if I can help." She made the pretense of lifting and scanning a well-loved copy of *MUGUMBO — Saga of the Pride and Passions of the Old South*. Her eyes moved back and forth, but they wobbled in a way that made me think she wasn't actually reading a single word. The nervous type, I guessed.

So I nosed around, idly appraising a glass relish dish, Huck Finn statues, old sewing machines, and a complete, encased collection of thimbles bearing the official flower of each state in the union. Did you know the goldenrod is the state flower of Nebraska? Feigning disinterest in the object of my desire, I finally picked my way around, giving the bird the once-over.

Loons are large birds, and when at full attention the way this one was, it looked like a small emperor penguin. It stood nearly thirty inches tall, its tiny eyes wild and red. Male or female, they both have the same black head and black and white striped neck. Its head was turned slightly, as if the loon sensed a wolverine's approach. The white feathers had turned tan, badly in need of cleaning. Big black webbed feet and legs betrayed no peeling and appeared in good condition. They were firmly attached to a rather good fake rock. Beached between the feet was a taxidermied perch — a nice touch.

But something was amiss with the long, sharp beak. It was a tad transparent and, upon close examination, had begun to peel apart. What at first looked like sawdust was visible inside the beak, so I turned the bird, produced a penlight, and looked into his head.

"Damn," I muttered, despite myself.

"Whatsamatter?" my hostess barked.

"The price tag on the bird says $250."

"I'll let you have the penguin for $150," my ignorant hostess said, nodding.

"Well, if you look inside the bird's

14

head, you'll see it's full of bug shucks."

"Bugs!" Cola Woman grimaced.

"Larval shucks. Frankly, I'd be afraid to bring it home for fear the moths would get into my clothes." Or my polar bear. Or my puma, my lynx, bobcat, foxes, beavers, owls, marmots . . .

I brought the loon over to the register and tipped it so that some of the shucks fell into my hand. "I thought they were sawdust, but look. . . ."

She recoiled. "Awright. Twenty bucks."

Ah, the rarest and most beautiful bird in my forest: The Copper-Crested White-Eyebrowed Pushover. I dusted my hands off over a waste bin. "Do you have a bathroom I could use, you know, to wash my hands?" It was then that my eye focused beyond Cola Woman, to a gray squirrel mounted in a glass case. My keen attention to detail alerted me to the fact that this was not your garden-variety trophy-case squirrel. Attached to the paws were thin black sticks. The eyes were unnaturally large and cross-eyed, the front teeth hung down below the chin, and the pink tongue stuck out to one side. A seam at the back of the jaw betrayed that the mouth was articulated. A sudden realization made me lose my dealer's savvy.

"That's Pipsqueak!" I pointed. "Pipsqueak the Nutty Nut!"

Cola Woman set her jaw and with visible force of will didn't turn to look at Pipsqueak.

"Not for sale. Bathroom's through the curtain, on the left."

"That can't be *the* Pipsqueak," I said with a nervous laugh. "Perhaps if I could speak to the shop owner?" I tore my eyes from the squirrel only to encounter Cola Woman's rock-hard visage. I was a little taken aback, as much by her stern manner as by the fact that I noticed her freckles were painted on.

"I'm the owner. Not for sale. Bathroom's through the curtain, on the left."

Raymond Burr with a wig was telling me — in no uncertain terms — that I'd better go toity. So I did, but found it on the right, not on the left.

There wasn't a thing in the bathroom that didn't have some kind of plush, cutesy cover. Even the spare toilet paper roll was covered with the hoop skirts of a southern-belle Kewpie. I gave my hands a quick rinse and dried them on one of those wimpy embroidered hankies polite society calls guest towels.

Was I still tucked in bed, drooling on my

16

pillow, Mr. Sandman working his magic? Nothing at Tiny Timeless Treasures made sense except in the bent, id-laden realm of Dreamland. All this froufrou merchandise should be the wares of a dowdy, daisy-frocked maid with a penchant for scented soaps. Cola Woman should be riveting B-25 wings over at the Grumman plant, not soaking up sappy romance novels and mending doilies. Pipsqueak the Nutty Nut was the tip-off that this might be a dream. You know, one of those childhood icons that loom inexplicably large in the subconscious.

I looked in the mirror and gave myself a pep talk. "Well, so what if Cola Woman defies pigeonholing, Garth? The loon is only twenty bucks!"

Even if I could get the bugs out of it, I wasn't entirely sure I could salvage the bird. The beak looked beyond repair, and I'd probably have to replace it with an artificial one. You'd be surprised what extraneous and mundane animal parts taxidermy suppliers manufacture. Otter noses, beaver teeth, elk septums, peccary tongues, widgeon lips . . .

The other option was to take it home for parts. There was always the possibility that I could Frankenstein it to another loon with a good head and bad legs. There was also the possibility that I could use loon parts in conjunction with another piece in a diorama, like as fresh kill for a fox.

But my desires drifted back to Pipsqueak. A real piece of taxidermy too, only made into a puppet. The genuine Pipsqueak, I figured, would be found at the Museum of Broadcasting. This one was probably a promotional double or something. Then again, Pipsqueak may have loomed large for me as a kid but was ultimately the product of a dinky two-bit program. This could be the Real McCoy.

The front door to the shop went *ting-a-ling:* another customer. I was a little surprised to overhear Cola Woman greet the visitor in a harsh whisper: "You son of a bitch!"

"Gimme the squirrel!" a male voice boomed. Glass shattered. Probably the front display case.

I held my breath, hand hovering over the bathroom doorknob. To my mind, this had the makings of a domestic dispute. You know, the kind you read about in the papers where some do-gooder tries to intercede and gets a gut full of lead for his trouble.

"Bastard!" Cola Woman screeched.

There was a shot, the bathroom mirror exploded, and I dropped to the floor, trying my best to curl up into a ball behind the commode. A rip in the wallpaper betrayed where the slug had passed through the wall on its way to the mirror, Sheetrock dust still hanging in the air. The buzz of that lead bee still resonated in my ear; it had passed close enough that I could hear its wobble through the air. I tried not to think what it would have been like had I been stung.

Out in the shop, the struggle progressed, staggered, stomping and grunting, lamps crashing to the floor, the case of thimbles rattling.

"Help!" Cola Woman wheezed, and I think she meant me.

"Squirrel!" the man barked.

Sure, I'd trip a fleeing purse-snatcher anytime. Or throw stones at a mugger to ruin his day. But Superman and bullet-proof I'm not. Even so, to do nothing but cower behind a toilet rowels the conscience and paints a yellow stripe down your back.

I crawled over to the bathroom door, pushed it open, and stuck my head around the corner. Through a part in the curtain, I caught a glimpse of the happy couple in their spastic waltz, a sizable black gun waving in my direction. The echo of that bee sent me scrambling back into the bathroom, where my yellow stripe and I were quite happy, thank you very much. But I picked up a shard of the broken mirror and angled it to keep tabs on the action. All I could see clearly were their feet: her modest white tennis shoes, his black motorcycle boots. They lurched out of view and there was a tremendous crash.

The gun went off again, I heard some grunts and groans, but it sounded like their little mambo had come to an end. I couldn't see anything with the mirror. On my belly, I squirmed over to the curtains to take in the outcome — and to see if I might be able to scoot out the front door.

Black motorcycle boots stuck out from behind the collapsed display case, the toes swaying slightly. Outside, I heard a car start, rev, and the distinctive growl of a hemi V-8 trail off down the road. Cola Woman making her escape, probably in the Chrysler.

Glass crunched underfoot as I cautiously advanced into the room. Biker Boy, decked out in matching black jeans and T-shirt, was sprawled on his back, his hairy bare arms badly glass-gashed and responsible for a lot of extraneous blood. He had long messy dark hair, sideburns, and thick black-framed glasses half wrenched from his face. I scanned the floor for the gun: zip.

There was a canvas folder tucked in his belt, a small shaft of silver metal sticking out of it. I thought it was a knife at first, but then recognized the metal for what it was: a tuning fork. Hell's Piano Tuners?

The loon lay in front of the counter, legs broken, head pulverized. But the perch and fake rock still looked useful. On the wall behind the counter there was only a dust shadow where Pipsqueak had been.

I stepped over a smashed porcelain poodle lamp. Biker Boy was still breathing, barely, but had stopped moaning or moving. My idea was to try to bind up some of his leaks before calling the cops, so I grabbed a stack of linen commemorative Bicentennial napkins from the floor, took the biker's hand, and lifted his arm. That's when I saw another, more dramatic wound near his armpit. Though I couldn't get a good gander at it through the tear in his T-shirt, it looked very nasty, with meat or something sticking out of it.

The room suddenly got a little dim and began to twist. I dropped the biker's arm and braced myself against a bookshelf.

Without having much of a chance to be grossed out, I realized I was about to faint and struggled past the bathroom and into the small efficiency dwelling beyond. I sat on a nicely ruffled bed, slapped myself a couple times, and picked up the phone.

Chalk one up for steering clear of strangers' driveways.

Chapter 2

Back in the dark ages when I was but a lad, back before the felling of rabbit ears in favor of the kudzu of coaxial cables and the gibbous shadows of satellite dishes, TV audiences were limited to a "broadcast area." Afternoon programming was provided by the three networks airing soaps, soaps, and more soaps. All other after-school programming emanated from cinder-block bunkers dotting the outskirts of town; the independent stations scraped together what they could to tap into the local ad market. In my area, we had Station 10, which ran saggy-scripted B flicks interspersed with an unctuous host pulling postcards and phone numbers for lucky daily winners. The prize: dinner-theater tickets to what had to be the longest-running *Brigadoon* in North America. Another station, Channel 3, had soap reruns from caveman days when TVs were round. Another was VHF, Public Television Station 22, which due to vagaries of the stratosphere or something couldn't be tuned in until after my bedtime.

Though the sun might be shining and the lawns might be freshly mowed invitations to a rousing game of capture the flag, kids' bicycles in a thirty-mile radius were tossed aside for the rec-room sanctuary offered by Channel 8: *The General Buster Show*.

In a word, this homegrown program was a five out of ten on the *Captain Kangaroo* scale. I think we even knew that back then. But at the same time, I think we were keenly aware that *The General Buster Show* was broadcast only in our area and, for all its technical and talent shortcomings, it was *our* show. It helped that we were encouraged to send in artwork and postcards, which eventually got shown or read on TV. In return we got on the mailing list and were kept abreast of local shopping centers where Buster and cast would be making appearances.

Now, I don't mean to upset all the General Buster fans out there. Buster put a lot of heart into the show, I'll grant him that, though he was clearly a middling clown/ventriloquist who didn't know when to quit. Valiant, too, were the writers, designers, and crew, despite lousy equipment that constantly tripped up their best efforts. There were collapsing sets, klieg fires, and miscued cameras that accidentally showed the puppeteers, or Buster adjusting his gargantuan white muttonchops.

The premise was a mélange (some might say rip-off) of many contemporary cartoon and kiddie shows. General Buster commanded Blast-Off Air Force Base in some remote location called the North Woods. He wore a red uniform, a cascade of medals, a white gun belt complete with a gold-plated .45, and a white pith helmet with a red parrot named Gussie on top. His retinue was comprised of three puppet pilots: Howlie the Wolf, sidekick Possum, and Pipsqueak the Nutty Nut. The set looked like the inside of a Quonset hut, a painted canvas airfield outside the window. Inside were the Magic File Drawers, the Milkshake Saloon, and Sergeant Desk, who spoke in squeaks that only Buster could understand.

Each show would open with a bugle sounding retreat over the roar of a jet landing. Buster made his entrance as though he'd just come back from a flight. He'd take off his parachute and greet the live kiddie audience. Gussie the red parrot would then say hello to the kids and hit the General with a lame knock-knock joke. The rest of the cast then popped up in the window and matched wits with General Buster. Without fail, each episode's suspense centered on Howlie and Possum's scheme to eat or annihilate Pipsqueak — if only they could: a) get Buster to fall asleep; b) send Buster off to fly a wild-goose-chase mission; or c) prove Pipsqueak was a traitor so that Buster would have to shoot him. The result was usually that: a) Buster woke up in the nick of time (kid audience screaming, "Wake Up!"); b) Buster returned in the nick of time (kid audience screaming, "Come Back!"); or c) Sergeant Desk or the Magic File Drawers would produce evidence clearing Pipsqueak of treason. Howlie and Possum would be sent to the Brig without a milkshake. The End.

And how's this for a little Cold War nostalgia? Buster's troop had a greater nemesis, simply referred to as "the Enemy." This thinly guised Slavic empire inspired air-raid drills on the show during which kids at home were supposed to duck and cover.

And of course, there were low-rent cartoons on the show. *Roger Ramjet* was the main ingredient, plus a portion of *King Leonardo*, a dash of *Ruff and Reddy*, and a pinch of *Crusader Rabbit*. *Clutch Cargo* cliff-hangers were the garnish to the show's end.

Barring nuclear winter, the show went off every weekday with the not-so-subtle mission of promoting Gutterman's Taffy Cremes, confections so gooey they peeled from their wrappers like slugs from hot macadam. Every kid I knew found the cremes themselves utterly horrible, as well as the company name, which made us all think of sauerkraut or pickles. But against all odds, the entire cast of *General Buster* worshipped Gutterman's Taffy Cremes. Pipsqueak naturally favored Gutterman's Peanut Butter and Jelly Taffy Cremes, and his dopey likeness even appeared on the package. Predictably, we kids caved in to the pressure of advertising and bought the chews regularly, despite the fact that we made "yechh" faces as we scraped the taffy from our teeth.

Perhaps the most novel aspect of *The General Buster Show* was that a taxidermist had made the puppets from real animals, though I think Howlie must have been fashioned from a coyote rather than a wolf. Possum was a stuffed opossum, looking fiendishly like a rat. Terribly un-PC by today's standards, granted, but this was the dark ages, when a bacon-and-egg breakfast was de rigueur and TV drunks were funny.

Our happy hero — Pipsqueak — was

made from a real squirrel. He was a good-natured goof, who through sheer luck managed not to get killed between the hours of three and four-thirty every weekday afternoon. And for some reason Pipsqueak riveted us kids.

In many ways, I'd have to say the puppets on *The General Buster Show* inspired my appreciation for taxidermy, perhaps because the five-and-dime plush replicas of Pipsqueak never did the genuine puppet justice. The closest I ever got to meeting the real Pipsqueak was at the grand opening of a new Buster Brown shoe store. But thanks to my little brother's penchant for petty crime (he'd siphoned and sold the gas from our car to local go-carters), the parental bus ran late and a sizable herd of kids kept me separated from the Nutty Nut by several hundred feet.

So when I saw Pipsqueak in that glass case, a flood of boyhood aspirations instantly disarmed me. Was it possible that I could — not just touch, not just manipulate — but be *the sole possessor of* Pipsqueak? Alas, it was too good to be true.

Chapter 3

The local Sussex County papers dubbed it *The T3 Murder*, and the best efforts of the state police were to no avail in solving the case quickly, although I give them credit for finding Marti Folsom, the actual owner of the little curio shop, in a coat closet at the store. A hook-nosed woman, fifties, with blond beehive hair, she was trussed with duct tape, gagged, and bound by the wrists to the hanger rod. She was very much alive, especially after being unbound. I was still there when they found her, and you haven't heard such screaming and wailing in all your life. "Thieves! Violated by thieves! What kind of country do we live in where people tape you in a closet! Where are the police? Sleeping in their cars, that's where they are!" Like that.

Biker Boy was identified as Tyler Loomis, alias Gut Wrench, former punk-rock devotee, Greenwich Village roust-about, perennial record/poster store employee, and more recently a card-carrying sonopuncturist (that is, an acupuncturist who doesn't puncture, using tuning forks instead of needles). His activities and association with Cola Woman — presumed murderess — remained a mystery. However, had he not arrived when he did, the cops surmised that Cola Woman might have done me harm.

As you can imagine, my ordeal with the police was lengthy. I had to go down to the state police barracks. That is to say, they asked me to come down and recite my statement again. Now, you don't have to go if you're not under arrest. But the cops have a really annoying way of insinuating that if you have nothing to hide, you'll go. I don't know who trains them in this skeezy tactic, but they're very good at it. It's as rudimentary — and effective — as saying, "Chicken?"

So you go, kidding yourself that if you do, the whole thing will pass by like a sun shower. They act all chummy, give you coffee, chitchat about sports, and sit you down in the room with the glass wall, behind which stands a platoon of assistant district attorneys and other animal behaviorists ready to judge your performance. One thing they knew for sure was that whoever did the crime had to be there to do it, and I was there.

Yeah, well, I know from past experiences with the law — and just from reading the papers — that the innocent can royally botch such interviews, inviting unwarranted suspicion and time in the jug. They want a statement at the precinct, fine, but the right thing to do is get a lawyer, if only to keep you from having an anxiety attack. Sure, the cops will give you the "Chicken?" treatment again, but give them a "Pound sand!" smile and drop a dime on your barrister.

It helps, of course, if you've got one to call. I didn't. But a New Jersey friend, Bob Martinez, recently sued his garbage collectors and was therefore tight with his lawyer. Dammit — he wasn't in, so I left a message and hung up. I noted someone standing behind me.

"Waiting for the phone?" I frowned.

"Go ahead," he smiled. A shortish brown man, he had a leathery complexion, high cheekbones, silver hair pulled back in a ponytail, and a bolo tie. Large features and button eyes betrayed a kindly spirit. I guessed him to be Native American.

"Thanks." I started punching the two dozen digits for my calling card and a line home to Angie, when the man behind me tapped my elbow.

"Sorry to bother you, but I couldn't help

but overhear. You looking for a lawyer?"

"Yup. You know one?"

He smiled again, and I looked at his shoes. I've got a theory about how to size up people's characters. It's all in the smile. And the shoes. I liked the beneficent smile. Who wouldn't? I followed his bowed legs down to the shoes: suede cowboy boots, the lived-in kind, not the line-dancing kind.

"I'm an attorney," he said almost bashfully. "Not in Jersey. In New York. But did I hear right? You just want someone to sit in on your statement?"

"That's right."

"Well, I can advise you, you know. It's not like you're going before the Court." His voice was soothing, but deep and soothing, like the distant hum of a lawn mower on a summer day.

Yikes, would this be convenient or what? "How much?"

"You from New York? The City?"

I nodded, expecting that his price had just jumped.

A slow shrug worked up his body and spilled over his shoulders. After a slow blink, he said, "It's a freebie. Maybe in the city you'll need a lawyer sometime." He handed over a card, which read: *Roger Elk,*

Attorney, 115 East 23rd St., Suite 403, N.Y., N.Y.

"I couldn't ask you to take time out to —"

He waved away my objections and led me by the elbow away from the phone. "I'm only here to report that someone backed into my car in a parking lot. And, you know, once in a while you have to commit random acts of kindness. I may have read that on a bumper sticker, but it's true."

"Well, this would be really, really good of you, Mr. Elk, really."

He winced. "Call me Roger, er . . . ?"

"Carson. Garth Carson."

"So, Garth Carson, tell me what happened and then let's talk to the police together, hmmm?"

My lucky day.

Chapter 4

While my profession as taxidermy broker doesn't seem the obvious fulcrum on which crimes would pivot, it has nonetheless happened twice in my past. Those episodes were both the result of my tangles with black marketeers who deal in such items as bear gallbladders, gorilla remains, and rare Asian wild bovids.

With Roger Elk's help, I managed to stay out of the hoosegow this time, proving once again that the best thing about advancing years is wisdom. Okay, so I'm only forty-five and a half, but it feels (and is) a quantum advance over thirty-five and a half.

I'm not some kind of intrepid paladin or do-gooder, and I do my best to avoid trouble. But I keep being drawn into the designs of some inexorable fate. The T3 murder of Tyler Loomis was a third strike, a blow to the law of averages, a less-than-subtle suggestion that Garth Carson is jinxed. What were the chances that stopping at a Podunk shop would turn so perilous? By the same token, and after much reflection, I did an admirable job trying to convince myself that the chances of ever running into such a calamitous situation again were astronomical.

Of course, in the back of my mind, obtuse reasoning nurtured fresh doubt. Based strictly on the law of averages, auto insurance rates should go *down* after you have an accident, not up. I mean, if you have an accident once in ten years, it stands to reason that you probably won't have another one for about ten years. If the universe is merely an entropy chowder, with no kismet chunks lurking in it, then the insurers should actually be raising their rates for those who've never had an accident because they're obviously due for one. As I stare into my own bowl of soup, I suspect Mutual of Omaha must have a special insight into the cosmos that they're not sharing.

Anyway, it was months after T3, late October in New York, and the time when street trees take their turn to rob the citizenry of fall colors. Sorry, pal: green to brown, no fancy stuff.

On this particular October evening, Angie had her back to me, hunched over her jeweler's bench in the cubicle across the room. She was annealing some titanium earring components. The strap to her goggles fanned her sassy blond hair, and flickers from her torch popped like blue flashbulbs. As a professional jeweler, Angie does piecework at home for various manufacturers, gem setters, and art jewelers. Her current order was for the latter, a hoity-toity bauble involving rose diamonds and brown biwa pearls that to my discerning eye were dead ringers for Raisinets.

At my own workstation, I was putting my head into a lion's mouth. Well, practically. My forehead rested against Fred's nose while I made final adjustments to a newly installed tongue. I not only collect taxidermy but also spend a good deal of time restoring stuff acquired on the cheap. Fred (so named for the sidekick in the *Super Chicken* cartoons) has been in the family since I was a kid, a venerable member of Grandpa Carson's trophy collection who wasn't earning his keep. To rent my stuff for photo shoots, stage productions, TV, and the movies, a piece has to be presentable. My lion Fred is one of the early full-body "lunge" mounts, his hind feet planted on a wheeled base, his front paws extended and bristling with claws. Fred was mounted by a renowned British taxidermist in the fifties but suffered from shrinkage in the lip area, as many cat mounts do over time. Also, the phalanx folds on his claws were flaking and most of his whiskers were gone. It was time to update his choppers, resculpt his lips, cut back those cuticles, plant new whiskers, and darken his eyeliner.

"Anyway, Peter is being completely asinine about this thing for Madeline." Peter was a jewelry auteur and working for him always made her a little batty. "He drove the pearl suppliers bananas over matching pairs. He keeps bringing them back, wanting to look at the ones he saw the day before. 'No, not those, those other ones. You know the ones I mean.' And of course, they don't, and neither do I. Peter actually had me pop some pearls out and try to return damaged mabes. And I've shaped, reshaped, and de-shaped enough titanium settings to build a nose cone for an Atlas rocket! Yoo-hoo, Peter! I'm being paid by the piece, not the hour! Idjit."

Angie's default expression most often centers on a smile, though I'll grant you, she isn't always happy. I'd venture to say her smile just has a lot more versatility than most people's. Put a hard squint with it, and she's turning mordant. With one eye almost closed you've got chagrin. Forehead wrinkled: the smile of incredulity. Lopsided: tenderhearted. Eyes closed, breathing deeply, a gentle curve to her lips? Angie sleeping.

"One heck of a purple Atlas nose cone, though," I said, trying to lighten her mood. Anodizing titanium brings out some stunning colors.

"A blue nose cone that he can shove up his" — her left eye tweaked closed — "nose."

While facially expressive, Angie is one of those rare types who can't bring themselves to make a lewd or untoward remark. And she won't tolerate it from others either. A plumber came one day to clear a drain, and every other word from his mouth had four letters, most beginning with *F* and rhyming with *truck*. Angie shamed him into editing his language, and without his copious though limited modifiers, he was effectively a mute. It's not like Angie's a prig. She's just principled and more than a little intrepid, a combination I find endearing and companionable.

"I assume you'll charge him not just for the final piece but how many times you made it."

"Doubtful." She squinted. "He gives me

the vaguest of direction, drawings done on cupcake liners, and expects me to read his mind. I try to call, to talk, to discuss it further, to show him some sketches, but he's too bleepin' busy planning his spiritual Khmer 'liftoff' trip to Angkor Wat. Then I bring him the piece by his deadline and he says I did it all wrong. I won't even start about how long it takes to get a check out of Peter."

"Then why work for him? You've got plenty of other clients, and it's the busy preholiday season."

"Two words, Garth: Princess Madeline." Her grin tightened, eyes twinkling. "Earrings made by Angie, worn by royalty."

I shrugged. "Yeah, but Mocano isn't even a country, it's a principality, for Pete's sake." I wiped my hands on a rag and took a step back from my work, giving Fred's chops a critical once-over. I bowed before the finished product.

"Hail, Princess of Mocano! Hail, Viscount of Pago Pago! Hail, Exchequer of Walla Walla!"

"About ten minutes ago, Garth, you said you'd make coffee," Angie sighed, forehead wrinkling, smile growing up one side of her face. "So how about it, Sugar Lips?"

I shrugged at Fred. "Want coffee, Marquis de Fred? Oh, that's right, it keeps you *lion* awake at night." Angie groaned from somewhere behind me.

I exited my cubby into the living room, which is also the kitchen, sort of. We live in one of those funky old New York City apartments folks rhapsodize over without realizing how drafty and cranky they really are. Remember soda shops, the kind where bobby-soxers slurped malteds and swooned to Dion 45s on the jukebox? No, not like the lame *Happy Days* set: older, the kind that looks like an old bar but with a big marble counter, black and white checked floors, and booths by a storefront window. That's our place. We sleep in what once was a storeroom, the soda bar is our kitchen/dining room, and the booth in the window is our meal nook. The center of the room, where Angie and I broke our backs removing the decrepit black and white tile, is reserved for a colossal collection of taxidermy and some overstuffed furniture acquired on Park Avenue. Not in a store on Park Avenue but actually on the street, a common foraging ground for those of us who want real furniture (as opposed to IKEA breakaway stuntman furniture) but not the accompanying price tag.

Every now and then, in good weather,

we cruise Park Avenue, maybe Gramercy Park or the low teens around Fifth Avenue, looking for discarded furniture either to upgrade or add to the crew. We luck out often enough, particularly on Sunday evenings when the building superintendents put the stuff on the street for Monday trash pickup. No cat-piss sofas here. We're talking primo castoffs from those who buy new furniture every year or so to fend off the charity-ball blues. (Many supers in doorman buildings have exquisite furnishings, more than they can use or give away.)

Behind our soda bar, there's a whole array of stainless-steel built-in containers that once held ice cream and toppings. Now they hold coffees, sugar, cookies, crackers, etc. And where the Mixmaster probably sat is the coffee grinder and coffeemaker. I scooped, ground, filled, poured, and grabbed two mugs from the forty or so we have lined up in front of the huge, discolored mirror behind the bar. Why so many mugs? Ask the people who think they make the perfect gift.

"A guy stopped by looking for you today, Garth," Angie yelled. "Forgot to tell you."

"Who?"

"Said he'd stop by again. An old friend, he said."

I didn't like the sound of that. "What'd he look like?"

"Tweed suit, short hair. A slicker, that's for sure."

Didn't ring any bells, except on the phone, which rang. I let the machine pick up.

"You've reached Carson Critter Rental. Leave a message and we'll get back to you. Thanks. *Beep.*"

"Hello, this is Janine Wilson, Warner Brothers, and we're doing a shoot over in Brooklyn? We're kind of in a jam, and I was hoping —"

A distressed damsel with deep pockets? I picked up. "Sorry, I just walked in. This is Garth Carson. How can I help you?"

"Hi. We're doing a picture up in Park Slope, and we've got this sporting-goods-store scene. You rent taxidermy, right?"

"Yup. Lemme guess: You're looking for a stand-up bear, a deer head, a boar head too, perhaps, and then maybe something to sit on the counter like a beaver, otter, or wolverine?"

"Uh, yeah, something like that, you know, to make it look like a sporting-goods store."

"Rental rates are structured by big, medium, and small. Full-body mounts like a stand-up bear or sailfish are big at $250. Most heads and fish under four feet are medium at $100. Squirrels, weasel, birds, and so on are small at $50. We rent by the day (or portion thereof) or by the week over five days. You can tell me exactly what you want or have me put together a variety based on how many you want of each category."

"Thing is, we sort of need this right away. Do you deliver?"

I started untying my smock. "Delivery is included in the five boroughs with orders over two-fifty. But there's a ten percent one-day surcharge for same-day service."

"Whatever. How about two of each?"

"No preferences? Mammals, fish, birds? Mixed bag?"

"Mixed bag."

"How many days?" My pen was poised over a pad.

"I dunno. Let's just say a week."

Zowie! $2,500 + 1,000 + 500 + surcharge = four thou and change. "Address?"

Minutes later, I brought Angie her full mug.

"Thanks." She swiveled away from her bench, slid her goggles atop her head, and took the coffee. "Got work?"

"Warner Brothers, in Brooklyn, Park

Slope." I drained my coffee and went to the closet for some moving blankets and polystyrene logs.

"How many pieces?"

"Six. Two each, for a week."

"Not bad!" Angie toasted the air with her coffee mug. "With the dreaded sur-charge, no less."

"You bet. Gimme a hand?"

"Sure."

In about forty minutes we had the trailer loaded with the standing black bear, though we had him on his back on polystyrene logs and blankets like he was tucked in for the night. In bed with the bruin was a nasty full-body wild pig. In the wild, they go after snakes, so I always bring a snake mount to put in the pig's mouth — no extra charge. Arranged among blankets in the Lincoln's backseat I had a ram's head, a barracuda, a twin squirrel mount, and a wall-mount pheasant.

Angie brushed some blanket fluff off her sweatshirt. "You're set. Be home in an hour or so?"

"Not if I can help it," said a tweed man sauntering toward us.

I was just a little thunderstruck. You know, just a little, like atop a castle in a storm holding a steel rod. I found no words, so the tweed man turned from me to Angie.

"Hi." He put out a hand. "The name's Nicholas. Nicholas . . ." He gave me a sly look. ". . . Palihnic. Garth and I go way back. Childhood friends."

Angie sensed my shock but shook his hand cordially. "Hi. I'm Angie. You'll have to excuse Garth, he's just on his way —"

"Still with the dead animals." Palihnic surveyed the car's backseat and locked eyes with me, nodding. "Garth never really was much one for words, were you?"

"Hi, Nick," I finally mumbled. "Where you been?"

"I don't want to hold you up, Garth. You headed out somewhere? Why don't I ride along, and we can catch up."

"Yeah, sure." I answered Angie's stare with a glance and a wink to let her know nothing was wrong. "Let's go."

"Fine." Nicholas paused before opening the passenger door and admired the Lincoln. "Still got your dad's old car." He gave me one of his big smarmy smiles. "He'd be proud."

My little brother got in, shut the door, and we drove off toward the West Side Highway.

Chapter 5

Both as a brother and as a person, Nicholas had always harbored ulterior motives, a secret agenda that made him feel smarter than everybody else. It also made him a charming son of a gun, replete with a dash of freckles and farm-boy features. But now he looked a little too smooth for his own good, perhaps betrayed by the short, slick, dark hair with a little widow's peak "flip" or the bags that had started to form under his eyes.

I'd not seen this incarnation of Nicholas. The tweed seemed out of character, but maybe that was the idea. I hadn't heard from him in over fifteen years, and the last time I saw him was before he entered the Peace Corps, of all things. That had been just after our father's funeral. Dad was a professional butterfly collector and finally succumbed to emphysema and congestive heart failure while chasing down spangled fritillaries in a field of marigolds. My father and I were kindred spirits, both possessed by a passion for collecting and identifying. As a kid I collected bugs by the thousands, and now I collect taxidermy, which is sort of the same thing, except on a much larger scale. And we shared a fondness for big convertibles, like the Lincoln he left me in his will.

Anyway, Nicholas was often as not the object of Dad's disapproval. He was not born with the scientific ethos that Dad and I shared: Rather, he seemed hatched from the egg of avarice. Even as a fledgling, Nicholas took a shine to the persuasive, psychological ploys of commerce. He couldn't have been more than five before he started setting up all manner of stands out in front of the house, from which he proffered whatever he thought he could sell. We're not talking about lemonade and cookies. Stock in trade was more like gold (rocks painted that way), the neighbors' cats, dead batteries, worthless stock certificates, etc.

I most vividly remember an early venture in which he made shoes out of cardboard. They were painted with watercolors, garden twine for laces. Some male teens came by his shop and laughed themselves sick, ridiculing him. Assuming he'd been humiliated, I went to console Nick after they left. He turned on a big sly grin and held up a crumpled dollar bill in his little fist. He didn't care what they thought of his shoes or that the reason they bought a couple of pairs was to parade around in front of his stand. "Chumps!" was his reply to my compassion. Nicholas couldn't have been more than seven then, and I'll admit to being a little bit frightened of him ever since.

So it had been plain to see that Nicholas was destined for Vegas, Wall Street, Sing Sing, or worse. He had his share of high-school troubles, pummelings, and suspensions: a pyramid scheme here, an applejack racket there. Rather than college, Nicholas used the bankroll he'd accumulated (which some of his varsity henchmen hinted was in excess of twenty-five grand) to buy into real estate. Using a shoebox full of Visa cards, he financed New York property deals that he turned to profit rapidly enough to pay off the creditors before incurring massive financing charges. Yeah, that gimmick they once advertised on TV. Well, it worked for him, and he became an overtipping hotshot and a club-scene fixture. Then he developed an obsession with penny stocks, around 1987, just before the market crashed. The brokers went to jail with all Nicholas's pennies. And just after that, the New York real estate market slumped, and Nicholas found himself with creditors he couldn't pay. A judge made him hand over the shoebox.

This would have been all well and good had Nicholas not convinced Dad to invest with him, to allow Nicholas to make good on all the trouble he'd been. I was out of town while much of this happened, and if I'd got wind of this I would have tried to talk some sense back into Dad and some shame into Nicholas.

"It's not just for me, or for yourself," Nicholas told Dad, "but for Mom. You guys aren't getting any younger, and what if something happens and you or Mom needs a long hospital stay? You can't pay the hospital with butterflies." Little did Nicholas know the old man was having lung trouble.

Dad was sucked into the scheme and became an eager, willing participant. Anyway, he took the loss hard, and even though I offered to kick in what little I had, Dad insisted on an absurd quest to earn back his lost nest egg. Any idea how many butterflies he'd have to sell to make a couple hundred grand? That's how he died, a septuagenarian run amok with a butterfly net.

Well, I was contemptuous of my brother

for bedeviling Dad. And while Nicholas acted like he was devastated, I was too jaded by that time, as I think Mom was, to believe he was upset about anything but his own financial calamity. In a bizarre bid to prove his sincerity, he enacted his own redemption by way of the Peace Corps. (The Foreign Legion had turned him down.) That was the last we heard of Nicholas. Well, almost. Mom and I each got a postcard from him that first year, strictly factual stuff with no indication he'd had any moral or ethical awakening. Nicholas sounded bored out of his mind. After that, we got several inquiries from Peace Corps officials wanting to know if we'd heard from him. Apparently, he'd gone AWOL in New Guinea. I rather fancied cannibals had made Nicholas Stew, though I imagined he'd have wangled a pretty fair price per pound for himself before climbing into the pot.

I'd never told Angie much about Nicholas, except to say he was a black sheep. Angie's the inquisitive type (to say the least), and for a time she urged me to track down my lost brother. "He'll show up one day, Angie," I said. "Then you may be sorry."

"Garth, you look good behind the wheel of Dad's Lincoln, you really do. It's right where you belong, like a captain behind the wheel of his ship. And still with that rockabilly blond hair the girls like so much. Little cool for the top down, don't you think?"

I didn't say anything as I made a sweeping left onto the highway. Then I looked him up and down, his left elbow over the seat back, the other over the door. "Palihnic?"

He winced and shrugged in one motion. "I like anonymity. Besides, I like the sound of Nicholas Palihnic. It's a name people remember."

"And New Guinea?"

"Some parts were okay, others were hard." Nicholas surveyed the Hudson River and the distant lights of Jersey City, his voice tightening. "I survived."

"Redeemed?"

He laughed like he'd rolled craps twice in a row, his eyes sharp. "Hard-ass, that's what we always liked about you, Garth." Nicholas would substitute *we* for *I* to give his sarcasm a royal sting. "Let's you and me play nice. We're big boys now. I don't call you a chump, and you don't call me a scoundrel. Role-playing is dull stuff."

Ha. That was good, coming from him. "I'll take that as a no, then. What brings you to town?"

Nicholas threw his arms out. "This is my town, Garth. I live here, I hang my shingle here. I have for — what? Six years or more?"

The Lincoln slid into the Battery underpass. "So, what's written on your shingle, Nicholas?"

"Professional Killer. International Jewel Thief. Food Stamps Accepted." He snorted at my pained expression. "Lighten up, Garth. I'm not here to borrow money or steal your wife. But then, Angie's *not* your wife, is she? What do they call it? She's your 'Cohab,' your 'SigOt,' your 'DomPart,' your —"

"Companion will do." I didn't like Nicholas talking about her.

"And I haven't come looking for any pointers on taxidermy either. Christ! You know, you may not be very proud of your little brother, but it isn't easy telling people your big brother deals taxidermy." Nicholas raised an eyebrow at the animals in the backseat. "To think you could turn that hobby into a buck. A lot of people find that dead stuff just a little creepy, Garth."

We pulled up to the tollbooth, and I handed the attendant a ten. She handed me a receipt and change, giving my backseat passengers a double take.

"Been following up on me, Nicholas?"

"Yup. I'm a regular Columbo with the Yellow Pages."

"They have my marital status in the book?"

"I asked your landlord this afternoon while he was sweeping the walk. Talkative fellow."

"So, what is it you want, then?"

"Garth, I am not El Diablo," Nicholas sighed. "Isn't it possible I just wanted to drop in and catch up with my disapproving big brother? You know, like old times, maybe I just wanted to come by and push all your buttons, watch you bristle?"

I didn't say anything.

"See, like that! You're bristling!"

"Am not."

"Well, what do you call that?"

"What?" I sat back and unbugged my eyes, steering the Lincoln onto the Prospect Expressway.

"That's better," Nicholas chortled. "Relax, Garth, my baby-eating days are over. These days I undo other scoundrels. I'm an investigator."

"Investigating what?"

He tucked a card into my shirt pocket. "Thefts. Art, jewels, valuables. For insurance companies." He searched his inside jacket pocket and came up with a pen, which he held up for me to see. "I even have my own promotional pens, so people can write me checks and get the name spelled right." He slipped it into my inside sport-coat pocket. "Sorry, all out of air fresheners."

"An insurance investigator? What's the angle?"

"I get a percentage of whatever I recover. Mostly, I try to locate the thief and bargain for return of the goods. Other times, I arrange to take back what was stolen."

"*You* apprehend criminals?"

"There's no money in *apprehending* anybody, especially if you end up with a knife in your neck. No, I just go for the item. You'd be surprised how reasonable a lot of these thieves can be when properly motivated."

"Sounds more like you're a fence." I veered the Lincoln onto the Tenth Avenue off-ramp and came to a stop sign. "Should I ask how you got into this business?"

"Er, probably not."

"Should I ask again why you've chosen now to reappear?"

"Maybe once we unload your 'critters,' we should drop in for a drink somewhere. I know a bar over here . . . no, that place is *too* Brooklyn. I know another place."

At a traffic signal, I gave him what he used to call my X-ray-vision look, my Amazing Kreskin glare, my sodium pentathol stare. The glow from the stoplight shone red on his face and eyes.

"I really think you want to hear this over a drink, Garth."

"Tell me."

Nicholas took a deep breath, and his face turned green. "I'm looking for Pip-squeak."

Chapter 6

"Beck's." Chin in my hand, I grinned faintly at the young blonde in a midriff.

"Macallan on the rocks. Double twist." Nicholas smiled at the bartender. "It's Kelley, isn't it?"

She smiled back quizzically, tossing coasters on the bar in front of us. "Yeah. How you doin'?"

"Just swell, thanks."

She went about getting the drinks, and Nicholas pulled from his pocket a pile of newspaper clippings with various phrases highlighted in yellow. He put on a pair of wire-rim specs, with too much flourish, I thought.

Unlike the few pubs I'd been to in Brooklyn, this bar wasn't your typical outer-borough place where strangers are ogled like invaders from Alpha Centauri. It was akin to the comfy taverns in Manhattan: dark, with an ornate wooden bar-back proscenium and mini-spots lighting the bottles.

Nicholas pointed a clipping at me. "So

it's like this woman who took the squirrel was in a costume?"

"Read that in the papers?"

"Who's Columbo now? Yes, in the papers, Garth."

"And you've been hired by . . . ?"

Nicholas smiled, wagging his head.

"Can't say. Client confidentiality."

"An insurance company, then?"

"Could be. Point is, Pipsqueak was stolen from somebody and ended up in Tiny Timeless Treasures as part of an estate sale."

"Here y'go." Kelley placed our drinks and Nicholas handed her a twenty. He held out his drink to mine for a clink. "Auld lang syne?"

I clinked without relish, and Nicholas wagged a finger at me. "Grumpy Garth. You'll have to show a little enthusiasm if we're going to rescue Pipsqueak."

I hiccuped. "Rescue? We?"

"I need your help to find Pipsqueak, Garth! You're the only one who'll recognize this woman."

"You know what she looks like from [*hiccup*] the papers. Red and white checked shirt, blue jeans, red lipstick . . ."

"Right. Elly May Clampett driving a Packard. Good. I'll get right on it, Garth."

"It was a Chrysler. That I'd recognize."

"But not Elly May."

"She was in that costume with painted freckles. I seriously doubt anybody goes around dressed like a *Hee Haw* refugee. So how am I going to [*hic*] — damn hiccups — recognize her?"

"You saw the way she moved, her speech patterns, the look in her eye. The indescribable."

I lowered my brow, looking up into Nicholas's eyes. "I'm not one of your 'chumps,' Mr. *Palihnic* [*hic*]."

"You don't care about Pipsqueak, object of even *my* desire as a youngster?"

I smiled grimly. "Except you desired to kidnap him and ransom him back to General Buster."

"Is that much worse than the schemes you must have been considering when you saw him in Tiny Timeless Treasures? Let's see, maybe you aimed to pay the shop owner a fraction of what he was worth. By a factor of, what, ten? Is that ripping someone off? Is that stealing?"

"I won't debate this with you, Nicholas. The point is, I don't want to get involved with the criminal element again."

"Again?"

"[*Hic.*]" I thought about that a second

and decided I didn't really want Nicholas to have the satisfaction of savoring sour morsels from my past. I didn't want him getting any ideas that he and I were in any way alike. "I, uh, once turned in some black marketeers selling bear gallbladders. Had to go [hic] to court, waste a lot of time. It's not my racket, Nicholas."

"You don't say?" He took his glasses and pointed them at me. "Fair enough. I wouldn't want you in on a crusade you don't believe in, and I certainly wouldn't want you to waste your time. Like any other subcontractor, I'll pay you."

"Pay me? To do what?"

"One evening, maybe two, but that's all. I'll pay you thirty bucks cash an hour, off the books. We go to a few clubs, look for Elly May. I think I have an idea where she might hang out."

"Tiny Timeless Treasures is way out in New Jersey. You think she's in New York?"

"Might be. There are clubs that cater to people who dress up. I'll need you to make a couple of hundred easy bucks to find out."

I was suddenly interested. But then I noticed the eyeglasses in Nicholas's hand: His index finger was protruding through where the lens should be. They were fake glasses, a prop, which for whatever reason put my thoughts on Dad. My mood darkened. "Easy money, huh?" I finished my beer, stood up, and started working my pants pocket for loose bills. "It's always about easy money."

Nicholas flushed. He knew I was reflecting on Dad. "Gimme a damn break, Garth. Just what makes you so perfect, so good, and so true of heart that with a clear conscience you call me a monster? I'll play our damn childhood game if it's the only one you know, but I'd kinda hoped you'd grown up a little. Life's not checkers."

I almost said something, but felt any retort would have no greater effect than my silent disapproval. Turning from my stool, I went through the door. Outside and walking to my car, I heard him yell after me.

"Life's a game of chess, Garth, and the moves you make aren't always your own."

I'd forgotten that. It was never enough for him to have the last word. He had to have it twice.

Chapter 7

The apartment was dark when I got home, and by the look of things Angie had turned in. So I quietly shouldered the front door shut, flipped the bolts, took a step forward, and placed the parking sign on the soda bar. This was the curbside parking regulation sign from in front of our home, which I'm compelled to manipulate so I can park with impunity.

Maryland is for Crabs, and Virginia is for Lovers. But as you enter New York City, the welcome signs actually greet you with: PARK LEGALLY AND AVOID TICKET AND TOW. Our city motto should read, *Don't Get Mad, Get Even.* And I get even by switching the signs in front of my building. When I'm not around, the NO PARKING ANYTIME sign holds my spot. When I get home, a little quick work with a cordless drill and the sign suddenly reads, NO PARKING M–W–F 8 AM TO 6 PM or NO PARKING T–TH–SAT 8 AM TO 6 PM, depending on the day and time.

Anyway, my eyes were adjusting to the

gloom as I walked behind the soda bar to the refrigerator. I grabbed a beer and turned to open it on the counter. In the folding wedge of light from the fridge, I caught a glimpse of two hairy, naked feet. I froze. Someone was lying on the bar.

From the darkness came a lilting, Slavic drawl. "Eh, Garv, it's lookink, my friend, yes?"

"Otto."

"Yes, Garv, eetz Otto, old friend. How's looking?" Otto's silhouette was suddenly sitting upright on the bar, his oaken grasp pumping my wilted palm. He flicked a lighter, and his impish goateed face glowed with happy wrinkles. "Ah, you lookink, Garv, very lookink."

Lookink is just one of Otto's vernacular inventions that can mean many things, one of which is *looking good*. He's a Soviet émigré with a unique brand of pidgeoninski English, one of these fellows who is like a stray dog you ultimately regret bringing home but can't bring yourself to ditch. Angie discovered him fixing watches in the subway some years ago and drafted him into her service for jewelry production work like soldering and polishing. I found use for him cleaning and repairing taxidermy. Then he left us to fulfill a lifelong dream: to become part of the American beach subculture, preferably at a nude beach. That was over a year ago.

"Otto, I thought you were in Maine. Selling hot dogs on the beach."

"Garv, December, very bad hot dogs sell. I go Calivornia. Burritos, very nice. And veemin! Nice, not like burrito. Maybe like voodchuck, soft, round, eyes big, but teeth, maybe not so big, and —"

"Must you sleep on the bar, Otto?" I turned on a deer-foot lamp. "We have a perfectly nice sofa right over there."

He flashed his steel dental work. "In gulag, Otto sleeped at floor. When KGB punish Otto, make to sleep him on vooden pole, eh?" He showed me with his hands how wide the pole was, and I remembered his previous rendition of the story. Apparently, when he was in the gulag, one of the punishment devices was a horizontal wooden pole no wider than your wrist, upon which a prisoner was required to stay for days at a time. This was more difficult than it sounds, and if your foot touched the ground or you fell off, guards would beat you and throw you into an isolation box towed out onto a frozen lake where you'd likely freeze to death. Otto perfected a technique of lying on the pole, his spine perfectly aligned so that he could sleep balanced on the rod.

"Back like rock," he continued. "Bed like bosom. Very nice, but no good to sleep, Garv. Tell to me: Yan-gie, she say may for you work at Otto, yes?"

I poured some beer into mug number thirty-seven and handed it to my friend the mutt, whose pajamas were Lakers sweats. "I guess, maybe. But why did you leave California?"

"Have come New York to see Luba." He slurped foam.

"You're not still married." Apparently, Otto was married, in a fashion, to a woman named Luba. He'd go back to her for a while and then get thrown out again. We'd never met her, but by piecing together Otto's reports she was a veritable gorgon who didn't put up with any of his nonsense.

"But of course."

"Luba will take you back, after you left her?"

"Otto go to beach, not leave."

"Well, how come you're not with Luba tonight, then?"

Otto put an arm around my shoulder. "Garv and Yan-gie not married, yes? Veemin, when marry, animal not same.

64

Not like rabbit, or voodchuck." He squinted in thought at his beer. "Luba like bear. When vinter stop, like bear very angry. Except Luba not bite, she throw. Maybe deesh, maybe chair, maybe knife, and —"

"I get the idea." I slid out from under his arm and the stench of tar plus nicotine. "She threw you out. But you can't tell me you came all the way back here to see Luba."

Otto stroked his pointy little beard, grinning to himself. "Ah, Garv, I miz my friends."

Smiling, I patted him on the shoulder. "See you tomorrow, Otto." I put my empty mug in the sink and headed for the bedroom.

I sat on the edge of the bed, and Angie said sleepily, "Guess who's back in town?"

"Our favorite Russian gnome?" I peeled off a sneaker. "Yeah, I found him stretched out on the bar. Like the good ol' days." The other shoe dropped.

"Well, I couldn't turn him away, Garth, could I?"

I stared up at the woolly buffalo head facing the bed.

"Could I?" Angie kicked me from under the sheets.

"You? I guess not."

Chapter 8

Of course, I was up half the night explaining all about little brother Nicholas, and Angie was afforded plenty of time to digest the whole story and formulate an opinion by the time we sat down to one of Otto's breakfasts the next morning.

While Otto isn't what I'd call a chef, he is a fine cook of various Slavic and a few Afghani dishes. This morning it was paprika poached eggs in a cheese sauce on potato pancakes. On the side were freshly baked biscuits resembling scones. And no Otto breakfast is complete without fruit piroshkis, little dumplings bursting with berries. Decked out in my red and white barbecue apron that said CHEF, DAMMIT, he swirled around the kitchen stirring, mashing, frying, serving, clearing, and finally washing, all the while humming one of those noble, soaring Soviet anthems.

While Otto has a myriad of less endearing traits, these are almost evenly offset by his agreeable domestic functions. When in our employ, there are no tasks he disdains. If he sees that we are running out of professional jewelry/taxidermy duties for him, we soon find him waxing the floors, cleaning windows, regrouting the tub, ironing shirts, or cooking dinner. He even rotated the tires on the Lincoln. After a couple of weeks of that, you wonder how on earth people live without full-time domestic help.

Angie and I'd finished our meal and were dawdling over coffee.

"So?" Angie said, apropos of nothing of which I was aware.

I glanced up at her from my latest Yasco Taxidermy Supply catalog and sipped coffee. I didn't answer.

"So, what about Nicholas?"

"Nothing about Nicholas," I shrugged.

"He's your brother, Garth. You have to talk to him."

"Nope."

"Darling —"

"Angie, this is not open to discussion." My coffee cup landed on the table with a thud. "If I want to shun my brother, that's my right. I don't tell you how to deal with your siblings."

"As an orphan, I never had the luxury."

"Yeah, well . . ." My phone rang, and I jumped up to get it.

"Got your blue jay ready," a voice boomed. "Wanna come git him?"

"Sure, Dudley, be over right away."

"Got the ring?"

"I've got the ring."

"What you waitin' for, then?!" He hung up.

"Blue jay ready?" Angie asked. I grabbed my sport coat.

"Yup. He needs me to come over right away to get it, before he goes, uh . . ." I snapped my fingers, searching for the destination. ". . . back home to ol' Virginny." I stood behind Angie's chair and kissed her on the head, giving her shoulders a reassuring squeeze.

"Last time I checked, Dudley's hometown, Memphis, was in Tennessee." She pushed her head back into my chest and looked up into my eyes. "Garth, please, I want you to think about Nicholas. You can't afford to discard family."

She put her face back into the morning paper. "Don't forget the ring box."

I palmed a tiny black velvet box out of the armadillo mail basket next to the front door. "See ya, Sweetums."

Dudley lives about twenty-five short blocks from me. Using the gridiron conversion factor, that's about twenty-one football fields. Though with metric the new standard, I suppose we should start converting to soccer fields, which would make Dudley's, uh . . . Anyway, he's walking distance on a nice day, due south, near the corner of Renwick and Canal Streets. He's got a studio loft in a narrow, white brick carriage house, one of those landmark Federal-style buildings sandwiched between grimy postwar warehouses and auto repair shops. Two wooden barn doors form the building entrance, and the ground floor is Dudley's garage and workshop.

By profession, he's an electronics whiz, high-end auto security being a recent specialty. The "alarms" use space-age resources once the sole province of the NSA, NORAD, and the Strategic Defense Initiative. One or two of which, as it so happens, are Dudley's former employers. He can't talk about it, and elects not to talk about what goes into his most popular product, Shadow Box. Made of some exotic polymer (in either flat black or white), these sleek little boxes the size of radar detectors are adorned only with one cryptic blinking blue diode. No knobs, buttons, wires, dials, displays, suction cups, hook/

loop fasteners, attachments, or switches. Just the little blue blinking light and the embossed words *Air Freshener.* He installs it on the ceiling of your vehicle next to the dome light and clips a chip to your car key, and Shadow Box knows when an intruder has entered the vehicle.

What exactly happens next is open to conjecture — Dudley won't say. I've never seen it in action, but apparently there's a blue flash and the intruder is "strenuously repelled." It's my guess Shadow Box produces a static charge of some kind. In any event, the intruder is zapped like a June bug, after which he usually stumbles out of the vehicle and crumples to the ground, presumably the victim of the *narcotique du jour.* (The "zap" effects are supposedly temporary, but I don't think the motorist owners of these devices would lose any sleep if the thief were irreparably brain-damaged.) Back at the Bat Cave, Shadow Box has communicated with the chip in the car key, which beeps and blinks blue light. The next course of action is up to the individual motorist. Theo in the East 70s might call the cops and have the "drugged-out" bounder arrested, while Joey out in Sheepshead Bay might just acquaint the intruder with the business end of a Louisville Slugger.

A legal device? Nope, which is why Shadow Box is labeled *Air Freshener*. But it fills a demand among victimized, frustrated, and ultimately vindictive New York motorists with a hankering to kick a little butt. Motorists, that is, with five thousand dollars to spare and the patience to stand in line up to a year for installation. Dudley doesn't advertise or discuss details over the phone. It's all word of mouth and all cash.

Upstairs in the studio is where Dudley practices his hobby — avian taxidermy — and that's where I found him after he buzzed me through the front door. Songbirds are his specialty. Not only is his trade illegal, but so is his hobby.

Most songbirds are protected under both federal (the 1912 Migratory Bird Treaty Act) and New York State law. In some cases, a particular bird might also be listed as Endangered and Threatened as per Title 50, Part 17.11 & 17.12 (Subpart B), by the U.S. Fish & Wildlife statutes. And it's also possible that a particular bird might be on the Convention on International Trade in Endangered Species of Wild Flora & Fauna (CITES), Appendices I, II, & III, Title 50, Part 23, Subpart C. What all this means is that it is illegal to be in possession of, say, a bald eagle *living or dead . . . and all parts readily recognizable as parts or derivatives thereof.* . . . Exceptions are made in some cases if you are (or supply) an accredited institute of learning, in which case you have to fill in a lot of confusing paperwork — confusing because much of it is scripted for housing live animals. I've done it for many of my mounts that are endangered or protected species, and it requires crossing out and correcting the language of the form itself. While I have sold to various museums, I also have mounts like Fred that are permitted based on the provision of proof they were harvested before 1972 when CITES went into effect.

I support the protection of endangered, protected, and migratory bird species; Dudley does too. But as anybody who watches the evening news can tell you, the law is often nonsensically inflexible in some areas while alarmingly permissive in others. For example, if you find a dead chickadee — one that croaked on its own — you are not permitted to keep it, much less have it mounted. If you find a hawk feather or a gull skull, you may not keep it. Strictly by the letter of the law, these items must be turned over to the authorities so they can be destroyed, even if you can provide documentation that you just found them. And birds, like all animals, die quite regularly as a matter of course, completely free of human murderous intent.

Like most of the citizenry, I'll go along with the law as long as it makes common sense and as long as it is enforceable. In New York City, we've got only a couple of special cops out there policing almost eight million potential violators of Title 50 and CITES. They're kinda busy busting folks hustling bins of fresh tiger penises and rhino horns. Chances of their getting around to tracking down that blue-jay feather in your curio case are exactly nil. And I think if you tried to give them a dead hummingbird for a proper government-approved disposal, they'd tell you to give it a flume ride to alligator land.

Which all brings us to last January, when Angie and I found a dead jay lying peace-fully on the snow, waiting to be molested by the next passing house cat. Damn pretty bird too, so I brought it to Dudley for mounting. It's mainly for our permanent collection, and I can't see getting in dutch as long as I don't try to sell it.

Dudley is fifty-one and looks like a bulldog. Brown and bowlegged, with big forearms, a prominent jaw, and furrowed brow, he is completely oblivious to his canine appearance. Unlike a bulldog, though, his forthright demeanor is mostly attributable to his whiz-kid brain. He made a hell of a foreman when we met at jury duty on a whiplash case eight years ago. But our friendship didn't really take off until we met again at our next tour of duty. See, since they drag you in to jury duty every so many years, it's not unusual to see some of the same people caught in the same cycle. This time, we weren't on the same jury, and it wasn't taboo to eat lunch together (they're afraid you'll gab about the case — a no-no).

"Best jay mount you'll ever see, you old rag-picker!" Dudley pointed a thick finger at me from his workbench as I entered the loft. He was at his computer, which was neatly arranged with all its hardware — modems, zip drives, zap drives, what have you — on a rolltop desk. Reclining in an old wooden four-caster I got for him on Park Avenue, his outfit made him look something like a bulldog would as a southern sheriff: red suspenders and matching Dickies khaki work shirt and pants.

Wainscoting encircled the room, and it

was topped with a ledge boasting perhaps fifty domed songbird mounts. Above them, dozens of framed photos and paintings of songbirds crowded out the bare walls.

"I'll be the judge of that, Dudley. I have seen a lot of bird mounts in my day." I put out my hand. Oops: I forgot. He's a tactilophobe and doesn't shake hands with anybody. In fact, he tries to avoid touching anything he doesn't have to. The way he sees it, New York is a hotbed of influenza. Dudley's paranoia has some validity in fact, once you start to look around at the infectious threat of everyday things — elevator buttons, ATMs, doorknobs, handrails. Whenever possible, Dudley uses his pinky finger to operate ATMs, elbows to push elevator buttons, and he'll shoulder open whatever doors he can or time his entry with someone else's exit. Gloves? "They just collect germs," he says.

"Voilà!" With a flourish, he whisked a white silk hanky from the blue-jay mount.

Perched on a birch branch nub, the jay sported an erect crest, his beak parted and his wings partially open. Not like he was about to take flight, rather like he was warding off an approaching rival with bluster and a long chatter.

I beamed, turning the birch log so as to

admire the mount from all sides. "Very nice indeed. Truly, one of a kind."

"And where's mine, ragpicker?" He tried to fold his arms, but they were too bulky.

"Voilà!" I put a small black velvet ring box in his paw, and he eagerly snapped it open with the silk handkerchief. "Three-quarter-carat pinkish oval, flanking aquamarine baguettes, platinum setting. Here's the supply invoice." Bartered services, the tax cheat's best friend.

"I de-clare!" He gasped. "It's stupendous! I tell you, Carmela is going to go ape!"

I swallowed a burp of laughter. Only the other day Angie remarked that Carmela was hairy as an ape. "When you going to pop the question?" I thought of adding "You dog, you!" but behaved.

"This very eve! Today! Maybe right now!"

"Down, boy!" I heard myself say. "Take her to a candlelit dinner tonight and do it then. Romantic, you know?"

"Says you. What do you know about it, Romeo? No ring on Angie's finger." He squeezed the ring onto his pinky and admired it at arm's length, alternately giving me a suspicious look.

"Can't go wrong doing something romantic. Besides, it's the way they do it in the movies, a reliable touchstone for what women hope men would do if, in fact, men weren't fundamentally insensitive louts."

"Carriage! A carriage ride, maybe? Or the Empire State observation deck!"

"Corny as all get-out, but probably win you points in the long run."

Dudley struggled to get the ring off his pinky. "Now, how come that clever gal of yours never compelled you to bend your knee and look longingly into her eyes?"

"Marriage? She could just as well propose to me, thank you very much."

"Hilarious. Really, Gawth, how come?" He grunted, then smiled in relief as the ring came off.

"I guess I never felt she — or I — had to be conscripted into marriage in order to commit."

"Unusual." Dudley shuddered the subject away and pointed at the jay. "Now, this mount can be put on a table, like it is now, or hung on the wall. See, I flattened the back and installed a recessed hanger. Wanna cream soda or a Fab Form?"

"Fab Form?"

"Health drink."

"Right. That stuff from the billboards."

"It's quite tasty! Here." He snapped

open a can, poured me a shot. I gave it a try, suspicious.

"Bleck. Tastes like Kaopectate and mango juice. Quick, a cream soda to cleanse my palate."

"Been ads for it on TV, and I like it." He waved the Fab Form can at me, opening the fridge for my soda. We toasted the air and took long sips.

"Dudley, you have an encyclopedic brain. I got a real-life brain teaser for you, something that's got me puzzled."

"Do your worst!"

"Remember that trouble I ran into out in New Jersey?"

"TV-squirrel mount, Cola Woman, dead biker, loon full of bugs."

"Well, a squirrel puppet," I corrected.

"Ah, a squirrel puppet!" His eyes lit up, and he pointed a knowing finger at me. "I can tell you about animal pelt puppets. It's very interesting, actually. . . ."

"Well, that's not what I was going to ask. What I was going to say —"

He wasn't listening. "There are some places in Siberia where the natives make puppets from native animals. Lemme see. Is that the Yakuts that make those things, or the Evenk? Anyway, it's taxidermy, made into puppets. A handicraft. They use them to tell stories to their kids."

"Really?" I tried to look interested. Once you uncork Dudley's brain, it's tough rebottling the trivia genie. "Yeah, well, what I wanted to know was what you know about the downtown club scene. You see a lot of the club hoppers around here. What kind of club would you see Cola Woman at?"

Dudley finished his Fab Form on the third gulp. "Retro." At first, his accent and enunciation made it sound like he said "Jethro."

"Where's that?"

"It's not a where, it's a what. From your colorful if curious description, Cola Woman had an affected old-fashioned look. Retro people dress up like that."

"Retro people?"

"Dress like FDR is still president, hang around swing clubs. Lotta former punks, but they sometimes dally with current punks or rockabillies."

"Got it, the swing craze. Rockabillies being . . . ?"

"You know, people who take rockabilly very seriously. The Sun Records, 'Yes, sir, Colonel Parker' look. Giant Dep hair, black leather jackets, cuffed jeans."

"Greasers or Elvis impersonators?"

"Bit of a country twang in it," he cautioned. "Eddie Cochran, Gene Vincent, Stray Cats, like that. But some are more rudimentary. Some are more hilly-billy."

"I'm with you."

"Then again, many are also into swing, early fifties, and forties jive. Crossovers. Dressing up as a hilly-billy, Cola Woman could be a rockabillette. What makes you think this character frequents a New York club?"

"Hot tip, don't know what to make of it. They dress like this just to go to the clubs or . . ."

"Hard-core ones dress the part full-time. What kind of punk — retro or otherwise — would you be if you didn't cop the look daily, get the odd looks, define your rebel place in society?"

No matter what the context, I always find something slightly sinister in the way southerners say the word *rebel,* or maybe it's just the way some of them work the word into sentences as if to bait Yankee paranoia.

"So they don the painted ties, two-tone shoes. Fifties rebels in ties and fedoras? Jitterbugging?"

"They prefer *lindy hop* to the word *jitterbug.* The point is, purple mohawks were crazy, but everybody got used to them and the shock value went *pfft*. Now dinner jackets, tie clips, hair cut high over the ears, and white sox get the reaction. Let's not forget the stray zoot suit. Retro is the next big thing, Gawth. Where you been? They're in Gap ads, even."

"I'm a newspaper, magazine kind of guy. TV ads got too noisy." I sat on the edge of the table. "So, where do you find these retro clubs?"

"Remember Vito Anthony Guido?"

"Could anybody forget a name like that?"

On the second tour of jury duty, Dudley and I palled around during lunch breaks with Vito, who as it turned out was one of Dudley's glass-eye craftsmen. Sure, chickadee eyes may be all the same to you, but to Dudley, there is glass and then there are diamonds. When confronted with taxidermy, people stare at the eyes first. If the eyes aren't sized right or aren't set correctly, that lifelike effect isn't achieved. Conversely, eyes that have depth and sparkle reinforce the illusion of life.

It's all custom stuff, passed on to Vito as a hobby from his dad, a former Venetian glassworker, though the prosthetic human eyes are what brought his family renown.

He's a horn player on the side. After duty one night, Dudley and I went to hear him play cornet with a jazz band at 10th Avenue Grill.

"I'm still in touch with Guido. Mostly through his band's mailings. I stop in on him now and then. He plays in both a swing band and a rockabilly band."

"I find it hard to believe Vito is a retro." We used to kid him about his trademark moth-eaten sweaters.

"Naw. Career musicians are adaptable. They play the music that sells. Bet you didn't know he plays a trumpet at the Renaissance festival in Tuxedo, upstate, every year. Doesn't mean he goes around wearing a codpiece to the feed store."

"He playing anytime soon?"

"Tomorrow night at the Buckboard Bar, a rockabilly venue. But lemme get something straight here, Gawth. You have a mind to have Vito hound-dog Cola Woman?"

"Sort of."

Dudley crushed his health-drink can like so much plush toy. "May I ask why?"

I made a face, thinking.

"You want that squirrel, now, don't you?" he said.

I purposely ignored his last statement

and snapped my fingers. "I know. We'll celebrate your engagement at the Buckboard, couples, the four of us."

His pug face wrinkled up into a smile, and he barked a laugh. "Gawth, like you say. What I like about you? Always something crazy going on up underneath that wild blond hair."

Chapter 9

When I think back on Dudley's "crazy" comment, I have to concur. What in the hell was I thinking? And ultimately I come back to the same answer: I fancied I might still have a shot at owning Pipsqueak. I mean, there he was in that shop, and had I skipped a leisurely Scranton breakfast, I might have arrived there before Cola Woman and bought him. At the time of the T3 incident, I tried to ask Marti Folsom, the shop owner who'd been locked in the closet, how much she would have sold him for had he not been stolen. But my tactless approach was for naught. She was beside herself, alternating weepy hysteria with reproach for the police. I couldn't get an answer.

So at this stage of the game you'd think I'd have had all the warning signs I needed to steer clear of Pipsqueak. Alas, I'm not without my foibles.

Pipsqueak represented a certain magic, a time of life back when the most important thing in your life was today. The Nutty Nut epitomized my youth. There's a special appreciation you acquire for those feckless days of youth as you approach midlife and the long, slow slide. You know, the slide to a time when the most important thing in any given day is a good bowel movement. Yeah, okay, I'm a half year shy of forty-six and the more deeply middle-aged scoff. But there's a noticeable deterioration from ten years back that probably (gads, let's hope not) won't be as profound in the next ten years. Gone are the days when I could eat jalapeños, for example. So long to dependable, nightlong slumber. Bye-bye to hair-free nostrils and ears. Hello, allergies, two-pint hangovers, lower-back pain, and a size-36 waist.

Then there's the dealer's natural competitiveness, the need to score. What a coup that would have been! I mean, I see a dirty old buggy loon in a store window, reluctantly investigate, and discover the find of a lifetime, a piece with a history, like a penguin mount that belonged to Admiral Byrd or the pelts worn by terriers in *Attack of the Giant Shrews*. Or were those beatdown rugs? Nutty as it sounds, other devout collectors — whether of stamps, Barbies, or striptease highball glasses — find there's something special about a storied piece. In the fine-art world, they call it *provenance*. Yeah, I know Pipsqueak ain't exactly Mr. Ed. But the only mildly famous piece I have is a crow that used to be in a wax-museum display accompanied by the paraffin likeness of Alfred Hitchcock.

What if Marti had sold me Pipsqueak for sixty bucks? The knees go wobbly at the thought.

But what chance did I have of getting Pipsqueak once the *Grease* desperadoes had absconded with him? Well, I kidded myself that I might be able to at least locate him, call the cops, stand witness against Cola Woman, and then Marti would give me Pipsqueak in gratitude for nabbing the hooligans. Then there's the matter of Nicholas, who says it belongs to someone else, though he might (almost certainly) be lying. Then why does he want it? I mean, how much is a puppet from a lousy local sixties cartoon show really worth? A couple thousand? Why did Cola Woman kill a biker just to steal Pipsqueak?

I figured it couldn't hurt just to see where Pipsqueak had been all these years since *General Buster*. I couldn't even recall when he went off the air.

So rather than go directly home, I headed to the Broadcast History Center. Angie and I'd gone to an event there a few months before. I walked from Dudley's over to Avenue of the Americas and the A train, the no-nonsense subway that by-passes lesser stations and puts you uptown but fast. Twenty minutes after stepping on the train, I was face-to-face with a skinny young woman with hideous black-framed glasses, bright green dress, and matching three-inch rubber clogs. She looked like a giant starving frog, one that happened to work the sleek but elegant front desk at the BHC.

I told Frog Girl what I wanted, she had me fill in a little card, and I was soon seated at a computer terminal in a research cubicle. Now, I don't own a computer, or a PC, whatever. I still organize my life with 3x5 cards and file drawers. I suppose I could bar-code all my taxidermy and scan them prior to renting, but that would be pretty elaborate for a couple of pieces a week. I'm one of those who still use phone calls and postcards rather than e-mail or personalized annual desktop-published newsletters. Oh, I could do my taxes in twelve-point-five minutes and play the markets with my expendable income. Sounds great, but until I bank my first million, I'll just have to squander the *full* two hours that it takes now to do my finances on a calculator. Dudley says I'm a technophobe, but mostly I'm just not that interested in gadgetry or enhancing my day-to-day infrastructure with Internet providers, modems, and flashy screen savers. My car doesn't "think" about the brakes locking, ignition timing, or fuel mixtures, and my limited intellect does the navigation without benefit of orbital transponders. Viva Thoreau: *Our life is frittered away by detail. Simplify, simplify.*

Angie, on the other hand, has a computer, and she's beginning to fall prey to its wiles. How can I tell? Not normally much of a cardplayer, she's now a solitaire junkie. (The phenomenon seems pandemic: Computer solitaire has replaced baseball as the national pastime.)

Cro-Magnon though I am, an encounter with the museum terminal did not spook me back to my cave. It was very similar to the ones in libraries that are perfectly simple, helpful machines. User-friendly, if you insist. And yes, I still go to the library to check out books, though I'll admit that whale seems doubly harpooned by Web crawling and superstore book lounges.

I filled in the Subject blank on the screen and depressed the Enter key. The following jumped onto my screen:

The General Buster Show aired from September 1964 to June 1972 with almost 2,000 episodes broadcast locally. While at its inception the hosted "cartoon show" format was already well established by others, the show's creator and star player, Lew Bookerman, was the only one to base his show on Cold War themes that by today's standards seem quite dark. Bookerman's show was largely entertainment rather than educational, with some morality themes. Each show promoted a "duck and cover" segment, and playful treatments of espionage and treason were common elements. Puppets were a common element in children's programming of the day, but *General Buster*'s puppets had the distinction of being made from real animal fur by Mr. Bookerman himself.

General Buster broadcast to a limited audience and met with mediocre reviews. Lew Bookerman was never interviewed regarding the style and content of his show. Recent e-mail from production staff indicates that Bookerman was a Russian émigré who claimed to have credentials as a puppeteer from a Soviet circus. The show was canceled in favor of comparable and more economical syndicated programming (*Banana Splits*). Lew Bookerman's last known residence was in Illinois, where he owned a holistic healing shop and a line of health foods.

No video on file.

Chapter 10

Angie was arguing with the phone when I got home.

"Peter, darling, this doesn't make any sense!" She pulled the phone from her head and gnashed her teeth at Otto.

"Very nice! Yan-gie face like Fred." Otto glanced up from grooming the lion's mane. "Ah, Garv, Fred, he's lookink, yes? I careful very brush all to nice."

"You need an argon atmosphere to solder titanium, Peter. . . . Well, that kind of solder on titanium is crappy workmanship. You want the platinum beads popping off Madeline's ears into the champagne at the Savoy Revue benefit next week?" Angie aimed a withering "Peter" sneer my way. "What I'm trying to say is that unless you want to contract Lockheed to solder the beads, it's got to be cold connections. How do you feel about rivets?" Angie clenched a fist of her hair and squinted at the ceiling. "No, Peter, I don't know anybody at Lockheed."

I slipped behind the soda bar, checked

the answering machine, and obeyed the wink of my blinking diode. At the same time, I obeyed the need for a cup of coffee from the Krups.

"Guess what, Gawth? I did it! I proposed to Carmela right there where she works, at the DMV lunchroom. Said yes. And Gawth? I got a call back from Vito. He's playing a swing set at the Gotham Club tonight. What say we do the foursome celebration tonight? Nine-ish."

Beeep!

"Mr. Carson, this is Janine Wilson at Warner's. Do you have any more snakes? Kevin O'Brien — our director — he wants some more snakes. Please give me a call ASAP. It's about nine-ten a.m."

Beeep!

"Oh, forgot to mention. It's dress-up night at Gotham. Vintage duds, you know? See ya."

Beeep!

"Hi, Mr. Carson, Janine Wilson again. Kevin wanted me to ask about any other reptiles you might have. Like lizards, big lizards? It's about nine thirty-five a.m."

Beeep!

"Mr. Carson, this is Cat Taylor calling from Kenzie Taxidermy Supply? About your recent order? The Sal Soda, horn stain, magnesium carbonate, Permatex, cedar oil, and Sculp Stix are on their way, but we're back-ordered on the bird tongues and beaver teeth. They should come in in the next week or so. Just to let you know."

Beeep!

"Professor! It's Stuart, Sharp's Antiques. Look, I just came across the most gawd-awful thing, thought you might want it. It's like I dunno what. A giant weevil? Stands about two feet high on a square of wood. Ugly. But weird. Thought maybe you should come up here and have a look at it. Also have some kind of bone thing. Dunno what that is, either. Ugly. Gimme a call."

Beeep!

"Hello, this is Stage & Set Marketplace calling to see if you want to renew your ad. Call Andy Poole. Thanks."

I dialed up the customer first and told Janine what I have in the way of reptiles.

"Four-foot spectacled caiman (like an alligator), alligator heads, a crocodile skull, an anaconda skin about twelve feet long and mounted on a board, eighty-pound snapping turtle in a glass case, a three-foot monitor lizard on a Crea-Stone rock, a couple of garden-variety freestanding iguanas, four or five striking rattlers. That's off the top of my head, of course. I could fax a complete list."

"Uh, no time. Just bring over your three biggest lizards and three biggest snakes. Any live tarantulas?"

"No live stuff. But I have a friend, Pete Durban, who wrangles tarantulas."

"Yeah, we lost him. A camera dolly squished one of his bugs and he walked out on us."

"Well, I know a guy who might help you out. Alan Peden, he's at Middle Village Exotica, in Queens, snakes and bugs a specialty. But can I ask why there would be a live tarantula in a sports shop?"

"Oh, different scene altogether. Dream sequence."

"Ah, I see. So anyway, I'll bring the stuff over right away."

Next call: the Big Weevil.

"Hi, Stuart, Carson here. Let's hear about this whatsits."

"Gotta see this thing, Professor. Come on out." He always wants me to come charging out to New Hope every time he gets a piece of taxidermy, and he's never able to identify even the most rudimentary of animals. I once went up there to check on what he said was an eagle only to find it was a turkey. Then again, he drew me out

94

there with a story about a mean-looking black chicken and it turned out to be a capercaillie, an exotic Siberian game bird I scored for a mere thirty bucks.

"A big bug, huh?" Could he be talking about a *Dynastes hercules,* world's largest beetle? Approaching seven inches long, the olive-colored males have a pair of long pincers as big as a raven's beak. They originate in Central America, and as a kid I was forever searching bunches of bananas at the supermarket in vain hope of finding a stowaway. Needless to say, young Garth never did collect a Hercules beetle, a critter I reckoned big enough to qualify as taxidermy. "You open tomorrow?"

"At eleven."

"Maybe Angie and I'll pack a picnic, make a day of it."

"A day of what?" Angie said as I hung up.

"Stuart's got something. . . ."

"And he doesn't know what it is, I'll bet. Wants you to come out to New Hope to look at it. Now you're thinking picnic, right?" Her smile was pained, teeth clenching her lower lip.

"Right."

"Forget it. I'm stuck showing Peter what the gosh-dern beads will look like posted to the titanium." Angie has the cutest ways with expletives.

"And tonight?"

Angie gave me a sidelong look. "Tonight?"

"Yeah, I told Dudley we'd go out to celebrate his engagement."

"Engagement to the Beast?"

"Uh-huh."

I got a knitted-brow smile, and I clasped her shoulders.

"Save your bad humor, Angie, for Peter. Look, we're going to hear music, a swing band at the Gotham Club."

"Dancing?" The clouds began to part.

"Yes indeedy. And it's dress-up night. We're supposed to dress forties or fifties or something."

The clouds darkened Angie's brow again, and she struck me a blow to the shoulder.

"Ow!"

"How could you, Garth?"

"What?"

"You know I don't have anything to wear to something like that."

I reflected on the two closets filled with her clothes.

"Surely, Sugar Cube, you have something you could throw together —"

"Ha!" Angie stalked to the back room and I heard the closet door almost fly off its hinges. Angie's usually very even-tempered, really. Just Peter drives her nuts. Which meant my next move was to assemble the best-of reptile squad and run them out to Brooklyn.

"C'mon, Otto. Help."

Otto dropped his brush and scurried after me into the basement. "Vhat I help, Garv, please, tell to me?"

The snakes are pretty fragile, so we put them in an oversize Rubbermaid storage tub in a vat of styro peanuts, squares of shirt board to separate them. The caiman and monitor I bubble-wrapped and rolled into moving blankets. A crocodile skull the size of a small dog I merely wrapped in a blanket, and we put a couple of iguanas in a box of shredded paper. I have to store not only the critters but all the supplies for transporting them. Packing is one of Otto's talents. He has a near perfect sense — esoteric as it may be to some — of how to fold paper, bubble wrap, or cardboard over toes, claws, and muzzles in such a way that a rigid cocoon is formed around the delicate bits most likely to get snapped.

"I ever tell you you're good at packing, Otto?" I knew what the response would be but decided to see if his story changed any. Otto claims to have done things and been places that I sometimes don't completely believe.

"Otto, of course, pack very nice." He waved a piece of newspaper at me, rather resentful that I might even question his talents. "Tall ago, like young man, home in gulag. Ve not just play card, drink tea day into night. Guards take us to factory, I wrap package night to day."

Otto picked up his tub of snakes and I hefted the rolled blankets of lizards. I unlocked the cellar door to the sidewalk. At street level, we emerged and aimed at the Lincoln. I put the top down and we loaded up the backseat with all the wrapped beasts. Once the cellar doors were locked again, Otto took the opportunity of being out in the fresh air to light a cigarette. I paused before getting into the Lincoln.

"Otto, how'd you get out of the gulag, anyway?"

He paled, the circles around his eyes darkening. At first I thought the smoke had caught in his throat, but the peaty vapor came out in a long, thoughtful stream as his eyes narrowed sharply toward the Hudson River.

"How is Garv see man die? Knife?

Kalashnikov? Rope? Hand? Teeth?"

"Uh, what, you mean like on TV? The movies?" Naïveté is my specialty sometimes.

The sun glinted off his steel dental work, the smile of hard knocks flickering on his scruffy jaw. His gray eyes met mine.

"Otto, he is not knowink how seeink many men die. Very much, Garv. Eetz not good place, maybe, God put to man." Cryptically, he drifted off toward the roar of the West Side Highway, smoke rising, arms folded, silhouetted by shimmering afternoon sun on the Hudson.

I got in the Lincoln and drove past him to the highway. Did he misunderstand my question? Or had Otto killed someone to get out of the gulag? Was there a massacre of some kind? Had he witnessed carnage? There was a grim story that he wasn't keen to tell, and I was slightly queasy just from his innuendo, not so much for what the particulars might be but for all my vast ignorance of and ultimately indifference to the systematic brutality seemingly endemic to far-flung places.

In that he slept on bar tops, aspired to sell hot dogs on a nude beach, smoked too much, and babbled, I didn't take Otto very seriously. Quite the contrary. But I was beginning to think there was a lot more to him, that maybe his flip everyday persona was the result of some very difficult times. Times in which he learned that all is fleeting and perhaps meaningless.

As I drove south to the Brooklyn Battery Tunnel, I looked around me. A Rollerblader had fallen and scraped an elbow. A taxi had a flat tire. A couple argued outside a restaurant. A Lost Our Lease sign. An enraged motorist honking at someone who'd cut him off. A woman limping along with a broken heel. A shabby man slumped in a doorway.

The problems of Mall Age America seemed somehow paltry in comparison.

Chapter 11

As usual, the male of the species had little trouble choosing a wardrobe. My choice was made easier by having only two options for the occasion: the blue pinstripe or the ivory cruisewear. With the remarkable foresight of a collector, at the tender age of twenty I had rescued four seriously dated suits from my late grandparents' wardrobe before my parents sent them off to the Salvation Army. (The wardrobe, not the grandparents.) In the midst of gargling, I had turned from the image of my sleep-tousled hair in the bathroom mirror in time to see the SA truck pull up in front of the house. I had sprinted down the stairs in a towel and half a faceful of shave cream. Catching the Salvation Army man as he was going down the front walk, we got into a bit of a tussle, much to the dismay of my folks. To peeping neighbors, the tableau must have looked like a missionary in hand-to-hand combat with a Watusi savage right there on Red Robin Road. I'd pretty much got the suits out from under his arm when I made a bonus grab for a bunch of ties in the box. My towel dropped, I coughed up the Scope, and he let go. The rest is history. (Mr. and Mrs. Vogel from across the street probably still bend the postman's ear about it.) Anyway, the suits fit like tailor-made — tails, tux, pinstripe, and cruise — and I've kept them around for twenty-five years and only had occasion to wear them each once in that time. Since it wasn't summer, and I wasn't waving a hanky from the deck of the *Piscataway Princess*, my choice was reduced to the pinstripe. In the pocket, I found a cocktail napkin from my dad's funeral.

Angie's closets were not devoid of fashion. She found a black, calf-length, off-the-shoulder bridesmaid dress loaded with pleats. (Yes, a black bridesmaid dress. This is New York, after all.) With the matching black pumps, the ensemble wouldn't have gotten her much more than a shrug at the Gotham Club. But it was her jeweler's eye for accessorizing that got her the nod: elbow-length black satin gloves, seamed stockings, crushed velvet wrap. With a curling iron, she sculpted her shoulder-length blond hair. After much angst, she'd decided that even a small hat was too much, so acorn-sized red costume earrings and matching lipstick ended the ordeal.

Standing before the mirror, she smiled, then turned to me with a frown. "I look terrible. Don't I look terrible?"

It only took fifteen minutes to convince her otherwise, and another fifteen to get us out the door and into a cab.

"You look good, Sugar Plum." Angie squeezed my arm. "Though maybe it needs to be let out in the middle a little."

I sucked it in ever so slightly, about to protest.

In ten minutes our cab delivered us to the Gotham Club, an outwardly unremarkable venue in the low 50s, and we went in.

Beyond red velvet drapes we emerged into a cavernous blue-tiered ballroom, concentric rows of candlelit tables making a bull's-eye of the obsidian-tile dance floor. There was enough headroom to bone up on your model rocketry, though they'd opted to use the extra space to keep the velvet industry solvent via curtains billowing down from the apex to the floor. Diamond-shaped sconces dimly defined ledges in the plush walls that were balconies.

The muted light was yellow, dampening colors so that a navy suit wasn't that far off from the red pillowy walls.

Thick and red as pimientos, every woman's lips were laden with lipstick.

Sharp eyes darted to competing fashions. Hair spray — layers and layers of hair spray — stung the nostrils. With a laugh and the self-conscious wave of a cigarette holder, one woman put a hand on a man's forearm to make a point.

Chiseled jaws, beetle-wing hair, and a dreamy look were the men's ideal. Hands wanted to go into pockets, but it ruined the look of the double-breasted jackets. A few had attempted the pencil-thin mustache, but the Gable mojo only worked for the swarthy ones, and looked itchy anyway. Breezy, but uneasy too, they checked their surroundings for familiar faces.

Swank cliques, positioned in archetypal clumps, cast sardonic looks on the inauthentically attired.

"Timex . . ." Miss Cat Glasses whispered to Miss Corsage.

"Chess King . . ." Mr. Tux said to Mr. Briarwood.

". . . tie clips that don't go the whole width, you know what I mean?" Mr. Boutonniere muttered, his pals chortling commiseratingly.

"Your hat, sir?" A finger was tapping my shoulder. I pivoted toward the coat check. "Check your hat?"

"Yes." Angie swapped my fedora for a

ticket, smiling tightly. "I could see the cheapskate look coming into your eyes."

"Wisenheimer." I put out my arm and Angie hooked her gloved hand through my elbow. We walked to a railing overlooking the tiers and dance floor.

"Have I told you how exquisite you look tonight?"

"Yes, but it never hurts to hear it again." Angie gave me a skeptical smile, the one that knows the compliment is contrived but appreciates the thoughtfulness anyway. She did look great.

"Gawth!" Dudley was waving us toward his table on the second tier with the gusto of a crewman on a carrier flight deck. "Angie!"

"Congratulations, you guys!" Angie chimed in.

"You big palooka!" I jabbed Dudley in the shoulder. He looked dapper in a fifties suit with shoulder pads big enough to disqualify him from the NFL. A sizable pink flowered tie covered his chest. He stood behind Carmela's seat, hands on her shoulders and grinning like Teddy Roosevelt at a Sunday picnic. (That is, he was holding her shoulders with the thumb and forefinger lifted and safe from contamination. Dudley is quick to point out the thumb

and forefinger's complicity in viral trans-
missions.)

Carmela, of course, sported her usual
hangdog expression.

Angie and I exchanged a glance. We
were merely reiterating past thoughts along
the lines of "How the hell does Dudley get
all puppy-lovey for Carmela?" It's not that
she's just gaunt, stooped, ashen, and
beetle-browed. The killer is that she has all
the personality of a brooding log. And
she'd gone easy on the primping this fes-
tive eve: green sack-cut dress, poppit necklace, unshaven legs, and black flats. Well,
there was a bow in her hair, one of those
clip-on plastic thingies, and it must have
been Dudley that got her the corsage. But
both accessories looked ridiculously
droopy and out of place, the way they'd
look if you put them on a borzoi.

Angie made a stab at girlish camaraderie.
"So, Carmela, let's see how the ring
looks?" The bride-to-be dropped her hand
on the table like a bad banana and blushed
ever so slightly.

"Wow," Angie said, and touched
Carmela's shoulder. "You must be so excited."

"Yes," Carmela grunted.

I easily resisted the temptation to give

the lucky girl a peck on the cheek. As an alternative, I waved. "Congrats. Got yourself a fine man in Dudley."

"Yes."

I pulled a chair out for Angie and hailed a waiter. "I guess this calls for a toast, hmm?"

"A toast indeed!" Dudley trumpeted, resuming his seat.

Angie launched into conversation by explaining the fine points of the ring she'd put together for them.

I ordered the cheapest bottle of champagne in the cellar and proceeded to reexamine our surroundings at the tier tables. Many of the same sorts as in the gallery by the bar, though not the hard-core types, by my reckoning. There were a few Mom 'n' Pops in the tiers too, looking ready to revive golden ballroom memories. So I took to scanning the railing and gallery beyond, noticing irregulars. For example, there was some rumpled fellow in a cardigan wearing a skimmer and sucking on a pipe. He was all of twenty-something and trying desperately to look like Bing Crosby at fifty. Next to him was another youngster in a greasy pompadour and black bowling shirt. On the back were two red dice and the words *Lucky's Speed Shop*. Bing and Bowler surveyed the crowd like a pair of vultures. On the other side was a spoofy flapper chick in a gelled hairdo with big black feathers fanned out in back like a turkey tail. Tiny black-frame glasses circled her eyes. In one hand, a cigarette holder that could double as a yardstick; in the other, a martini that could double as a birdbath. From what I could see of it, her dress was a cascade of black feathers. Perhaps she'd just auditioned for some Broadway musical version of *H. R. Pufnstuf.*

From the mannerisms of these and most of the rest of the gallery people, I got the impression that they were the hard-cores. They didn't act like this was a costume ball. Even while being sociable among themselves, they continually lapsed into serious postures of folded arms, confidential whispers, and meaningful glances. It was as though this gathering of wine and song had some grave import to them: less Benny Goodman, more Brahms.

The lights dimmed and the champagne arrived. Curtains parted at the back of the dance floor, and applause drowned out the pop of our cork. About ten band members in red blazers, white shirts, and red ties sat at attention in two rows of bandstand stalls monogrammed with *GC* (for *Gotham*

Club). Piano, bass fiddle, and drums flanked the stalls. The drummer's base had *The Swell Swingers* stenciled on it in gold glitter. The bandleader was in shirtsleeves with red arm garters and a red bow tie hanging undone. He brandished a grand smile but was unshaven and had black rascally locks hanging in his eyes. Possibly a little stoned.

"Gawth! See Vito? First row, all the way right. Cornet."

I nodded. There sat Vito in a neat red blazer, shaved head shining in the multicolored stage lights. His shaded eyes sparkled beneath hooligan black eyebrows, the kind that shake hands at the nose.

With a wave of his red baton, the bandleader charged into a round of familiar swing numbers that got the crowd dancing. When the bottle of champagne was history, Angie and I hit the dance floor for two numbers, and I was relieved not to notice any hypercritical stares from the technically accurate dancers. At this point, I really couldn't say whether what we were doing was a Lindy, East Coast or West Coast swing, jitterbug, jump, or what. In fact, it's certain that we abbreviated the steps. But I figure as long as you can swirl the girl, dip your doe, flip your chick, and not drop the dame, you're doing okay. I'll take panache over persnickety any day.

The applause from the last number stumbled to an end as Angie and I resumed our seats.

"Thank you very much, ladies and gents, thank you!" Wiped from exertion and free radicals, the bandleader took a long drink of ice water. He drew a hand across his head, pulling the sweaty locks from his face. "I'm Rob Getty, and the Swell Swingers are certainly glad you could make it to the Gotham Club tonight." While the audience applauded obediently, he stole the pianist's cigarette from an ashtray on the Steinway. "And now we'd like you to give a warm welcome to Scuppy Milner and his Wailing Voice of Gold!"

From stage left, an aquamarine tux jogged onto the stage filled with the night's singer, a man with a forehead twice the size of his face. And atop that sat a rigid triangle of reddish-brown hair. Tiny blue eyes glinted above a smile as wide as his forehead was tall. I'm not completely sure he even had a nose. Scuppy (Scottish puppy? Schoolhouse guppy?) was a caricature of himself, an amalgam of outsize features, and his pugilistic hand gestures made it clear that he was rarin' to go mano a mano with Buster Poindexter. The very thought: like a Godzilla flick, two giant foreheads locked in battle, swinging at each other with their titanic hair ledges, buildings toppled, Greenwich Village laid waste.

The teeth flashed. "Who's ready for some new stuff, huh? Shake it loose, people!" The gallery exploded with applause for Scuppy, obviously a local fave.

The band fired up again, this time with a boogie-woogie beat, flaring horns, and hoodoo jungle drums. Scuppy lit up a smoke, winked at the audience, and made a fist around the mic.

I didn't catch all the lyrics, but I picked up a Swell Swingers CD later that spelled them out. And the song — "Blinking Light" — went:

Baby, step away from that screen
Now let go, jive and scream
Tomorrow's not a day to waste
The future's past as bongos race

Blinking light commands
That you never ever understand
All to own and not to breathe
Bar codes, access, shopping TV

Listen up and dig the sound
It's your mind coming 'round
Light me, baby, eyes of fire
We'll wail away the techno mire

Baby, step away . . . [refrain]

Tongue that tastes complete
Isn't junked with the obsolete
Dance with me, leave your mouse
Wall of numbers, crumbling house

Doctor says we're not lookin' well
That we're dancin' to certain hell
Electron gun shot his hypothalamus
Red blue green — now he's not
  one of us

Baby, step away . . .

I got the gist of the lyrics during the performance, if not the complete swing libretto. Maybe it's just me, but the sentiments seemed a little odd — certainly a far cry from "Jump, Jive, and Wail." I looked back to the gallery while Scuppy belted it out. Some were cutting the rug in earnest. Meanwhile, Bing, Bowler, Feather Lady, and their cronies hung over the railing popping fingers, howling, bobbing heads, and generally going bananas.

Peppy, contemporary swing music is to my liking, and I must say that I was pleased to see it come to the fore, especially as swing seems to be edging out the seventies revival. So I have a gut appreciation for this swing craze. But I have to say that the music coming from the stage at the Gotham Club had a dark element that was both alluring and sinister.

The Swell Swingers finished their set a few numbers later, trombones swaying and horns blaring. Angie and I barely had time to quiz Dudley and Carmela about their wedding plans before a pair of hands grabbed my shoulders.

"Hey ho, whadda ya know?" Vito came around from behind me, grinning, and pulled out a chair.

"Hey, nice set, Vito." I stood, shaking his hand. "Angie, this is Vito."

"This is your woman? Can it be true?" Vito the charmer.

Angie put out a hand; Vito kissed it.

"You know the swankiest people, Garth," Angie quipped.

Vito turned to Carmela. "And can this flower of loveliness be Carmela?" She stared balefully up at Vito's waxed head. Without hesitation or pensive blink, he took her hand and squeezed it. "I get to be flower girl, am I right?"

Dudley guffawed. "Oh, siddown, you cad!" He waved over a waitress, who replaced the empty bottle.

After some reminiscing about jury duty, what Angie and I were up to, a sentence on Carmela's job at the DMV, and what Dudley was into, we got around to Vito.

"So, come up with any innovations in the glass eye?" I asked. "I'm in the market for some goat eyes."

Vito pointed at me. "You know the new contoured eyes with the offset scleral band, with the corneo-junction?"

"Scleral band?" Angie said.

"With the white around the side," I explained.

"Have you seen any prerotated, with exaggerated veining, using powdered production gold?" Vito thumped the table for emphasis. "Can you imagine how stunning that is for photography, the way the eyes light up instead of looking like black glass? I suppose you'll be looking for some slot-pupil models that would work for a goat. What size?"

"Maybe twenty-seven millimeters? Maybe not even that big."

"Call me, I'll see what I've got. Would

you believe how busy I've been with the music scene that I haven't filled any orders lately?"

"Swing?"

"Yeah, swing has got every horn player in high gear. Used to be, I'd have three solid gigs in a good week, but now? Forget about it." His fingers tapped out a triumphant drumbeat on the table. "Would you believe that if I wanted to work more rent-a-band shindigs, this big bad wolf would be blowing down the piggy's house seven nights?"

"So you play in more than one band?" Angie asked.

He nodded gravely. "Doesn't everybody? I mean, you got your main gig, but you sit in with other guys, pickup bands, you know? A few studio musicians, a couple fellas from the symphony, we pull up chairs, and what have you got? A band, so what do you name it? I play in the Buddy Phelps Hepsters, the Hell's Kitchen Irregulars, Pistol Pete's Mob . . . Sometimes we make up the name when we get to a club or when we put in at an agency for a listing to play private parties."

"All swing?" I asked.

"Variations. One bunch does twenties stuff, another is very zoot suit, while another may be more jump, rockabilly, or tra-ditional. How many flavors fit on a snow cone?"

"Gawth wants to know about retros, Vito," Dudley interjected.

Vito nodded thoughtfully, waiting for me.

"Well, I guess I'm curious about these people back up at the bar. I understand that this isn't just dress-up."

Vito pursed his lips. "I'd say not."

"What's behind it?"

He shrugged. "A fad, a craze? Maybe in two years I'll be back to playing Dixie-land."

"That's it, huh? I was listening to the lyrics in that first Scuppy number. Not the usual crooner fare."

Vito suddenly looked impatiently at his watch. "They gotta write songs about the war, you know?"

"War?" Angie injected.

Vito stood up, looking toward the band-stand, where one musician was working spit from the valves on his horn. "Before: Hitler, Vietnam. Now? Would I say it was like lifestyle wars? Technology will be the ruin of us all. Hey, nice seeing you guys. Gotta get backstage for the next set."

Angie and I exchanged glances, but

Dudley didn't seem to register anything from Vito's sudden departure.

"You didn't get to ask him about Cola Woman," Dudley noted. Angie and I exchanged a different kind of glance.

Candle flicker made Angie's sly look menacing. "Now, why would Garth want to ask Vito about Cola Woman?"

Dudley drummed his pinkies on the table and looked at the ceiling, realizing he'd goofed. Carmela stirred her soda with a finger, mollified, I think, by the tinkling sound and golden-brown flash of ice light.

Now, some people believe you should share every thought with your mate, and under ordinary circumstances, I'm one of them. But as I've intimated before, some pretty extraordinary circumstances have presented themselves over the last couple of years. More specifically, dangerous circumstances, those that I don't necessarily go looking for but seem fated to encounter. Obviously, I knew that looking for Cola Woman — a de facto murderer — had certain risks. At this point, I was just nosing around to see if I might be able to spot her while filling a social obligation to my friend Dudley and taking Angie out on the town. You know, based on Nicholas's hunch.

I'm sure that in a lot of relationships, it's the gal who frequently bemoans her man's predilection for dangerous activities. You know, like "You're not going to try to fix the roof yourself!" or "Skydiving? I don't think so!" Yeah, but Angie ain't that kinda girl, which is just another reason I love her so. The trade-off is that she is an inveterate puzzle person. Crosswords, Jumble, *Win Ken Kleine's Money*, and even TV whodunits, like that. And she's good at it too, whipping through the *Times* crossword over a cup of coffee and unwinding movie plots while the title credits are still rolling. Penetrating tenacity is her hallmark. She gets hold of a crossword and won't let go until it's done. Forget about breezing past an incomplete jigsaw in a bed-and-breakfast parlor. Something about her psychology drives her to pounce on and unravel a puzzle. In the past, she's injected herself into my "extraordinary circumstances," and despite my better judgment I stuck my neck out to satisfy her quizzical reflex. In the process, she's nearly been shot and blown up. I've nearly been assassinated and crushed by a boulder.

Call me overprotective if you must, but I didn't want Angie getting involved with Cola Woman or my burgeoning Pipsqueak search.

Nicholas was one puzzle she'd already got hold of, and I didn't think she'd really let go of the T3 incident, either. God forbid she saw a connection. Of course, it was too late now, about Cola Woman anyhow.

"I just mentioned to Dudley that since Cola Woman was dressed kind of old-fashioned that, you know, there might be some kind of outside chance that we might see her here." I must have shrugged ten times. Darnedest thing about cohabitation is that you become so transparent to your mate.

"Ah." Triumph curled on her lips. Angie saw a pattern and was starting to stir jigsaw pieces in earnest. I wouldn't hear any more about this until later, so I excused myself to the gent's room before the band started up again.

As I ascended the plush steps from the tiers to the gallery, I kept my eyes peeled for Cola Woman — not that I really expected to see her. She certainly wouldn't be dressed Elly May–style at the Gotham Club, so I probably wouldn't recognize her anyway. Then again, as I looked around, she might not be so out of place at that.

It was much more crowded in the gallery than when we entered, the late-night crowd filling up the joint for the second set. And the fashion demographic was becoming proportionately wackier. I noted a pair of black-leather rockabilly boys sporting giant pompadours and cigarettes behind their ears. Variations on the jive costumes were myriad, ranging from men in coats with palm-size triangular buttons and string ties to women in their grandmas' flowing black nightgowns with matching marabou slippers. I was beginning to detect direct themes and influences to ensembles too. Blaze-orange capri pants and silver-sequined camisole: Laura Petrie goes deer hunting in Vegas. Sharkskin suit, black shirt, crew cut, and El Presidente cigar: Dobie Gillis morphing into Jerry Lewis. There was the woman with the Veronica Lake hair, red flannel shirt, porkpie hat, baggy pants, clodhoppers, suspenders. Her girlfriend was in a black suit, white shirt, narrow black tie, Debbie Reynolds hair. It was all making me a little woozy. I made a point of not looking too closely at the gals in line for the powder room as I made my way to the men's room.

As usual, the men's room wasn't that crowded, and I took my place at the urinal.

I don't know about the rest of the country, but New York has gotten out of hand with advertising. Walk four blocks and take every handbill for porn or cheap suits. You'll have a full ream. Leave your car parked on the street for a couple of hours, and the windshield is covered not only with parking violations but handbills: Zoom Lube, Go-Go Moving Company, and Barney's Fried Chicken. Enter your apartment and the entryway is carpeted with Chinese, Indian, and sushi menus. Messenger bikes now have tiny billboards on the back of the seat. Whole sides of buses shill for TV. Mobile-billboard trucks drive the street hawking vodka, and taxis are painted up as ads for the latest Broadway show. Every mundane item that might hold your eye for a millisecond — cups, fudge-bar sticks, cocktail stirrers, bottle caps, gum wrappers — assaults you with an important message about another consumable. And how could you help but notice the two-fers? Cola cups/bottle caps that promote not only the cola brand but the latest blockbuster or the NBA with some lame "peel-off" game. I challenge anybody to find a soda container from a fast-food chain — or most other places, for that matter — that doesn't cross-promote. *Sorry, try again!* I don't think so.

And some Madison Avenue Einstein recently decided that public bathrooms are the "it" venue. As you wait in line, there are racks of free postcards that are actually liquor or car ads. At the urinal, I was faced with a foot-square billboard for Fab Form, that soapy health drink. And then there's the plastic cage for urinal cookies. Commercials are found posted on the bull's-eye, so now (particularly if you're male) you can piss on the product they want you to buy. This one, though, had a good-cause message, perhaps a belated warning for many. *Say No to Drugs.* I don't know about you, but I think in their avarice, the Larry Tates of this world have so inundated us, so overstimulated us with their blaring flash-frame TV spots, that we no longer see any messages at all. Really take a hard look around at how thoroughly immersed your life is in ads, and you'll feel like you've been snapped out of a trance.

I noticed that the images of the healthy couple chugging Fab Form had been scratched (using keys, I guessed) with messages from fellow whizzers. *Access Is Submission. Black & White. No Codes. Smoke & Degauss. Who's monitoring whom? Hello, dick breath.* Except for the last, I found them more interesting than whether I could measure up without Fab Form. Unlike ads, cryptic sloganeering is at least thought-provoking.

I gave myself the once-over in the mirror — just to make sure my wayward hair was still frozen under the spell of ULTIMATE CONTROL, Level 6, hair gel — and made my way out past the women's room line. I squeezed my way through the gallery of jive lost boys and was just taking a step into the tiers when I turned. I'd passed someone I thought I recognized, but now she was gone. I turned forward again, saw Angie giving me a curious look from our table, then decided I wanted to see who it was I'd maybe recognized.

As I approached the bar, my eye zeroed in on a figure over by the hatcheck. I saw a red dress, small stature, full figure, and yellow beehive hair, but it was the chunky legs that had been imprinted on my memory. She was talking to that Bing Crosby wannabe while collecting her wrap. He put a hand to her flabby elbow and they moved off into the red velvet folds of the exit. Dodging Feather Lady and a zoot suit, I got to the hatcheck just in time to see Bing and the Red Lady step outside. They paused, him offering her a light from his Zippo. I zoomed in on her profile. I knew her from somewhere. Then it hit me like Moe's fingers in Curly's eyes. As the door closed, I heard her kvetch: "This better not take all night."

Angie's hand grabbed my wrist. "Garth, what's going on?"

"It was her!" I handed over my hatcheck stub.

"No way!"

"Definitely."

"Cola Woman?"

"What? No, no . . ." I grabbed my hat and guided Angie to the front door.

"Who?!" Angie implored.

"Marti. Marti Folsom. You know: the owner of Tiny Timeless Treasures."

Chapter 12

I hid my face with my hat as we exited, as if I were checking my head size or something equally absurd. But the blind was unnecessary. They were halfway down the block and stepping out between parked cars. Bing's hand shot in the air, and brake lights flared on the back of a passing cab.

"Marti?! I don't get it, Garth. Are you sure?"

I gave her a cross look instead of an answer. "They're getting a cab, dammit."

Angie and I darted into the one-way street, searching the oncoming traffic. No white For Hire lights headed our way. "C'mon."

With Angie holding my arm, I started hustling toward the intersection where Bing and Marti's cab had come to a stop at the light.

"Hang on!" Angie yanked me to a stop, plucked off her shoes, and dashed ahead of me, her trailing velvet wrap flapping in my face. I had no idea how we could hope to follow them and, if so, what we would do when we caught up with them. My only thought was to grab the next available taxi and give the driver the line every cabbie yearns to hear: "FOLLOW THAT CAB!"

The light turned green, and the cab went straight across the intersection. We dashed across too, but Angie suddenly veered, hopping into the back of an available cab. Only this taxi wasn't the prerequisite yellow, and it didn't have a NYC Taxi & Limousine Commission medallion. What it had was a tall, sandy-haired man in Italian cyclist hat, spandex racing jumper, and Tevas poised over the engine. It was no ordinary cab; it wasn't even a hansom cab. It was a bright green pedicab. You know, like a tricycle on steroids, the modern rickshaw and latest addition to New York's traffic snarl.

"Get in!" Angie gestured frantically at me. I hesitated.

"Where's the fire, guys?" The sandy-haired cyclist drawled.

"Follow that cab!" Angie pointed.

"Sure, toots. Mind telling me which one?"

Of course, like any midtown avenue and side street on a Friday night, the roads were chockablock with yellow cabs, all hired.

"Make a right, it's halfway down." I jumped in. There were about a dozen cars between our target and us. "Twenty dollars says you can't keep up with it."

Sandy gave me a scorching look, bit his lip, and said, "They'll eat my dust, buster."

His bell ringing madly, Sandy pumped the pedicab up the pedestrian ramp and onto the sidewalk, yelling, "Pregnant lady! Out of the way! Pregnant and in labor! One side!"

Angie — always the quick study — rolled her velvet wrap into a ball, tucked it under her dress, and fitted it onto her abdomen. She assumed the last-trimester slouch and gripped her belly, moaning loudly.

Chinese-food delivery boys on bikes wobbled from our path, herding scurrying pedestrians onto car hoods and into doorways. That's not uncommon in and of itself, mind you, except that for once it was the result of someone *else's* recklessness.

"I think you're overdoing it a little, Sugar," I yelled to Angie.

"Keep it up, girl! We're gaining," Sandy growled over his shoulder, his bell jangling like that of a Good Humor man during a grand mal. "Pregnant, one side! Move it, mister: baby on board!"

The next intersection loomed. Bing and Marti's cab turned right, heading downtown. Sandy was closing.

"Hang on, Pregnant Lady!" Sandy leaned on an air horn; it was so loud I almost blacked out. Folks crowding the street corner froze, stagger-stepped, and ultimately dove from our path as the pedicab parted the pedestrians, jumped the curb, and careened right onto Broadway after our target. Another jounce and we came back down on all three wheels.

Sandy ran the light, zipping past Bing and Marti's cab.

"You're ahead of them!" I prodded.

"Cool it, Pinstripe. We're on Broadway. The cabs only use Broadway up here when they mean to go downtown, way down. Gotta stretch it out here a bit, may need the extra furlongs in the home stretch." Sandy glanced back at Angie. "Okay, sweetheart, cool it with the moaning. Give birth to your wrap like a nice girl, and I don't want no velveteen placenta messing up my cab," Sandy cackled.

Sure enough, we played leapfrog with Bing and Marti's cab all the way downtown, me with my hat over my face like I was sleeping and Angie with a disinterested look. We went all the way to Houston

Street, a busy crosstown boulevard, where they hung a left. We followed about a block behind, Sandy having worked up a considerable sweat despite Broadway's gentle downgrade. Way east, past the usual club areas, pool halls, and a famous kosher deli, Bing and Marti's taxi made a right into a commercial area that's deserted at night. But they didn't penetrate far before pulling over, which gave us the opportunity to hang back at Houston Street.

Sandy groaned, drawing an arm across his forehead. "Whew! So, Pinstripe, what's that worth to you?"

Angie and I climbed out, and I gave the cabbie four ten-dollar bills. "Nothing but tens from the judges. You get the gold medal."

Sandy pocketed the bills. "Just the gold, thanks." We left him at the corner sucking on his water bottle as we turned down the side street in time to see the yellow cab zoom away. A beacon wedge of doorway light folded into black as Bing and Marti disappeared into a building. Angie put on her shoes and we assumed the pace of any normal retro couple on a late-night stroll through a desolate part of town.

"I don't like this." I scanned our perimeter: just a sparse archipelago of streetlight atolls in a sea of urban gloom. "We note the building they went into, we go home. Tomorrow, in the daylight, we maybe come back and explore."

Angie nodded, and I hoped she meant it. I figured we could sprint back up to the bright lights of Houston Street in a trice should things get scary, though we'd probably be sacrificing Angie's shoes in the process.

It was a canyon of grimy, defunct storefronts on the ground floors of old redbrick buildings. *Goldfarb's Millinery. East Side Remnants. Lenny's: MATZOH, GEFILTE. Max's Haberdashery — We Steam Felt. Moshe Trucking. Bederman's Wholesale.* To a height of four stories above the storefronts, windows were boarded, shuttered, or dark behind the black zigzag of fire escapes. Traffic, radios, shouts, and honks — New York's equivalent of waves at the shore — faded as we walked, beckoning us back to the relative safety of urban bustle.

The building they'd entered was obvious by the seam of light under the door. *Gunther's Thread* was spelled out in peeling gold on the store glass, specks of light visible where the black paint had flecked. The hubbub of voices, of a crowd, was audible within, but deep within. In fact, our ears directed us toward the metal sidewalk cellar door, where the crowd was louder.

"They're in the basement." Angie pointed, getting down on her knees to put an eye at the latch hole.

"C'mon, let's get out of here." I snapped my fingers.

"Wow. I can't see much except a few elbows and some folding chairs. Sounds like quite a crowd."

"Angie: time to go," I whispered. "We can't crash this shindig. Marti will definitely spot me."

Angie stood, brushing off her knees. "So what if she does?" she whispered back.

"I dunno. What if she thinks I'm following her? I mean, it seems pretty obvious that somehow she's mixed up in Pipsqueak's kidnapping."

"Theft. Assuming this isn't just some kind of coincidence."

"How about 'squirrelnapping'? 'Puppet-napping'?"

Angie rolled her eyes. "What's she going to do about it? There's a whole lot of people down there. I can't see her pulling a gun. Besides, you've caught her off guard. She'll probably think it's coincidence or something. But she'll have to think about it awhile before she does anything."

Light suddenly poured from the front entrance. Like possums in the headlights, Angie and I squinted at the forms of two men standing in the open door. A retro man in a wide-striped suit stepped past us, gave us the once-over, and moved on up the block. The big silhouette in the doorway boomed, "Well?"

Chapter 13

"Hi!" Angie chirped.

"We were just —" I chortled.

"Password?"

"Nobody told us about any password," Angie snitted.

"Nobody *who?*" Silhouette leaned defiantly on the door frame, the shadow of a toothpick waggling in his lips.

"You mean who told us to come? Garth, who's that friend of yours? The one that told us . . ."

"Friend of a friend, really." I shrugged. "Jeez, Angie, whatsisname . . ." I snapped my fingers.

"Hardy har-har," Silhouette boomed, standing aside. "Get on in."

Before I could grasp what he meant, Angie glided into the speakeasy. "Thanks!" Angie nodded to the silhouette.

I followed, tipping my hat and bestowing a nervous smile up at the doorman. Out of silhouette, he was still looming large in what must have been a size-58 jacket. His neck and head were shaved close over cauliflower ears, a nasty-looking scar on his forehead arcing up into a streak of white hair on his scalp. A shoo-in nominee for the Heavy of the Year Award. He didn't give us a second look.

Directly inside was a dusty, vacant shop, walls lined with empty spool pegs. A cracked glass counter on our right was piled high with hats. Attending was ennui personified as a bobby-soxer. She said nothing as she took my hat and held out a ticket.

Angie and I bounced eyebrows at each other and continued toward the only obvious route at the back of the room, where we went through a set of curtains. I heard Mr. Heavy open the front door and growl, "Password?" Snapping fingers followed, and the next group entered. So that was the password. And to think but for dumb luck we'd have been safely on our way home to call Dudley and explain our disappearance.

Skirting a room of aging crates and scattered excelsior, Angie and I descended a narrow stairway to the left, a rush of cigarette smoke and convivial murmuring rolling up at us.

I put a hand on Angie's shoulder. "Take it easy with the small talk down here, okay?

Don't say anything if you don't have to, not our names . . ." And I reflected that Angie had said my name in front of Mr. Heavy. Angie patted my hand as if to calm my nerves. As if.

We emerged into a large industrial basement, complete with cast-iron pillars. Nobody had gone to too much trouble to doll the place up. Stray crates, pallets, and dangling bare-bulb lighting constituted the decor, along with about twenty rows of folding chairs in a variety of different materials and vintages. At the head of the rows was a podium, and behind that a makeshift bandstand with musicians. We were about the last to arrive; only standing room was left available. Much of the congregation was smoking. We were too, of course, by default.

A dude in an extralong pencil-thin mustache handed us each a program as we entered, and we drifted to the far back corner of the room. Busy scanning the room for Bing and Marti, I didn't look closely at the program but saw that the cover had a cartoon of a wolf in a zoot suit twirling a chain.

"It's like church," Angie said under her breath.

"Not like the churches Mom and Dad

135

took me to, I'll tell you that. Check that out." I pointed with my chin at the far side of the room, where Bing, standing, gestured in earnest to a fellow with white hair, white dinner jacket, and a white Panama hat in his hands. I didn't see Marti.

"He's just a kid," Angie whispered. "Kind of a silly boy smoking that pipe, wearing a straw boater. Who's he trying to look like? Bing Crosby?"

"That's my guess. You're right, he is young, too young to be hanging around with Marti. She's fifty plus if she's a day."

"You're sure it was her?"

"Positive. The hooked nose and voice are a giveaway. Hey, that's Vito. In the band!"

"Oh, my gosh! You're right."

A fat, older man in a loud checked suit, goatee, and a classic example of male-pattern baldness stepped up to the podium and tapped the mic. The musicians stubbed out their fags and gathered their instruments. The lights dimmed and a smoky spotlight beam snapped onto the podium. All eyes turned forward and the crowd lowered the volume to a murmur.

"Gang," Checkers began, "Scuppy is running a little late. I — oh, here he is!"

Scuppy made his entrance from somewhere at the back of the room, and I wondered where the other entrance to the building was. In an alley? A freight elevator? The audience jumped to their feet, applauding.

Scuppy swaggered up to the podium, waving apologetically, and Checkers retreated. "Sorry I'm late, but my taxi was cut off by a pedicab rushing to the hospital with a pregnant lady." The crowd laughed. "No, really!" Scuppy laughed. "Anyway, listen up, people. Maestro?"

The audience sat, and the band laid down a sleazy, urban Peter Gunn rhythm, the drummer working a cymbal with a steel brush.

"I want to welcome you all back to the Church of Jive and to welcome any newcomers who've come to get the skinny, to open their eyes, to awake to the syncopation lost years ago but regained by you, me, and a growing number of others. How many people here remember black-and-white televisions?"

Some hands went up.

Scuppy nodded thoughtfully. "Well, you at least saw the last era of freedom. I never did. We had a Magnavox console TV, and I was placed in front of that thing as a baby. And I remember . . ." Scuppy picked up the microphone and stepped in front of the podium, the spotlight following him. ". . . I remember, one of my very first memories, I was very small and used to crawl up to the screen and put my eye right up to the screen." Pantomime began to accompany the narrative.

"I liked the little colored dots, the waves of red, blue, and green that undulated across the phosphorous inner coating, and wondered who was inside the TV. But it didn't take long before I stopped noticing all the little dots, and I stopped wondering who was inside the TV. I just sat there." He made a goofy face of someone stultified, and the congregation laughed.

"In the back of your eye, in a part of the retina called the macula, there's a tiny spot containing the receptors that give you color vision. There are as many as six million cones. Did you know that the signal induced from these sensors travels along the optic nerve — a bundle of one million nerve fibers — into the vision center of your brain's cerebral cortex? This is the same place where your ability to hear and understand and sleep are located." Scuppy whipped the mic cord authoritatively. "Now, do you think that way back in the 1960s — in the middle of the Cold

War — it was a coincidence —"

"No way!" someone testified from the audience.

"I don't think so," someone else added.

"— that the scientists at the Broadcast Standards Institute — an organization, mind you, rife with German, ex-Nazi scientists, and funded at least in part by the CIA — decided to have the red, blue, and green electron guns fire sixty scans a second in a frequency that sent waves along the optic nerve to the cerebrum and induced a kind of seizure? Now, I'm not talking about spazzing out." Scuppy acted like a spaz to get a chuckle, and got it.

"You know how flashing red lights can cause epileptics to have a seizure?" Folks in the first row were nodding. "They know what I'm talking about. And how about this?" Scuppy pulled out a news clipping and held it up. "There's a copy of this in your program. In Japan, a cartoon show caused children all over that country to go into seizures, to vomit. From flashing colored lights. And what happened? Did they pull the show? Did anybody even try to find out what that cartoon did to their brains? Or did our government look into the possibility that terrorists might be able to use this on Americans?"

Scuppy froze, a look of wonder on his face. The congregation hushed. Slowly, Scuppy pulled from his jacket a handful of clippings, holding them out for everyone to see. "Well, gee. Guess what, people?"

"What!"

"Speak!"

"Give us the word!"

"It has happened in America. It happens all the time in America, in fact." He plucked an article from his hand like the petal from a daisy. "May 1994 issue of *The Medical Journal of Sciences*. Says here that kids all over the United States of America have been experiencing seizures from video games. Repetitive, high-intensity, multi-colored flashes caused what they call complex partial and absence seizures. No spazzing, just" — he squinted at the article, as if reading — "impaired consciousness, intense memory recall, déjà vu, confusional episodes, and audible and visual hallucinations. Well . . ." Scuppy let that article fall to the floor, and pulled another. "July eleventh, 1995, *Mid-Atlantic Bulletin of Medicine*. A woman has blackouts and acts strangely when she sees a certain talk-show host." He let that one drop. "September 1996, a study by the Hecklen Neurology Institute reports someone who smelled bacon every time she saw a local TV sign-off video of the Stars and Stripes waving in the wind." That one dropped. "*River City Times,* 1999, residents black out after a local TV broadcast of *Oklahoma!*" He let the rest of the clippings fall to the stage. "And these are just the cases we know about. The government is all jazzed up over terrorism, over the prospect that someone is going to get us with poison gas or a thermonuclear weapon. Tell me: Why, then, haven't they gotten to this? Could be some foreign government, some towelheads, perpetrating this, practicing on small segments of the population before they go for New York. Tell, me: Why?"

He paused, letting the question hang long enough that the audience began to squirm. Then he put a finger to his enormous forehead. "But you see, our government already knows what it is. After all, they invented it. It's called color television, and they made it to insinuate itself into your brain and create a kind of conscious sleep. Who here has spent a whole day on the couch watching TV? How many kids spend the whole day, the whole night, playing video games? How many neighbors got their eyeballs riveted to that there PC monitor? Who here's been a potato? C'mon!"

Hands came up all around, and Scuppy nodded. "You just lay there, you just sit there, and the longer you lay there, the harder it is to get up. If that isn't a trance, gang, I don't know what is.

"Now, you ask me, 'Why are they doing this, Scuppy? Why do they want us in front of the TV? What is the purpose of putting an entire planet under a spell?' Gee, do you think it has anything to do with *power*, anything to do with *money*, anything to do with the so-called *gross national product?* Do you think it has *anything* to do with increased work hours, less leisure time, stymied labor organization, and an economic boom?" Scuppy's volume rose, working up to a crescendo, as did the riff from the band. "Do you think that just maybe it has *anything* to do with commercialism, with everybody wearing *ads* on their clothing, with *hyperconsumerism,* with a stock market twice the size it was ten years ago? Do you think it has to do with Internet providers cramming their screens with flickering icons and ads? Do you think it has to do with the *shopping mall* being the alternate center of everyday life when you *leave* the TV?! DO YOU THINK . . . it has *anything* to do with the fact that we are increasingly asked to stare at *color monitors* all day at work, only to spend our lunch hours on the same monitor *playing solitaire,* only to come home and tune in our *twenty-five-inch Sony Trinitrons* or *surf the Web?!*"

Scuppy's shout echoed into silence as he scanned the congregation with his pointed finger. No music. The audience was rapt.

"DO YOU THINK?" he shouted, spittle flying from his accusing lips.

The spotlight went out, and the band blared in the darkness for a few moments before the hanging bulbs slowly lit up and the congregation broke into applause. A chant started: "THINK! THINK! THINK!" Scuppy was gone, and ushers started to pass Folgers cans for a collection.

Angie was standing right up against me at this point and squeezed my hand. "That was almost like you when you get going on your Madison Avenue diatribe. Scary, huh?"

I nodded. "Can we go now?"

"Show's not over, gang," Checkers reassured us from the podium. "We're just getting warmed up. I think many of you know who I am. But for those of you who don't, my name is Doctor Henry Fulham." A projector screen was set up behind him, and one of the techies who'd been working the spotlight at the back of the room near Angie and me fired up a slide projector. "I am a neurosurgeon, and I was with the United States Army at Walter Reed Hospital in Washington, D.C. It's been my privilege, my duty, to serve the Church, to validate the dogma, to testify to what I know to be true about the single greatest conspiracy mankind has ever known. First slide."

The gang proceeded to be treated to a slide show documenting the history of the pursuit of world domination and the importance of en masse brainwashing techniques to that end. There were slides of Hitler, of Nazi anti-Semitic slogans and pamphlets, of Stalin. The Soviet Union, according to Checkers, was the last big push to try to manually subjugate a population through topical means. That proceeded into a lecture on what little is known about brainwashing, about how the Moonies, Scientologists, and scores of other cults can so easily manipulate people. "Stable, well-adjusted agnostic individuals," as Checkers said more than once, can in twenty minutes be convinced to abandon their entire life's possessions and "supplicate their lives before the Bible" simply through a twenty-minute discussion with a recruiter. Repetition, protein deprivation, excessive memorization, were the tools that could reduce the mind to a nonthinking organ. Slides included pictures of mass Moonie weddings, Tom Cruise, John Travolta before a Senate committee, recruiters working campuses, etc. He gave a few anecdotal case histories (with slides of the victims), then hit us with some of his work for the government on epilepsy and mind stimulation through the optic nerve and how 3-D movies were actually the brainchild of the Army. The 3-D glasses have one red lens, one blue, and the Army first devised them in an attempt to study the effects of flashing blue and red on the optic nerve while introducing flash frames of popcorn. We were, of course, treated to some eerie shots of movie-house audiences during the fifties in 3-D shades.

According to Checkers, the idea of "color flash" mind control was originally intended for troops, but the National Security Agency — "our CIA dedicated to sophisticated electronics" — took over the project, combined it with their color-television project, and rigged the Broadcast Standards Institute to perfect the technique and proper scanning rates to open the mind. The scanning rate, he explained, had an effect on the mind comparable to the repetition used in topical brainwashing, except now you had someone looking at the TV with "a full open mind, bereft of any apprehension or distraction from talking with a stranger, a recruiter." The entertainment worked as a sort of carrier signal for the color flash.

But this was only the first step. The next was to get as much protein out of the American diet as possible, which the government did by introducing a cornucopia of high-fat, high-carbohydrate snack foods. At the same time, beef, cheese, and eggs were vilified. So were snack foods to a certain extent, but they were so convenient and taste-enhanced that people ate them anyway. Commercials saw to that. Checkers showed charts and graphs of the increase in snack-food consumption since the introduction of the color TV, of insidious partially hydrogenated oils found on every snack label.

And finally he revealed to us the purpose of the color-flash brainwashing: money worship. The Soviets had it all backward, you see. They felt that if they could maintain total control over *supply*, they could completely control the people. In the West, however, we prefer the carrot to the stick. The government controlled *demand*, and that drove the economic engine, made people work harder for less real estate, more consumables. He cited the scarcity of condominiums before the advent of color TV.

"Next week, I'll go over what organizations are implementing the color-flash program, the size and breadth of the conspiracy. Following that, we have a guest speaker, formerly of the National Institutes of Health, to explain the mechanisms of how nicotine blocks color flash in the brain through dopamine enhancement, which in turn is the impetus for the government's efforts to abolish smoking. Included will be new information on how attention-deficit/hyperactivity disorder is a side effect of the Broadcast Institute's experiments, and how the drug Ritalin is being used in lieu of cigarettes to combat these effects. Thank you all, and please give as generously as you can to the Church fund. It goes into rental of this space, for organizing, for getting the word out. Maestro?"

The band struck up a riff, and the congregation all stood up at once. Angie and I weren't far from the door and slid out pretty quickly. I dropped a buck in the can of a guy next to the door on the way out.

And so we were some of the first ones up at Houston Street, where taxis had gathered. Like vultures, it looked like the cabbies had gotten wind of the meetings, and the ones in the know would stop down here at midnight to scavenge fares.

As we zoomed west on Houston Street, Angie cleared her throat. "Well?"

I gave a short laugh. "I've got to hand it to them, Angie. It's compelling, in its way. They've really brought a bunch of threads together, and it plays into a swell conspiracy theory."

"Think any of it is true?"

"Just enough. Going to continue playing solitaire?"

"I mean it, Garth. A conspiracy?"

I smiled, but not with full conviction. "Conspiracy theories are the ultimate in human conceit. Look at the Department of Motor Vehicles. Their task is perfectly simple. They just need a few facts, date of birth, name, address, then a photo. You get assigned a number, so does your car. Now it just becomes a matter of keeping the number straight with the names and vehicle identification numbers. Go to the DMV, what do you find? Chaos, huge lines, confusion."

"What's that got to do with —"

"If the government had the wherewithal to perpetrate a complicated conspiracy, you'd think they'd have the wherewithal to make the DMV the pinnacle of efficiency."

"Some would argue they're only as efficient as they have to be. What do they care if you have to wait in a long line? It's not like you won't wait."

"Even so, to pull off a conspiracy of this complexity you'd have to get a lot of people buying into the same principle without a religious dogma or beacon of hate to lead them. Hell, get six people together and you spend an hour and a half trying to decide where to go for dinner. And there's not even any power or money to be shared in that arrangement. Even so, it would have to be for something more than just the love of greenbacks."

"It is a tall tale." Angie sighed. "Then again, there seems to be no end to these loopy cults. You know, I was fooling around on the Internet the other day and came up with this Web page for some group that's convinced there's a global shadow government. You know who spearheads it? The Boy Scouts of America and their — what was it? — oh, yeah, 'Occult Symbolism.' I mean, these guys really think the Scouts are in cahoots with Amway to raise the Dark Lord and enslave the planet!"

"I could see Amway and the UPN network . . ." I grinned.

"But the retros: They have a lot going for them. I mean, they promote smoking and eating beef. Beats grape juice and white bread. And it wouldn't hurt anybody to have a lot less television and video games in their lives."

"Certainly cut down on the advertising exposure." I squinted.

"Yes, Sugar Lips." Angie gave me a pat on the hand. "Fewer ads."

Chapter 14

Our taxi pulled away from us and relit the For Hire sign. Angie and I walked around my black Lincoln parked in front of our digs and approached the doorway to our apartment. We use a side door that accesses all eight apartments in the building, even though there's a shop entrance into our living room that we haven't opened in years. It's not uncommon for a homeless person to curl up to sleep on our front stoop, particularly on windy, cold nights, and we don't mind so long as they don't wet the bed. Actually, the more common phantom urinaters are barhoppers. The Barbed Wire, a saloon that used to be around the corner, was a big B&T draw, meaning that "bridge and tunnel" kids from outside Manhattan — Jersey, Queens, etc. — came there to whoop it up in the Big City. I've got no problem with that except the B&Ts routinely mistook our stoop for a urinal on their way back to their cars. Don't ask me why they didn't use the trough at the Barbed Wire. This became so predictable for a time that I installed a motion detector and strobe light to scare them off. Inspired by Dudley's tinkerings, I schemed to deconstruct the components of a bug zapper, flatten out the charged grid, and slide it under a rubber mat on the stoop. I guess it would have been a "pud zapper." But Angie talked me out of that one because I might've electrocuted a passing pissing pooch.

Anyway, we didn't think anything of the person we could see curled up in our front doorway. Until we noted that said form wasn't dressed in the fashionable oily gray, navy, or brown coat of the indigent. The garb was red, and the outstretched hand had red painted nails. A strung-out transvestite? We drifted over for a closer peek. You have to be careful around sleeping homeless because they sometimes awake quite defensively. And whatever you do, don't nudge them with your foot or they can get violent — and not without some justification. Vigilante citizens have been known to fall upon the homeless while they sleep, literally kicking them bloody while they're down. The intended message? Don't return to sleep in and reduce the property values of our neighborhood.

A closer inspection revealed blood dripping off the stoop. We winced, but such spectacles aren't completely out of the norm in the Big Apple.

"Oh, my gosh," Angie gasped.

"Time to call an ambulance," I said as we backed to the building entrance.

Homeless die every day in New York, right on the street, and sometimes in the middle of a crowded sidewalk. They most often succumb to exposure in the dark, cold months. Huddled next to a building as if asleep, their body temperature draws down and they die quietly. Other times, they are the victims of their vices, isopropyl martinis causing gruesome public episodes of blood vomiting.

"Sure you wanna call an ambulance?" Nicholas had appeared, in a tan and brown suit. He was sitting on the Lincoln's hood, arms folded, a tweed goblin come to vex me.

"What the — Of course!" Angie shot him a cross look and unlocked the building door.

Nicholas straightened his green bow tie. "Okay."

Angie turned suddenly. "Oh, my Lord. It's not —"

"It's Marti Folsom, and she's dead." By his expression, Nicholas might just as well have told us our fridge was on the fritz.

"No bullet holes or stab wounds. Blood is coming from her ears and mouth. When the coroner gets through slicing up her brain and liver like so much Boar's Head, he'll probably find that it was an overdose. Not that she willingly took the overdose."

"But that's impossible. We just saw her . . ."

Nicholas raised his eyebrows and smiled. "Yeah? Where?"

I held my thoughts, but my eyes betrayed them.

"That's right, Garth. Someone's sending you a message. They know where you live, and they don't want you nosing around the retros looking for Pipsqueak."

"How long have you been hiding in the shadows here?" Angie asked.

"Not long enough to see who put her there, but long enough that I got here before you. So where did you two go after you left the Gotham Club? I just *happened* to see you there."

Again I held my thoughts. I learned a long time ago it wasn't wise to divulge anything while Nicholas was playing games.

"Well, you don't have to tell me, Garth. But you will have to tell the police. Er, you might want to make your next call to a lawyer."

My mind raced. Was there any way I could tell the police that I didn't know this dead person's name? What were the potential pitfalls? And if I did tell them who she was and that she was the owner of T3, where another murder had happened, might the police suddenly come to suspect that Cola Woman was "invented" by me and Marti? That somehow we'd conspired to kill Tyler Loomis, alias Gut Wrench, and blame it on a mysterious stranger who never existed? All to fake Pipsqueak's disappearance? But why . . . who . . . what if . . . ?

"Okay, *brother-in-law:* Just what are you doing here?"

"Sister-in-law Angie! I'm flattered that Garth told you about his little brother. I can see it all now. Christmas cards, Thanksgiving dinner. Hey, that's right. I don't have any plans for Easter!"

"Look, buster," Angie began, a finger of warning in his face, "I know you and Garth have some bad blood, but save that game for him. I'm a clean slate, and as far as I'm concerned you're family. And where I come from, family gets the benefit of the doubt, always, so I'm extending that to you." Angie poked his shoulder. "Don't bite my hand, Nicholas."

My brother displayed uncharacteristic contrition, real or not.

"Sorry, Angie, you're right." He held his hands up as if her finger were a gun barrel. "I'll cool it."

"That's better. Now I'm going to call the police."

"Think it through first," Nicholas advised. "Marti's dead, which means a lot of strange thoughts are going to go through the cops' heads when they get here and learn of Garth's connection to her. They don't cotton to coincidences. Garth's peripheral involvement in two murders means they're going to suspect him of complicity. Somebody did this to keep you two from playing bloodhound. If I were you, I'd tell the cops only the bare facts and wait to flesh it out in the presence of your attorney. I'm not sure you even want to get into the whole retro thing, if you can help it, much less that you think this has to do with a goofy puppet. Let them figure that out for themselves, if they can. Oops — looks like somebody already called the fuzz."

Flashing lights came down the block.

Nicholas started off on foot toward the West Side Highway but gave some parting advice.

"And whatever you do, don't offer to identify the body. Let the cops ask you to, and hope they don't." The ambulance and police car arrived simultaneously with Nicholas's disappearance around the corner.

Chapter 15

Sometimes I wish I could visit myself in the past and slap that Garth around. This stupid Pipsqueak thing was getting way, way out of hand, even as I had feared it might.

Two detectives showed up moments before the photographer. One was a wan white guy with black-frame glasses, a cratered, waxy complexion, and neatly pressed suit. To my eye, he'd have made a dandy embalmer. The other was a pudgy man of undetermined race. That is, he probably could have filled any or all of the Equal Employment Opportunity categories at the NYPD: sloe-eyed, short frizzy hair, thick black mustache, bright blue eyes, and skin that probably took a tan well. He handed me his card and asked questions; the Embalmer didn't. After getting our names, address, and phone number, Detective Tsilzer asked only six questions.

"When did you find her?"

"Just now, about ten minutes ago."

"Did you or anyone else touch or move her in any way from the way you found her?"

"No. We found her just like that."

"Who else was around when you discovered the body?"

"Nobody. Well . . ."

"Well?"

"Well, my brother was here. Nicholas Palihnic. But —"

"Where can we get in touch with him?"

I pulled out my wallet. "This is his card." Tsilzer tucked it in the back of his notebook without so much as scanning the name. He turned toward Angie.

"Do you have anything to add?"

"No." Angie shook her head.

"Awright, that'll do it for now." He smiled politely at us, looking from one to the other, in a way that might have meant "Have a good night" or "I'll find out more from you two later." Doubtless, Tsilzer intended it that way.

I guess we don't get the Good Citizenship decal for our window for this kind of mildly evasive behavior in the face of the fact that someone may have just been murdered. But as a garden-variety cynic, I have a fundamental distrust of those with the power to subjugate me. As a denizen of New York City, where the police are constantly out to impound or summons your car, distrust of the cops is endemic. And did I mention the hidden cameras? The police have taken to video surveillance of the citizenry at large, you know, for our own good. There are actually cameras installed at certain stoplights that take a photo of you running a yellow signal. Suspicion breeds suspicion. Some may prefer to see this as government mothering, but to my eye they're setting themselves up as zookeepers. Which by elimination makes me one of the caged animals. In the parlance of our times, "I'm not comfortable with that."

It might be different if I had any reason to believe that the NYPD had half the savvy of *Hawaii Five-0*. I'd put my life in Steve McGarrett's hands any day.

The whole dog-and-pony show folded up and was off our front stoop in a little under an hour. The NYPD have had lots of practice and are good at this sort of detail.

When they were gone, I called Dudley. He was a little put off by our Gotham Club disappearance until I outlined our predicament.

"There's a bad wind in the valley, Gawth. You need protection! You git yourself down here first thing tomorrow. I've got something in the personal-security department, something experimental. Just the thing."

"Experimental? I don't like the sound of that."

"You could be a test pilot."

The words *test pilot*, as inflected by a southern accent, have the most ominous ring. I see smoke rising from the distant high desert, heat-shimmering images of ambulances racing to a crash site where I've plowed into the ground at Mach 1.

"I don't think so."

"For Angie's sake, Gawth!"

"Look, I'm beat. Can we talk about that tomorrow?"

"Dudley's gonna get you wired one way or the other!"

"Sure, sure. Hey, Dudley, lemme ask you this. This business with the color television as, you know, a mind-control thing."

There was an uncharacteristic silence on the other end.

"Dudley?"

"Yes?"

"What do you think about the color-TV thing? Is it possible?"

"M-maybe. I really wouldn't know." Ordinarily, there wasn't anything on which Dudley would decline to opine, especially in the technology field. Except, of course, the particulars of his electronic devices. Or any of the "unmentionable" agencies he used to work for. Had I touched on something about which he knew a great deal but "couldn't talk about"?

"I see. Well, let's talk tomorrow."

"Yes, perhaps we will talk tomorrow," he said woodenly, and hung up.

The door buzzer sounded. Angie paused mid-pour from a jug of mountain Chablis and bit her lip.

"Should we get it?"

I went over to the squawk box. "Who is it?"

"KGB, eh?"

"Otto?"

"KGB, Garv."

I buzzed in the runt, and he burst into the room. He always shouldered the front door like there were a couple of Cossacks holding it shut from the inside.

"My friends, vhat you do? KGB, they here, I know I see." He took Angie by the chin. "You lookink, eh? Yan-gie, she good? I dunno. I very 'fraid my friends, maybe *pizdyets*." You don't want to know what *pizdyets* means precisely, but let's just say it's akin to the less vulgar *kaput*.

"Lego my chin!" Angie swatted his hand away. "We're okay, Otto, relax."

"Not okay. I know. I lookink, I see voman, red dress, and she not lookink, Garv!" He wagged his head morosely. "Voman dead! Not good."

"Not looking," I agreed, retrieving a beer from the fridge.

Angie flopped onto an overstuffed armchair. "Not looking," Angie agreed. "What are we going to do, Garth? They know where we live! And the police are going to come back. They're going to find out about Marti. Did you see Tsilzer's smile?"

Otto got excited again. "KGB smile? Oh! Oh, this very bad, KGB him to smile you!"

"Otto, cool it," I managed not to shout. "Let's remain calm. We can always call them, ask them about who the victim was, and then say, 'Who? Why, we know her!' And so on. I mean, we didn't get a look at her. We only have Nicholas's word that it's Marti. We're on solid ground." I wondered briefly if there was any possibility Nicholas was fibbing. For what reason? There was no telling.

"They're going to talk to Nicholas. What if his story —"

"We stuck to his story, remember? We made sure we didn't get a look at the body, we didn't offer any information. Besides, it was Nicholas who actually saw that it was

Marti, not us. We didn't touch her."

"Eetz good. Garv no voman touch to dead." Otto mumbled from where he sat cross-legged on the floor.

"But you're right," I continued. "We should probably just spill the Marti thing, tell them everything, let them work it out. Or not. But we've got to steer our way out of this."

"Garth, what if this warning means that we shouldn't tell the police anything either?"

"Well, you'd think they'd have sent a more explicit message if —" My eye suddenly caught the red blinking light of my answering machine. I went over and pressed the Replay button. It burbled like an angry gerbil, beeped, and played. There was just the ambient sound of a public pay phone, maybe in a bar. After a moment, a muffled nasal voice spoke slowly.

"Little Miss Muffet. Sat on a tuffet. Along came a spider. She called the cops. The spider bit her. Little Miss Muffet died. The spider didn't have to bite nobody else." That was it.

"Who Muffet, Garv, tell to me?"

"Woman on the steps, Otto." Angie and I shared a moment of dread. "I guess that answers your question, Angie. Now what'll we do?"

The phone rang and I let the machine pick up. "Yes, I'm calling for Mr. Garth Carson?" It sounded like a phone solicitation. But at 2:00 a.m.? "We're calling on behalf of St. Michael's Hospital. Your brother, Nicholas, has been admitted, and we need to talk with you just as soon as possible."

Chapter 16

Like most emergency rooms I'd seen in New York, this one was strewn with people in various states of disrepair. Folks with bloody towels wrapped around their hands (missing digits?), others puking into pans (cyanide poisoning, for all anyone knew), others flat on their backs groaning (acute appendicitis, perhaps). And as usual, the staff only seemed concerned with "processing" those who were actively dripping blood onto the carpet. I marched up to the admissions desk. Next to the desk was parked some poor son of a bitch in a wheelchair who looked like his face had hit the windshield. The nurse's station was vacant, and there was no bell to ring for assistance. Surprise, surprise.

"Don't thuppose you could thpare a drink for a fellow General Buster fan down on his luck?"

I turned once, then twice, to the swollen face next to me in the wheelchair. Realizing it was Nicholas, I flinched in surprise. The large hands of an even larger orderly on

Nicholas's shoulders kept my brother from escaping his seat.

"I know, not a pwetty thight. Thign me out, will ya, Garth? That'll make Mighty Joe Young here loothen his gwip long enough that we can get out of here and make last call over at Dew Dwop Inn."

"Jumpin' Jesus . . ." was all I could muster. His normally slim, angular face was all puffed out, red, and scratched. It was like a doll head had been snapped onto my brother's body and was mimicking Nicholas's argot. A doctor breezing through the room happened to look up from his clipboard long enough to register me talking to Nicholas, and he detoured.

"Are you Mr. Palihnic's brother?"

"Yes, I —"

"I'm Doctor Schumate. You should know that your brother is refusing an MRI scan." A ballpoint pen clicked nervously in Doc's hand. "There's a strong possibility that he's suffering from a concussion, or worse. Subdural hematoma is a distinct possibility."

"Yeth, but how'th my cholesterol, Doc? Maybe I thould cut back on the liverwurst, whaya t'ink?"

"This isn't a game, Mr. Palihnic." Doc waved an admonishing pen in front of

Nicholas's face, and turned back to me. "If you — I beg your pardon!"

Nicholas caught the orderly off guard, lunged forward, and grabbed Doc's pen in his teeth, growling.

"Mr. Palihnic! Please!" Doc struggled to get his pen back from my brother. "You're being childish, Mr. Palihnic!" The lifegiver's glance around the emergency room at the growing smiles among the wounded betrayed he was interested more in his image than retrieving the pen.

"Nicholas, maybe you should stay and have the MRI, huh?"

Those in the room who had an ounce of humor left eked out enough chuckles to make Doc turn red, let go of the pen, and storm out of the emergency room. "Nurse," his voice yelped from the next room.

Nicholas spat the pen on the floor. "Garth, I want outta here now. I need you to thtand by me." He looked up at the orderly. "You can let go now, Junior. To keep me here against my will is unlawful imprithonment, a cwime punishable by up to three years in a thtate penitentiary. I can get a cop, if you want. There's always one parked outhide a hothpital."

"I'll take him home," I reassured.

Joe rolled his eyes and stepped back. I helped Nicholas to his feet.

"I can walk, Garth, they only mamboed on my fathe."

"Excuse me!" A nurse burst into the room, nervously fussing with the front of her cardigan. "He's not permitted to leave!"

The first thing that popped into my mind was something akin to one of Otto's colorful Russian expletives. But I learned a few years back to count to three before replying. Five, better still.

"He can't leave until he's signed out!" she shrieked.

"I happen to agree with you that he should stay, but he wants to leave." She could see my slow burn. "So we're signing out. Now."

There was a taxi sitting in front of the hospital, and we interrupted the cabbie's Fab Form break. I folded Nicholas into the backseat and gave the driver my address.

"Belay that order, cabbie. Downtown, corner of Water an' Dover, next to the bridge." Nicholas held a hand up to my face. "I know, Angie wants to nurthe me back to health. Forget it. They know where you live, but not where I live."

"Who? What happened to your face?"

"Our fwiends, the retwos, happened to

my face. Real pwos, though, gotta hand it to 'em. Use the flat of their handth, with gwoves. No bwoken teeth. Lipth cut on the inthide, from my teeth. Nose is bwoke again, but what the hell. Didn't blind me or collapse my twachea. Mainly scwatches, swelling. In a coupla days, I'll look like a Tawwyton Thmoker, an' thath all." He widened one of his black eyes as if to prove it. The white was shot with bloody veins.

"I know the doc was an asshole —"

"Thow me one that ain't," he growled.

"— but you should see someone about your head. There could be bleeding."

His twisted lips coughed a laugh. "I doubt it. They held me off the gwound by the arms tho my head didn't hit the fwoor or anything. My neck, that'll be thtiff for a few days. And a headache? I've got the world's wortht. Tylenol and codeine? Plathebos. Cabbie? Pull over to this liquor store. Yeah, 'ere. Garth, you wanna get your little brother some scotch, please?"

"Is that a good idea?"

"Didn't you know scotch is an anti-coagulant, Doc Cawthon? Thins the blood, break up the clots you're so worried about forming on my bwain. Make it Macallan, huh? No thense in half meathures."

We pulled over and I paid way too much

money for the single malt. But it didn't take long.

"Recognize the guys who did this?" I asked once we were back on track.

"Maybe . . ." Which I knew from past experience meant he wasn't telling. "Driver? You know the car wash down here on the left? Let's go through the wash, okay? My tweat."

"Something *is* wrong with your brain. A car wash?" I said.

"Please, Garth, I won't tell you how to cwean a buffawo hide if you don't — Yeah, cabbie, over there."

In a few minutes we were in the car wash, sudsy rivulets flowing down all the glass. The driver didn't seem to think this was unusual. I guess some cabbies have seen it all.

"Here." Nicholas pulled what looked like a sausage in leather bondage from his torn jacket.

"What's this? A blackjack?"

"Take it. I didn't get a cwack at them. Maybe you will."

I pushed it away. "Where'd this happen, Nicholas? Near my place?"

"Naw. I went back uptown t'another retwo hangout." He sipped from the bottle and convulsed with pain. A wall of undulating felt strips approached the windshield and slithered like an octopus over the top of the car. "Thon of a . . . bitch, that thmarth! Damn! I know a girl, a waitress and singer. I asked for her at the bar. I got a note telling me to come backstage. I go into a woom, as directed, and there's four guys behind the door, in dinner jackets, crew cuts, and plaid cummerbunds like the frickin' Four Lads, 'sept they got Ace bandages wrapped around their faces."

"Like mummies?" The jet-nozzle rain frothed up soapsuds on all sides, the watery image of a phalanx of huge pink paint rollers fast approaching.

"Yeah, like mummies, Garth. Common pwactice in some circles. Beats wubber Nixon or Pluto masks. Better pewipheral vision too. Then they hustle me out back, into a van, and start driving an' hitting. Dropped me near the entrance to the Lincoln Tunnel, stupid schmucks." He laughed briefly before shooting back more scotch, whereupon he cursed bitterly for a few fractured sentences. The pink rollers drummed along the hood, fender, roof, and doors. It was raining again.

"I can't believe you can even chuckle about —"

"Cameras, Garth! They got camenas all

172

over the pwace to watch the traffic backup for the Lincoln Tunnel. I know people who know people. Might just be able to lift the license plate off the video. Too bad it wasn't daylight."

"I thought these types use stolen cars."

I got a disappointed stare from one of his bloody eyes. "Excuse me, Mr. Fwea Market, but just what do you know about *those types?*"

I shrugged.

"Well, I got a question for you, bwother. Just what kind of *types* are you familiar with that wear plaid cummerbunds and dinner jackets to a thumping?"

"Okay, Nicholas, okay." A wind tunnel had been activated in the car wash, droplets racing every which way on the glass.

"You know, mobsters, they don't thteal cars before taking thomeone for a ride. They take the family thedan. They got the juice, not like some Podunk jokers holding up a Piggly Wiggly, you know, those *types*. You ask me? Mummies in plaid cummerbunds are pwetty confident. They had juice."

"Just how — Oh, forget it."

"Out with it."

I gave him a hard look. The whole episode — from Marti's murder to Nicholas getting pummeled — was making me ill. My stomach was in knots. But it was the intellectual and emotional impact of this kind of violence and intimidation that had my mind floundering. I was in danger. Angie was in danger. They knew where I lived. The police were even a threat to me. The scenario was largely foreign and completely repulsive, and my immediate childish reflex was to reach out and stop it like a record on a turntable. Or maybe even spin the record back to the start and never let this wretched song be played.

"Is this what you wanted out of life?" I finally blurted. "Sleazing around bars, getting beat up, being on familiar terms with practices of the world's underbelly? Jeez. You were smart, ambitious . . ."

"I've changed my mind." He laughed bitterly. "*In* with it, big brother. *In* with it."

The watery windshield began to glow brightly as the taxi emerged from the far end of the car wash. "Cabbie? We're gonna duck down here under the seat. No towel dwy. Flip on your Off Duty light, and dwive down Broadway like you're goin' home, 'kay?"

The driver cleared his throat. "That's extra."

"Jeez, I already picked up the car wash. Five bucks, 'kay?"

The driver shrugged. "Yeah."

I lay down on the seat, my unruly hair catching on Nicholas's bristly scalp. "Why are we —"

"If we're being followed, they'll think we thkipped out of the cab in the car wash and ditched them."

"Hmm. Not so dumb, little brother."

"Well, gee whith," Nicholas snickered.

"Sorry. About the lecturing, I mean."

He didn't say anything, for once. If you knew Nicholas, a shrug was about the best response to an apology you could hope for. As we lay there, the streetlights flashed overhead on the cab ceiling, and I was reminded of backyard camping trips we did together when he was seven and I was ten. Headlights from cars passing on the lane would cut through the yard and reflect off the neighbor's side windows, shimmering across the rippling tent roof like aurora borealis. It would be fall — chilly enough, Mom said, so we wouldn't get eaten by mosquitoes or steam like ears of corn in our musty Army-surplus mummy bags. Lots of leaves were still on the trees, but dry and scratching together in the breeze, mimicking the sound of water falling on stone. Wafting leaves would pass across the headlight flickers in oddly shaped shadows.

Nicholas and I would imagine we were in the Yukon, sleeping outside our gold mine (Nicholas's idea), gazing at the northern lights, silhouettes of satellites passing through the glowing dust clouds. We'd talk about the mine, about how deep it was, how we'd have helmets with lights on them, eat nothing but hot dogs, french fries, and milkshakes, have our own jackhammers and use dynamite every day. Back then, Nicholas and I occasionally shared the boundless imagination all youngsters possess. And as brothers we were close primarily because we belonged to and shared the trials and indignities (bow ties, family photos, tea at Aunt Jilly's, dancing lessons) imposed by our parents. But the competitive wedge of the teen years was driven between us, and as older brother I had nothing to say that he cared to hear.

In the cab, I wondered how much if any of the youngster remained in Nicholas, a man seemingly devoid of any innocent past or any wholesome future. Even if there was some feeble morsel left, was that enough to reconstruct a relationship between us? I sensed that he wasn't the same avaricious scoundrel who took such a toll on Dad and Mom. That night he first reappeared —

when we went for a drink and "exchanged words" — even through the wisecracking veneer, I sensed some genuine hurt from my rebuff. And I savored that on the ride home, enjoying the flavor of revenge for what I felt he'd done to our family. He actually listened to me, I affected him, and he seemed to care what I thought. It had been a long time.

And what about Angie? When she castigated him, he seemed to react to the family angle.

I thought about the red, puffy doll head on the seat next to me that was my brother. No longer the young hotshot. I heard him groan slightly from exhaustion and was reminded that I was tired too. Hell, I was flat-out beat, and the streetlights rippling across the cab roof were lulling me to sleep. At that moment I felt there might be a way into Nicholas through all this. Maybe.

Chapter 17

I awoke the next day on Nicholas's couch. Through the open window came the thrum of cars on the Brooklyn Bridge and the faint smell of fish and briny piers. He lived on Water Street near the Fulton Fish Market, and an expansive brick wall at the intersection forms the anchorage to the bridge. I could tell by the slishy sound of tires on the cobblestone pavement below that it was raining. The sky was overcast, and I couldn't judge the time of day. I lay there and recalled arriving at Nicholas's digs. I was so beat that I called Angie and told her I was flopping at my brother's, adding that she shouldn't go anywhere without Otto, a brute of a man known during his wrestling career as the Moscow Mastiff. Kidding, of course. Otto looks like he was the runt of his litter, but I figured that as a gulag graduate, he might actually be able to put up quite a scrap. Ultimately, though, I felt the retros had done all the assaulting they were going to do in one evening. What sense would there be in coming after us again, after the recorded warning?

Nicholas's apartment had a decor familiar to anyone whose mailbox is frequented by Pottery Shed catalogs, although his furnishings were real. That is to say, they were actual twenties to fifties American antiques. Like the genuine Bakelite table radio, the brass wall sconces, the low red armchair with matching ottoman, the green-shaded desk lamp, and the stainless-steel–edged Formica kitchen table. The exception was the couch on which I was sprawled. It was probably from Macy's, and so were the drapes. They matched the dark large floral print. The apartment had a certain amount of style, but like most bachelor pads, it appeared to have been furnished in a hurry. He'd put some money into it, but to my eye, the mix of deco and fifties clashed a bit.

Footsteps were coming up the stairs, and I heard someone stop in front of the door. It opened and Nicholas stepped in, his hair soaked from the rain. His face was still red, but the swelling had gone down. Just not evenly. The baby-doll head had been replaced by the Elephant Man with black eyes. By the next day, he'd probably progress to the Uncle Fester look.

"Where were you?" I sat up.

"Went to my doctor. Brother, you should

see your hair. Look like a mad scientist."

"Have you looked in a mirror, Igor? What doctor?"

"I don't want to name names, but he's a Spanish guy over at the Pathmark drugstore. I mean, what do doctors do but size up your condition and give you pills? Or not, as is more often the case. I go to my amigo, cut out the middleman. I get the good drugs, the real stuff the doctors are too afraid to prescribe. You think there's anything but powdered sugar in Tylenol?" Nicholas ripped open a bag, and several brown prescription bottles rolled around the table.

I figured out for myself that this pharmacist–patient arrangement was illegal and didn't think he needed me to point that out. "Well, at least you're not slurring anymore. So what'd he say?"

"That I look like crap, but in Spanish." He started opening pill bottles.

"What about bleeding, in your brain?"

"Well, Dr. Welby, he concurs that I might want to get an MRI. Good news is I don't need a doctor, I just need an appointment at one of these outfits that do MRIs. He's got a friend named Rodriguez, an MRI technician, that he'll fix me up with. Tech guy reads the scans better than a doctor, says my amigo. Meantime, I got all this great stuff." He tossed back a palmful of pills and chased it with water from a tiki bar mug that had been sitting on the table. His neck was so stiff that he had to bend backward at the knees to accomplish this feat.

"You may not like this, Nicholas, but we had to tell the cops you were at our place when we found Marti."

Nicholas plunked into his red armchair. His one open eye was unfazed. "What'd you tell them, exactly?"

"They asked whether anybody else was there when we found her." I went to the kitchen sink for a glass of water. "We told the detective my brother was there, and he asked for your address. I handed him your card. He didn't notice there was only a PO box on it."

"That explains the message on my service. Tsilzer, wasn't it? I worked with him once. Just so you know, I don't give this address or phone number to anyone." He put his head back and closed his eye. "Feel privileged."

"What now, Nicholas?"

"What now? Well, the way I see it, you've got two choices. One, you join forces with me. Two, you don't."

"What about option three: going to the police and telling them everything?"

"Didn't you tell me last night, before you nodded off, that the retros left you a message warning you not to go to the cops?"

"Seems to me there've been plenty of cases where kidnappers warned their ransomers not to go to the cops, they do anyway, the kidnappers are caught and the victim saved." To be honest, I was back envisioning Steve McGarrett on the job.

Nicholas smirked. "They don't exactly go out of their way to publicize cases where the victim is murdered because of stunts like that. Besides, you're talking about federal cases. You trust this Detective Tsilzer like you would the FBI? I think you're going to have a hard time selling them on the idea that this is all about a TV puppet."

"And if you and I team up? Then what?"

Nicholas shrugged. "We get a message to these guys that we want to know what it will take to get Pipsqueak back. No questions, no hard feelings. A business deal."

"You mean buy him back? What if they want a lot of money?"

"I'm authorized by my client to go as high as $100,000. Client doesn't think they'll bite, though."

"Your client, huh? Look, Nicholas, if I'm going to throw in with you, you've got to tell me everything you know about this, including who your client is."

He was shaking his head. "Not about the client. Some of the rest, maybe. Like what Marti was doing in town. But not the client."

"Okay, what about Marti?"

"I can't tell you about her without giving you some background on Bookerman. Lew Bookerman is General Buster's real name."

I didn't let on that I already knew that. "Really. Okay, Nicholas, please tell your ignorant older brother more."

A sparkle entered his eyes, and I could tell he was bursting at the seams to share the whole story with me.

"I'll give you a teaser. Marti was staff on *The General Buster Show.* When the show was canceled, Bookerman's puppets were deemed property of the station, and though he tried to get them back, his contract had language that was ironclad. The whole concept and all creative materials belonged to the station. The management was a bunch of hard-asses. I mean, they didn't need the puppets, right? Anyway, Bookerman moved to Illinois. He was a hypochondriac with a budding passion for natural-healing techniques that got him into naturopathic medicine. So he opened a small shop selling assorted herbs, books, etc. Came out with a successful line of health snacks. Years pass, the station changes hands, and next thing you know they're clearing out all manner of junk, including the puppets. This was only a few years ago. Marti grabbed Pipsqueak, and two others got Howlie and Possum. Bookerman got wind of this somehow — maybe through a third party, a friend at the station — and went after his old puppet pals. One of the parties gave him Howlie, and he bought Possum from the other. Marti, however, wouldn't sell. Seems she and Bookerman once had a romance, and she still harbored malice for whatever transpired between them. That biker Tyler Loomis had been by her shop before, trying to convince her to sell the puppet to him, virtually begging her at all costs not to sell it to Bookerman."

"How did you come by all this information?" I asked.

"Secret." Nicholas waved a finger. "Let's just say I have an informer in the Church of Jive."

"You have an informer? Then why the hell did you try to recruit my help?"

"The problem with informers is you never

know when they'll be caught. And I have this feeling that Pipsqueak will surface and somehow you'll be there when he does."

"Nicholas, doesn't any of this sound, you know, completely wacko?" I stood up, flapping my arms in frustration. "My brain is spinning in my skull. So tell me: Why did Loomis want a squirrel puppet?"

"I've got theories on that, but I'm not going to say what they are. Anyway, Loomis warns Marti that Bookerman will do anything to get Pipsqueak, but she laughs him off, remembering Bookerman as a wimpy hypochondriac. Well, Pipsqueak is stolen, but she never tells the cops about Bookerman."

"Why?" I asked again.

"I've got theories about that too."

"Like?" I persisted.

Nicholas thought about that a moment and then shrugged. "I think she intended to shake him down. That's what she was doing in New York. Apparently, she sent a veiled threat to him through his health-food company."

I blinked. "General Buster is in New York?"

"Maybe."

I blinked some more. "Buster is with the retros?"

"Well, let's put it this way: Scuppy

185

Milner is his nephew and sole heir to Bookerman's budding fortune."

"Really? Then what are all these people really after? I mean, if Bookerman — or Scuppy — is psychotic, that's one thing. But now there are gangs in plaid cummerbunds and mummy wrap beating people up, a whole religious movement, all to protect Pipsqueak. It's nuts!"

One of Nicholas's black eyes widened. "Seems to me you know more about all this than you let on, brother."

I grinned. "Sure, and I'll tell you all about it once you tell me what your client has to do with all this. From my vantage, you're a joker in this deck."

Nicholas's eye closed. "Can't."

I started putting on my shoes. "I won't trust you unless you trust me. Doesn't sound like this is a good idea."

"My client pays for anonymity. That's a trust I have to keep. How could you trust *me* if I didn't?"

"Yeah, but your client probably knows why these retro people want the puppet." I put on my pinstripe jacket. "I mean, there's something about Pipsqueak, something other than the fact that he was a local kid-show hero. Come on, Nicholas, he's not worth $100,000."

Nicholas didn't say anything. He just peered at his knees, deep in thought. I headed for the door, but before I got out, Nicholas piped up.

"Is that the suit you wrestled away from the Salvation Army in the nude?"

"Yup."

"Thought so." He grabbed a notepad and jotted something down. "What are you going to do now, Garth?"

"I stand to gain nothing and lose everything by sticking my nose any further into this. It's no longer about Pipsqueak, it's about murder. These people play too rough. Angie and I are going to the cops, like any sane person would do, and let them sort it out."

"And if they ask where they can reach me?"

"We've got to tell them everything."

"Great." He sighed. "Look, here's my cell number." He handed over a yellow square of paper and gestured to one of those tiny black phones that clip to your belt. "Give the number to the cops if you want, though I'm hoping you'll call and tell me you've changed your mind. And do your little brother a favor? One little favor? Discuss this plan with your lawyer first."

Chapter 18

And so it was that we called upon our lawyer, Roger Elk. We found him dressed pretty much as I'd seen him last: suede cowboy boots, bolo tie, white western-cut shirt, corduroy jacket. His office was on the eighth floor of a narrow, dingy, industrial building, three floors of which still housed an artificial Christmas-tree factory. The elevator was more along the lines of a dumb-waiter, the unautomated kind that requires the elevator operator to physically heave on a cable to set the counterweight in motion. On the eighth floor, however, we discovered a neatly painted hallway lined with pebbled-glass doors, and we located the one stenciled *Roger Elk, Atty.* His two-room office had dark paneling, ceiling fans, and dusky wood furniture. Everything was old and worn but very tidy. A law degree from Northwestern, various Chicago civic awards, and a testimonial of some kind from the Aurora Corporation adorned his stately walls.

Angie, Otto, and I sat in an array of cushioned straight-backed chairs, the kind upholstered in old red leather and decorative bronze nails. Roger Elk sat calmly in his oak four-caster desk chair, hands folded over his potbelly and concentration wrinkling his brow. As he had instructed, I related the story from top to bottom, ending with: "And so here we are."

"Interesting story, and it's good you came to me first." There was something utterly reassuring in his manner, the propounder of conservative advice.

"My advice" — he loosed a broad, wise smile — "is *not* to go to the police."

I was confused. "But I don't get it, what about —"

"If they come to you, call me and we'll arrange to talk to them together."

"But —"

"What would you tell them, Garth? What you *know?* In point of fact, you don't *know* anything. You *suspect* many things. But the police have no interest in what *you* suspect. You don't know firsthand that the dead woman on your stoop was Marti Folsom, and even if you did, that doesn't have any direct connection to these retrophiles. You've not seen the 'Cola Woman' in their company and you have nothing to indicate that the retrophiles have anything to do with that puppet. You don't even know whether the puppet was the impetus for the Tiny Timeless Treasures murder. The anonymous threat on your phone machine will hardly impress them."

"What should we do?" Angie threw up her hands.

"My advice, Angie, is to steer clear of both the retrophiles and the police. Go near the jive crowd again and they may harm you. Go to the police with your suspicions about a puppet? Preposterous, and if the police discover that you are, however obliquely, attached to two murders, they will become suspicious. Forget about this whole episode, stop looking for the puppet, and go back to your normal lives. If you were being threatened, I can't see why those responsible would object and bring any physical harm on you."

"You think we can just do that and it'll be all over?" I laughed, slightly giddy at the prospect.

Roger Elk crossed his weathered brown hands on his blotter and leaned forward. "I believe so. Let's just hope the police don't approach you again. Now, I wouldn't want to be one to meddle in your family affairs, but your brother's involvement in this isn't helping you any. It seems to me that he's demonstrated poor judgment in dealing with some pretty rough characters. My advice to you would be to avoid him, at least until he's off this case."

"Exactly." I nodded enthusiastically, glancing Angie's way. "He's always been trouble."

We all shook his hand (Otto hugged him) and departed with spirits raised.

"Eetz good? No KGB? Eh?"

"That's right, Otto." I looked at Angie, and for the moment, anyway, she seemed resigned to let this puzzle remain unsolved.

"Maybe the police will figure it all out." Angie chuckled. "I mean, these retros are bound to step out of line again and get caught, right?"

"Sure." I shrugged. "It was a bit of an adventure, what with infiltrating the Church of Jive, huh?"

"Ah! Garv, Yan-gie, we must to go lunch, eh? Cey-ley-bration, yes?"

"Not a bad idea, Otto." I slapped him on the shoulder. We went over to a place on 22nd Street for haystack onion rings and beer.

Chapter 19

Two days later and all was well. My Brooklyn film rental was a wrap, and subsequent to that I'd sold the bison head (from the bedroom) and steer longhorns to a new bar opening where the Barbed Wire used to be. The former joint had been closed down for serving to underage kids, and the new place seemed intent on following the western theme of the former, probably to wrangle the same element to soil my doorstep once more. *Bull's Balls*, the new sign read.

Stuart Sharp had called again, and I had yet to visit New Hope to look at his giant weevil. I had been busy working with the Nassau County Science Museum to supply it with snakes for dioramas, which had me putting in calls to contacts in the Southwest. Diamondback rattlers and pit vipers are a cinch, but coming up with a scarlet king snake and either a western or eastern coral snake was proving to be a problem. They particularly wanted those two because they look very much alike, yet only the coral snakes are poisonous. It's one of those wacky natural-selection manifestations, like the monarch and viceroy butterflies, that make good visual aids. The two snakes are usually about the same sub-thirty-inch length, and both are variably striped with yellow, red, and black. But they aren't difficult to tell apart. Some prefer all manner of memory aids, like "Red touch yellow, kill a fellow." Or "Two-color tail, run like hell." However, I've never had any trouble identifying the one with the black nose as a coral snake. "Black = death." (By the way, a scarlet snake has a red nose. "Rudolph that wriggles, gives me the giggles.")

Lorna Ellison, my snake gal in Phoenix, had referred me to half a dozen people, and I'd resorted to looking for dead specimens that I could have mounted. Pete Durban, a guy I know from U.S. Fish and Wildlife, collects poisonous critters and owns a couple of corals, but I doubted very much whether he'd let me stuff one of his prized pets. I found myself calling Dade County Animal Control agents, asking if they'd had any calls to dispose of eastern coral snakes. Nope, just nuisance gators, the stray saltwater croc, and a pit bull or three. Hadn't had a snake call since a boa strangled its owner, an off-duty carnival performer called Sheena the Viper Girl. Texas has the next highest incidence of bites from corals, and I was about to ring up the San Antonio Animal Shelter when the front buzzer sounded.

As you can see, life was back to normal at our abode, and I was glad of it. My foibles were under control and I felt comfortably on track to forget all about General Buster and his pals. Even a hopelessly nostalgic dealer like me can be scared straight by a dead woman on his doorstep and his brother used as a punching bag.

The buzzer sounded again. It was about ten in the morning. Angie was up at Acme Crafts buying a hand piece for her flexible shaft and draw plates, which in itself wouldn't take long except she and Katie the salesperson talk a blue streak. Otto had gone to get his uniform for a part-time job selling hot dogs at Grand Central Terminal. "Veemin, milliontz of veemin, Garv! They go to verk, very much hurry, walk fest, eh? Veemin walkink fest: very nice, eh?" I think a Victoria's Secret catalog would put Otto into an orgasmic coma.

The day was sunny, but cool and breezy like the best of October days. The worst are rainy, cold autumn days when you realize May is the light at the end of winter's long tunnel. Most Americans seemed to have pumpkins on their porches, leaf piles burning in their gutters, and Thanksgiving on their minds.

"Who is it?" I hollered into the squawk box.

"Open up! Hurry," the box crackled back.

Boy, the Jehovah's Witnesses could be so pushy. "Who is this?"

"Dammit, open up, Carson. Please!" It was a high, wheezy voice, but I couldn't tell whether it was male or female.

"Not unless I know you."

"You don't know me, but I have an urgent package for you."

This was over the top even for a Witness, and the voice sounded earnestly troubled. So I went into the hallway and opened the vestibule door. Before me stood a soft-looking man with thick white hair, a narrow jaw, white eyebrows, and pale eyelashes, pale skin, full lips, and dark eyes. Not an albino, but definitely at the far end of the spectrum from George Hamilton. He had on a baggy beige suit, black shirt, thin tie, and two-tone shoes. A Panama hat was clutched in one hand, a wicker basket under the other. The basket was filled with crumpled paper and looked like a small wastebasket.

"Can I help you?" I picked up my mail from atop the radiator in the foyer as I watched him mop his brow with a polka-dot hanky.

He thrust the wastebasket to my chest. "Take this. Big risk, but there's nothing for it." He spoke quite loudly. "We've got to get it to safety. You know a man named Palihnic?"

I looked from the wastebasket in my hands up to the stranger. "What is this?"

Whitey peered up and down the block, looking to see if he had been followed.

"Don't be ridiculous. You have what you wanted. Is there a back way out of here?"

"Whoa!" I barred the way into the hall with my arm. "You're going to have to do some explaining before I show you the back way out. Now, calm down and tell me what this is all about."

"Can I at least come in, have a glass of water? I have to hurry back before they notice it's gone."

I considered a moment and thought it unlikely that Whitey had the gumption or the wherewithal to cause me much trouble. "Awright."

Whitey was momentarily flummoxed by the number of animals staring at him when he came into our living room — not an uncommon reaction. I've known people who can't sleep with a room full of taxidermy staring at them. He perched on a stool at the soda counter while I fetched water.

"You kill all these?" he mumbled nervously.

"I collect, rent, sell . . . here." I plunked down the glass and he drank greedily, eyeing all the birds of prey hanging from the ceiling. I noticed an envelope in the mail pile addressed to me that wasn't a bill and picked it out for closer examination. I felt a wallet-sized card inside. Probably my new bank card, I thought. "So, Mr. . . . ?"

"Sloan."

"Mr. Sloan, why have you brought me a wicker waste bin?"

"Don't be stupid, please, Carson," he gasped between chugalugs.

It was then that I saw among the crumpled paper what appeared to be an eye. Stuffing the envelope in my pocket, I stirred the papers in the basket, uncovering two bulging eyes. I shuddered, then spilled the paper onto the counter. Out tumbled Pipsqueak.

Yeah, I was a little surprised, and I think I said something like "Yak!" I gently slid a hand under the puppet and picked him up. He was surprisingly light, especially the head. I held the little black sticks to his hands and made his paws wiggle. Up close, I could see how much hair had been lost over the years and how his tail had probably been replaced at some point. His goggle eyes were actually purple painted pupils on a yellowed white plastic base. The India-rubber red tongue sticking out the side of his mouth was dried and cracked. The buckteeth were real but outsize for a squirrel, perhaps lower incisors from a deer or elk. A string on the back manipulated his mouth, and when I pulled it, the mouth fell open. I could see that the black elastic in the back of his mouth had broken many years ago. Pipsqueak's white belly fur was yellowed, and the whole pelt was in need of cleaning. He smelled strongly of mothballs.

It was hard to believe. Pipsqueak, in my hands! I wanted to savor the moment, and yet, to be honest, actually having him in my possession wasn't as satisfying as I would have thought. The emotion was a little . . . sad. Pipsqueak demystified?

And of course, after Marti's murder and Nicholas's run-in, I was a little scared at being dragged back into the retro imbroglio. Just days ago, I was after Pipsqueak. *Now he was after me.*

My thoughts and emotions tumbled over each other, but I managed to get the crucial question out first.

"What's so important about Pipsqueak the Nutty Nut?"

The look I got was vexed. "Don't toy with me, Carson. Surely you came looking for the puppet for the same reasons as Loomis."

I leaned in close to Whitey's face. "I'm outside the loop, Sloan. Tell me: What's with the squirrel?"

"It's Bookerman. He needs it. For the Church." Whitey was getting testy.

It took me a moment to register. "Fine, I can see why Bookerman wants his little pal Pipsqueak to comfort him in his later years. But what does the Church want with him? If it's not just a puppet, tell me what it is!"

I handed him another glass of water, and after he'd taken a long sip, he gave me a stern, penetrating gaze, the white eyebrows taut. I'd seen these Perry Mason eyes before, heard the loud squeeze-box voice, and I took a step back when I realized where. I probably made another one of my erudite exclamations, like *Gak!*

"You're Cola Woman!"

His eyes narrowed, but he said nothing.

"The woman at T3! But you're not a woman. You were dressed up like a woman!"

His eyes rolled slightly. "Got a problem with that?"

"You killed Tyler Loomis to get the squirrel! And I saw you at the Church of Jive the night Marti Folsom was murdered."

"Chill out!" Whitey wheezed. "Loomis was after the squirrel to stop Bookerman. He'd been trying to get Pipsqueak, the last puppet, just like me. I got there first, but you happened by, started fucking around with that penguin. It's your fault Loomis is dead. Well, his too. If you'd both just minded your own damn business . . ."

"What did he want with Pipsqueak?"

"You really don't get any of this, do you? This was a mistake. . . ." He got up and reached for Pipsqueak. I pulled the squirrel out of reach.

"Why did you bring me Pipsqueak, anyway?"

Whitey's gaze hardened. "A mutual friend said I should bring it to you and that you'd get it to Nicholas. I thought you understood."

"What mutual friend?"

"*Someone on the inside*, inside the Church, that's all."

Could this be Nicholas's informer? "Why do you want Palihnic to have him?"

"He's with the naturopaths, of course."

"Naturopaths?" I snapped my fingers. "Loomis, he had a tuning fork. He was a sonopuncturist, which means he was a naturopath, right? Okay, so you killed him to keep the squirrel from the naturopaths. Now you've had a change of heart and want to *give* Pipsqueak to them? Why?" I wasn't entirely sure what the heck I was talking about. Naturopaths? Puppet healing? Lamb Chop for lumbago, Beany & Cecil for neuritis?

Sloan's gaze drifted to someplace far away. "I thought . . . I used to think that Scuppy was on a righteous path. But now I know better. I thought you did too. The Church doesn't mean to free anybody. They just want to be the slave master!" Sloan's white eyebrows pinched together, sweat running down his cheeks. "I'll take that squirrel now, Carson." I could tell from his deportment that he didn't feel the matter was open to discussion.

Sloan was standing at the end of the soda bar, and I was behind it. No way out unless I jumped the bar, which I could do, but probably not fast enough to escape.

"So who'll you give him to now?"

"Most likely? The river. I can't find Palihnic, and if you don't understand any of this, it's obvious Palihnic couldn't trust you. So how can I trust you? You'd probably call the police. Then the NSA would get him. It can't go back to Bookerman." Sloan produced a sleek black pistol, as I was afraid he might.

The NSA? I could see myself asking Dudley if he knew why the government would want a squirrel puppet, only to hear his evasive mumblings because he'd personally worked on Ronald Reagan's billion-dollar Secret Squirrel Initiative.

"Hand it over, Carson. I'll do you like Loomis if I have to."

The Nutty Nut to be forever interred in the ooze of the East River? The child inside me wouldn't let go of Pipsqueak for anything. So when the adult handed it over, Sloan had to struggle to pull it from my grasp.

"Let go!" he wheezed.

"Sorry! Reflex," I mumbled, and let go. I wasn't as sorry as you might have thought. Having held him in my hands, having felt that fur, seen the cracked tongue — getting Pipsqueak back seemed somehow more possible once I'd actually held him.

Sloan backed to the door. "Better for

you, Carson. You don't want any part of this."

"That's what I keep saying." I flapped my arms helplessly.

He reached a hand back for the door-knob, just as a small man in a red and white striped jacket and cherry-red fez shouldered the door open from without. The door slammed Sloan's arm, which spun him around and flung Pipsqueak into the air. Sloan stumbled back, facing hot-dog man extraordinaire: Otto.

From that moment on, I abandoned the remotest inclination to buy a Rottweiler. Otto was surprised, but swiftly registered the gun, reacted, and lunged headlong at Sloan's neck, yelling, "Aiee!"

Sloan fell back, Otto on top of him, the gun waving in the air. A shot went off, a puff of feathers drifted off an owl over-head.

I saw Pipsqueak bounce off Fred the lion and hit the floor, the puppet's bulging eyes imploring me to come save him from Howlie and Possum. I also saw my chance to wrestle the dangerous gun from Sloan's extended hand. I hesitated.

Sloan hit Otto in the back of the head with the flat of the gun. That's when the attack dog made his coup de grâce. Otto slammed his forehead into Sloan's, the latter went limp, and I lunged for and snatched away the gun.

Otto got to his feet slowly, forcing a smile and rubbing the back of his neck.

"KGB *pizdyets, nah holidyets,* Garv."

Chapter 20

After dusting off Pipsqueak, I picked up the phone to call the police but heard Roger Elk's admonition echo in my brain. I called him first. He wasn't in, so I left an urgent message with his service.

"Now what'll I do?" I groaned, holding Sloan's gun by the barrel. Sloan was on his back, partially conscious, trying to blink his eyes open while Otto bound his hands behind his back with clear plastic packing tape.

"I dunno, Garv. Police, maybe, eh?"

"Okay, so I call the police and tell them this is the guy who shot Loomis, here's the gun." I nodded. "Right? This is probably the gun that killed Loomis. Of course, I'm holding the gun, it's got my prints on it now, and the police are sure I was there. They still might think I killed Loomis. And Marti, she's dead and can't identify Cola Boy Sloan. Now it's just my story, in which I say Sloan, disguised as a farm girl, struggled with and shot Loomis to steal a puppet and that Sloan may well have killed

Marti, or at least may know who did it."

"But why Garv kill Loomis?" Otto stood, satisfied that Cola Boy Sloan was well secured, and picked up his red fez. It said *Wiener King* across the front.

I handed Otto an ice pack for the back of his neck. "If I don't call the police, I'm obstructing justice, I'm harboring a fugitive or something . . ."

"I smoke." Otto slouched out the back door.

The phone rang. It was Roger Elk, and I explained the Sloan episode.

"Garth, don't do anything until I get there." He hung up before I could ask whether I should call the cops.

Sloan started to wriggle and cough and rolled onto his stomach with a low moan.

I looked Pipsqueak hard in the eyes. Obviously, there was more to this puppet than could be seen at first glance. Maybe something inside his head? There wasn't room anywhere else to hide something. The rest of him was just pelt, and I couldn't feel anything out of the ordinary there. But the back of his head had heavy stitching through the fur, and it had obviously been done hastily. It would have to be carefully cut so as not to damage the pelt further. Squeezing his head lightly, I tried to discern what might be inside, but under a layer of batting I felt only a hard, uniform core. The thought of cutting open his head made me slightly dizzy, but it seemed the only way to figure out what all this was about, since nobody would tell me. And ultimately, it was probably the best way to save Pipsqueak himself. The sooner his head was emptied, separated from whatever the contraband was, the sooner they'd stop chasing him. And, of course, the better chance I'd have of holding on to the squirrel.

But I was still conflicted, and mostly preoccupied with hiding Pipsqueak until I could get rid of Sloan. Lord knew who might pop through the door next.

I don't have a wall safe, but there are some loose floorboards in the living room that open into a cavity under the floor. Sloan was on the other side of the couch and his view was blocked, unless he could see through the narrow space under the couch. So I nestled Pipsqueak in a dish towel, wheeled my lion Fred off the carpet, lifted the boards with a butter knife, and wedged the puppet between the joists. As an afterthought, I tucked the gun in with him. It seemed a particularly sinister tableau. Squirrel puppet and a gun. From the way things were going, I'd have said Pip-squeak was the more dangerous of the two. With the floorboards back in place, I rolled out the carpet and wheeled Fred back into place atop the squirrel's hideaway.

The buzzer sounded. Roger Elk must not have been far off when he called. I buzzed the front door, and a moment later the apartment door swung open. It wasn't Roger.

"Well, howdy do?" Bing intoned, smirking at his friend Bowler as they entered. Bing was in a yellow sweater and bow tie, the skimmer tilted rakishly on his head. Bowler was still in his Lucky's Speed Shop shirt.

Great. More pistols, but mine (Sloan's) was under the floor. Like I would have done anything with it.

"Where's the puppet, son?" Bing sniffed.

"Not here," I said, hands half raised.

"Where?" Bowler prodded. His nasal voice sounded like the one on my message machine.

I thought a second. "Not here. If I do lead you to him, I need to be sure you won't kill me."

Bing adjusted his skimmer and ex-changed glances with Bowler.

"Let's go, champ." Bowler helped Sloan to his feet and shoved him out the door.

"After you, sport." Bing waved his gun at me. "We're going to take in the sights from your convertible. Top up, don'tcha know."

My Rottweiler was still out back, probably on his second smoke. I could only hope he wouldn't come barging into the room and get shot. And thank the Lord for the Acme Crafts yak sessions with Katie for keeping Angie away while this was going on. At least Roger Elk was on his way and knew the score. Between him and the cops, and maybe Nicholas, they might just find me. Assuming these guys didn't mean to kill me. Ransom? Me for Pipsqueak? They obviously knew Nicholas, but did they know he was my brother? I guessed not, so I wasn't sure whether they thought there was any leverage there for ransom. Ultimately, I think they grabbed me because they didn't think I was telling the truth and were going to question me further. Torture? I shuddered, turning my thoughts away from soldering irons and hobby tools.

Outside, I unlocked the doors to the Lincoln. Bowler shoved Sloan in the backseat, pushed him over, and got in behind the driver's seat so he could keep a gun on me. Bing rode shotgun — or pistol, to be more precise. I drove, and moments later we

209

were approaching the West Side Highway.

"Let's try south," Bing suggested. "Take the West Side to Battery Place, what say?"

I didn't say anything for a while, busy formulating escape possibilities, like bailing out of a car going thirty miles per hour or running a light in front of a cop to get pulled over. I didn't much care for the possibility that I might run myself over with the back wheels in the first scheme (probably wrecking the Lincoln), and the second was a long shot that would require finding a cop when you need one. I'll stick to lottery tickets. And then there was the really extreme option of orchestrating a head-on collision with a light pole. I was wearing my seat belt, but my guests weren't. That would have the advantage of sending Bing into the windshield, but the disadvantage of throwing Bowler on top of me with his gun. The doors would likely pin shut from the fenders shunting back, and I'd be stuck, unless the top popped open. Too much room for error, and besides, I hated the idea of wrecking the Lincoln.

"So where are you taking me?" I thought I might as well ask.

Bing's pistol sat in his lap as he stuffed Captain Black in his pipe. "Just drive, junior. We'll ask the questions." And they might as well not answer mine. "Take the left lane."

At Battery, we weaved around into the Wall Street district, which just prior to noon isn't overly busy with pedestrians, though by lunch the streets are swarming with humans on the feed. But delivery trucks cause minor backups on the narrow streets, which in combination with an infuriating number of one-way streets that always seem to be going the way you aren't cost us a good fifteen minutes getting four blocks over to William Street approaching Hanover Square. Not that I was complaining; the longer the better. Though in that whole time, I didn't see one good opportunity to make my escape. And not one cop.

"Make a Ricky." Bing pointed right, and I made the turn. "This driveway."

I stuck the Lincoln's nose into a narrow drive facing a garage door in the wall of a building. A plaque by the door said BANK OF IRAN. Bing got out, went to a squawk box next to the door, pushed a button, and spoke into it. The door opened and I drove the Lincoln into a low-ceilinged, circular, pale-green room. Bing walked in after us and the garage door clattered shut. The room jolted, there was a loud whirring sound, the grind of chains and the click of gears. We were going down in an elevator.

"Bank of Iran?" I said over my shoulder.

"We're no terrorists, if that's what you're thinkin'," Bowler sneered. "The Iranians, they don't use this place no more. This is a frozen asset."

I believe we sank two stories before the elevator clanked down to earth and a wall to our right rolled open. The room began to revolve toward the opening so that the Lincoln would be able to drive out. When it stopped revolving, Bing made like an airline-tarmac jockey and guided me to a parking space among a bunch of other vintage cars, mostly older than mine. The Chrysler sedan from T3 was among them.

While these sorts of vehicular transports may sound exotic, New York's parking garages — especially those in cramped quarters — have all manner of mechanical space-saving means to carry cars from street level to another elevation. Parking is such a commodity in Manhattan that people actually buy co-op parking spaces: patches of asphalt ten by sixteen feet. Elevators like the one at the Bank of Iran maximize the number of units for the developer. And for a bank, this lift had the added purpose of affording a secure egress for armored cars.

I parked the Lincoln next to a bulbous black Studebaker, and when I got out I realized my knees had gone a little wobbly on me. I was scared, but no less ready to bolt at any opportunity. At the moment, though, the only course of action seemed a bit of levity.

"Is this where they keep Lenin's brain?"

Bing and Bowler knit brows at each other, and finally the latter mumbled, "I thought Chapman blew Lennon's brains all over the Dakota."

Hangdog Sloan finally spoke.

"Listen, fellas, you gotta understand, Bookerman is nuts. You know what he's trying to do?"

Bing slapped him hard in the face and grinned. That was the end of that.

The basement corridor had pipes all over the ceiling giving off the ping and hiss of a nearby steam-heat plant. We reached a stairwell and went up one flight into a wood-paneled hall with fluorescent lighting. Pushing through swing doors marked GYMNASIUM, we passed into a white tile locker room, at the end of which were linoleum swing doors marked BATHS. They swung open, and in walked Vito.

Bowler put a hand on my chest. "Wait here." He handed his gun to Vito and followed Bing and Sloan through the BATHS doors.

I stared at Vito, who had the pistol trained on my chest. He was wearing a bowling shirt — you got it, identical to Bowler's. Uniform of the day. He was chewing gum so hard that he was working up a sweat on his shiny shaved head. Before I said something ridiculous, like how surprised I was, or how maybe he ought to let me go for old times' sake, he held up a hand to quiet me and took a step closer. His eyes were rimmed red, and he seemed under a tremendous strain.

"What happened?" he whispered hoarsely.

I shrugged. "Huhn?"

"Sloan brought you Pipsqueak. What happened?"

"Well, for starters, he pulled a gun on me, and so Otto came in and . . . well, we got Sloan taken care of when . . . I dunno why I should be telling you any of this."

"Garth, you gotta tell me where Pipsqueak is."

For some reason it hit me particularly hard, at that very moment, how absurd that sounded. I laughed and looked at the ceiling. I didn't even know how to answer that.

"Suddenly, after thirty-five years, every-body wants to know where Pipsqueak the Nutty Nut is, like it's the most important thing in the world where this third-rate puppet —"

"Look, Garth, I'm Nicholas's informant. You need to tell me where it is so they don't get it. Wherever you put it, it's not safe from them."

"Gee," I quipped. "Let me guess? You're a naturopath?"

Vito winced, seeing he wasn't getting anywhere.

"Look, Vito, I'm not telling anybody anything *until someone tells me something.* Like, what do naturopaths have to do with any of this?"

"Garth, they can't get hold of Pipsqueak again," he gulped. "It would give them the power to completely alter our society. They're fundamentalists, isolationists who want to turn the clock back, shun tech-nology and the information age. The spheres can't fall into the wrong hands — or any hands. The spheres must be de-stroyed."

"Spheres?"

Vito didn't get a chance to answer. Bing burst back through the doors, latched on to my arm, and dragged me into the baths.

A row of tile tubs was on my left, matching showers on my right. Dead ahead was Bowler, holding a gun on Sloan. It was muggy, and the place smelled like a root cellar. Pipes lining the left wall were attached to the tubs, which were filled with mud the consistency of giblet gravy. Wet, flatulent burps rose up in gloppy bubbles.

I unbuttoned my sport coat and pushed up my sleeves. Bing slapped a hand on my shoulder and turned me toward one of the tubs. I glared back at Bing with a quizzical eye. "What?"

I looked around and suddenly noticed two eyes in the tub of mud before me. Then the outline of a slathered bald head and shoulders jutting from the steaming gunk. A hand emerged, picked up a dirty washcloth, and drew it across the mouth to reveal pink lips. The eyes focused on Sloan.

"After all we've been through, you gave Pipsqueak back to the naturopaths?" I assumed that this must be Bookerman, but without General Buster's white mutton-chops and a pith helmet topped by a red parrot, I couldn't be sure. His voice didn't have the animated, announcer's bass that I remembered as a child.

Sloan's eyes were red with tears. He tried

to keep the sobs out of his voice. "What you're doing isn't right, I tell you! They use color, you use sound, and everybody loses!" He turned to Bing. "It's not about the music or nicotine! It's about the spheres."

"Enough," Mud Man barked. "Give him a bath."

Bowler and Bing hustled Sloan over to the next tub and, after a brief tussle, pitched him headlong into the mud, his hands still tied behind his back. Spatter flew from the tub, Sloan's sobs of panic burst from gooey bubbles, the tan of his suit quickly disappeared. I got a glance at Bookerman, his head turned from the fracas to keep mud out of his eyes.

Bing and Bowler backed across the narrow room away from the erupting mud tub, eyes averted, arms over their faces, and before me lay an open path to the door. Heart tight as a fist in my throat, I took two big strides, slipped on the mud, and pitched headlong toward the door. Behind me I heard a shout.

I bumped into the door and pulled myself onto my knees. Bookerman, a pillar of barking mud, was standing in his tub. He was pointing at me but yelling at Bing and Bowler. They were on the floor, trying to scramble to their feet. I skittered out into the locker room. My ears pounding, I ran toward the Exit sign and into the paneled hallway.

Bing and Bowler burst through the doors behind me, and I dashed around the corner, then up a flight of stairs and down another hall until I thrust through a set of swinging doors into an office area full of people. A woman in a funny little winged hat and a Speed Shop bowling shirt sat at a green monochrome computer monitor, typing. A man in round specs, slicked-back hair, and Speed Shop bowling shirt worked with colored markers on a poster at a drafting table. A hairy, bullnecked man in a Speed Shop bowling shirt was in a heated conversation on the phone. In a glassed booth filled with recording equipment were technicians — in bowling shirts with the red dice — making CDs and cassettes, the attached recording studio empty except for mics and music stands. Checkers, that professor or whatever from the Church of Jive, was there in his trademark suit, pouring himself a cup of coffee. They all went slack-jawed at my sudden appearance, and I vaulted over a low partition, aiming at an Exit sign on the other side of the room where sunlight spread under the door. Poster Boy lunged at me as I passed, but I shunted him off with my shoulder.

Past the doors was a wide, short staircase down to the building's street exit. There were two red-diced greasers guarding the glass doors, one sitting casually on the desk corner and the other leaning back in a chair at the desk. I had the advantage of surprise and was determined to use it. Instead of trying to skirt around them, I ran right toward the desk, screeching like a chimp on fire.

The one leaning in the chair fell back, tipping over a plant behind him. One down.

The other, unfortunately, sprang up and fumbled for his gun. I grabbed a brass lamp from the desk and flung it at him as I ran to the door. From the corner of my eye, I saw him dodge to one side. The shatter and clang told me the lamp had hit the marble wall. But it delayed his gun grab long enough that I made it to the doors.

They were locked, and I hit them like a bug on a windshield, a muddy brown smear. Office workers strolling to lunch outside looked up in mild alarm at my spattered shouting and pounding visage.

The driver of a cab across the street gave me an annoyed glance from behind his newspaper. A terrier heading for a hydrant ten feet from me darted away, his owner dragging him to the other side of the street.

"Mr. Carson, please —"

I spun around, stomach acid stinging my tongue and adrenaline blurring my vision. A crowd had gathered behind me on the staircase, a big gang of menacing people in black bowling shirts. It was like league night gone terribly wrong. The greasers had guns drawn, and Bing and Bowler stood glowering next to them. Checkers parted the crowd and approached. He crouched down next to where I'd slumped to the floor.

"There's no way out, Garth, but there's also no need to panic. Calm down, breathe easy, nobody is going to hurt you, we just want to talk to you, that's all."

"What about Sloan?" I gasped.

"He's fine, Garth. He just had a little accident, but he's better now. Come on, let's get you cleaned up, a shower perhaps, then we can talk and work this whole thing out." He chuckled, all friendly-like. "Boys, help Mr. Carson to his feet, all righty?"

I looked back out the doors as they

stood me up, taking a last grasp at hope that somebody out there would help me. The cab zoomed away, and I felt a sudden pain in my shoulder where one of the greasers was holding me.

And just before I went beddy-bye, I caught the fuzzy image of Roger Elk holding a syringe.

Chapter 21

It took me a while to make out that the bright light overhead was a bare lightbulb and not the sun or some alien abductors descending on me. I had no idea how long I'd been out or where I was. On a bunk in a windowless cinder-block storeroom. I rolled over to the wall, my consciousness still full of glue so palpable that my mouth felt like I had just drunk Elmer's. My eyes had no compunction to stay open, and I think I slept for a while before waking again, this time more definitively. Proof positive, I sat up and looked down at my shoes, then my pants, and then my shirt and suspenders. They'd cleaned me up and changed my clothes. I was now dressed in one of their Lucky's Speed Shop bowling shirts, baggy gray slacks with cuffs, argyle socks, and oxblood leather shoes. So much for the serenity of my sport coat, oxford shirt, chinos, and sneakers uniform. I looked ridiculous, of course, but reasoned retro clothes were the only kind they had around. I noted my wallet and the contents of my pockets in a plastic bucket by the bed.

They had been thoroughly searched.

While I suppose I should have felt betrayed, I felt mostly like a fool. It all made sense now. Well, sort of. Pretty big coincidence that Elk just happened by at the police barracks out there in Jersey, huh? Or, gee, could it have been that "Cola Woman" Sloan reported back to his superiors that there was a witness, and Roger swept in to do a little damage control? I suppose it turned out quite conveniently for the retro barrister that he could pull my strings from day one. My squirrelly friend and I were two of a kind: puppets. You might think being played for a fool would make me ashamed. What it did was fill me with resentment, anger, and, ultimately, resolve.

I looked beyond my shoes at the bucket. I picked it up and started to paw through my effects, numbly putting my credit cards, license, and registration back into my bifold. I picked up the *Palihnic Insurance Investigations* pen, eyed it thoughtfully, and clipped it into my shirt pocket. It must have been in my jacket, still there from our late-night car ride out to Brooklyn. I wondered briefly if Nicholas still looked like Uncle Fester and where his search for Cola Woman Sloan might have led him. Then I scooped out the change and picked up the envelope, the one I'd stuffed in my pocket before leaving home. It had been opened, and inside was a short letter, a wallet-sized blue card, and a small foil packet emblazoned with the words *FREE GIFT!* This was not my new bank card. The letter read:

Welcome to the Dudco™ Shoppers Club! Enclosed is your membership card, which . . . I tossed the letter aside. Just what I needed, junk mail in jail.

I got to thinking, and picked up the letter again. There was the symbol of a songbird at the top.

. . . entitles you to an electrifying array of discounts at local retailers displaying our emblem. Nobody wants to pay more than they have to, and this card is your self-defense against paying full retail. Each card is personalized and contains your secret code. Dudco™ is proud to be able to offer you this service and the security of knowing that we will protect your personal information from junk-mail lists. So enjoy the benefits of your membership, and with just two strokes of the card free yourself from the onslaught of price gouging like one, two, three. FREE! Also, please find enclosed the therapeutic shoe magnet insoles, free with this introductory offer! Put them in your shoes and enjoy immediate satisfaction and the therapeutic PROTECTION these magnets provide!

The postmark was New York, the song-bird cartoon at the top, *Dudco* — this was Dudley's handiwork.

I ripped open the foil packet and found two small brown plastic semicircles that felt like floppy refrigerator magnets. Didn't look very high-tech, but I dutifully took off my shoes and inserted them at the heels. After relacing the shoes, I stood up and found the insoles comfortable enough.

I picked up the blue card and held it up to the light. It wasn't completely opaque, and I could make out a matrix of micro-electronics under and around the magnetic strip. The card was so small and thin, I wondered if even Dudley could have packed a punch in such a small thingamabob. Then again, you hear tell of the inquisitive types who get electrocuted by tinkering with the innards of disposable flash cameras. And his little antitheft devices packed quite a wallop.

If the Dudco™ Card really was a weapon, I'd have to test it. I debated what to try zapping with the card. I decided against the lightbulb, not knowing what would happen if I put a static charge into a 120-volt AC system. An electrician I'm not, but for all I knew, the card might backfire. Likewise, I also decided against my bed frame, unsure of whether there was some taboo against metal-zapping. I mean, assuming it was like other Dudley products, it was meant to zonk people. I wondered how it was the card wouldn't buzz *me*, but reasoned it might have something to do with the insoles, which perhaps worked as grounding wires or something.

The cinder-block wall would at least absorb an electrical charge, so I decided it was to be the test subject. The underlined type in the letter — *just two strokes of the card* — indicated to me that I was supposed to draw the card between two fingers, count *one, two, three*, and then point. An arrow on the front of the card marked the electromagnetic muzzle. I hoped.

Understandably nervous, I gave it a try, the card trembling in my outstretched hand. The card was from Dudley, all right. It glowed blue for a second and then went out. But nothing happened. I assumed, I prayed, that the reason it didn't discharge was that the target had to be human. Then again, maybe the card was a dud, pun intended.

Footsteps clip-clopped down the hall and stopped in front of my door. I ditched the card in the pocket of my bowling shirt and sat back on the bed. A key turned in the lock and the door opened to reveal Roger Elk, with the speakeasy doorman right behind.

"Good, you're awake," Roger Elk chimed. "Time for a chat? Wait outside, Mortimer." Mr. Heavy went back out into the hall reluctantly, and Roger sat down next to me. "Let me just say, Garth, that I'm sorry for having to abuse your trust."

"Oh, hey, don't worry about it, Roger. What's an attorney for if not to put his client in harm's way at every turn?"

"You have every right to be angry, Garth."

"In case you don't get it, Roger, I hardly feel that I need your approval to be angry."

"Yes, you've been a pawn. But once you stumbled upon Pipsqueak and wouldn't stay away . . ." He shrugged. "You know, you didn't have to go to the Church of Jive. But what's done is done. You did what you had to do, and we've done what we had to do. But know this: There's a lot at stake here, Garth."

"Fine, Roger. You people are all worked up over a conspiracy theory whereby the government is brainwashing everybody with color TV and stealing Omaha cow anuses in late-night raids. Whatever. Believe what you want. But you're not getting

Pipsqueak until I know why you want him."

Roger Elk eyed me a moment, calculating. "Very well, Garth, I won't try to sell you. From your position, I'm sure it's hard for you to understand the scope and seriousness of what's going on here. Now try to see things from our perspective. We need that puppet to prevent a terrible threat to the lives and well-being of millions upon millions of Americans. Tell me, Garth. What lengths would you go to if you had the ability to stop a worldwide catastrophe?"

"I'm listening."

"Okay, let's get to the gist. I'll tell you why the squirrel is important. But first we need to know that you can take us to the squirrel."

My chest tightened. If they were willing to tell me the big secret, they probably had no intention of granting me parole. Options? Life in prison? More likely a mud nap. "I not only *can* take you to that goddamn squirrel but *will*. If you tell me."

Roger Elk nodded quietly for a moment and then slapped his knees. "I'll start from the beginning." He stood and leaned against the door.

"Good. But remember, I sat in on one of those 'church' services, so I know about the color-TV bit," I admonished. "Tie in why you need the squirrel to combat color-flash hypnosis and what this has to do with naturopaths."

"As you wish, but I will defer the technical aspects to Dr. Fulham. You know, the man who —"

"Right, the checked suit."

"The checked suit, yes. So I'll condense. While the U.S. and its allies were developing and perfecting color-flash technology, the Soviets were developing countermeasures using sound to cancel the effects. There is a long history in Asia of using vibrational medicine in place of the more invasive acupuncture, and the Russian experiments found that certain tones or compilations of resonant frequencies affect the sphenoid bone. This small bone in the skull cradles the sella turcia, a cup that holds the pituitary gland. A neural-hormone reaction is triggered in the hypothalamus — that's where sleep, body temperature —"

"I get the idea. You think you can cleanse the mind of the color flash with sound. The same way people like Tyler Loomis think they can cure nail fungus and migraines with tuning forks."

"Allow me to continue. The hypothalamus — while not necessarily the transmitter — is the emitter of the individual's chi or odic force."

"Life force?"

"Yes. These tones that we're trying to produce — the ones the Russians developed — can't be reproduced with tuning forks. The wave pattern produced by forks is wrong for the phonophoresic effect. But there are special tuning *spheres,* which, when toned in a particular sequence, create just the right tones at just the right frequency. They're made of a special hydrogen metal that only the Soviets were able to create."

"Hydrogen metal? It doesn't exist." I once asked Angie how come there aren't any solid forms of some of the other elements that jewelers might use. I suggested hydrogen, and she said that while scientists had tried, nobody had succeeded in making solidified hydrogen.

"At very low temperatures, hydrogen goes from liquid directly to a frozen liquid. At higher temperatures, it turns to gas. The Carnegie Institute failed in its attempt to use 'diamond anvils' to forge hydrogen using extreme pressures, and some said if it exists at all it may only be found deep within the gravitational crush of Jupiter. But, using controlled, underground hydrogen-bomb explosions, the Soviets succeeded. That is, after some underground tests, they discovered an abundance of perfectly round hydrogen globes. Spheres."

"Stable at normal air pressure and room temperature?"

"Yes. They are opaque, with a vibrational quality enhanced by their superconductivity. Bookerman was formerly a Soviet technician involved in tests of the hydrogen spheres on prisoners. He effected his escape from Russia in 1958 with three spheres."

"And immediately set about hosting a children's cartoon show? He doesn't even have an accent."

"Like any number of Russians involved in secret work, he was taught to converse fluently in English. He used to interpret clandestine recordings of U.S. scientists. Puppeteering was a folk art taught to him in Siberia by his father, a circus performer. Making puppets from animals and using them to illustrate folklore was a traditional pastime in his Yakut clan. When he decided to take the spheres and escape the Soviet Union, he hid them in the puppets to help get them out of the country. And upon arriving in the United States, he couldn't very well go back to his previous line of work. So he used his hobby and his family background in the circus to make a living as General Buster. Did you hold the puppet in your hands?"

"Yes."

"Notice anything, ah, unusual about it?"

"Head was very light. Bookerman hid the spheres in the heads of his puppets."

"Exactly. Three sizes of spheres, three sizes of puppets. This was not only a convenient hiding place but also ample protection from being struck by a hard object. The fur and batting acted as a cushion that would keep them from toning accidentally. The spheres are extremely light, and so nobody ever noticed anything unusual about the puppets. Because they belonged to him and were kept in his dressing room, this hiding place seemed ideal. When the show was canceled suddenly, he went to the studio, only to find himself locked out of his dressing room and the puppets confiscated. He tried to get the puppets in a legal battle but lost. That's where I met Bookerman. I'm his attorney." Roger Elk put his hand on my shoulder. "Satisfied, Garth?"

"But you already had two spheres. Why get so hot and bothered over the one in Pipsqueak?"

"The desired effect can only be obtained using all three sizes. The Soviets tested hundreds of spheres before they found that these three were perfectly matched. For the longest time, only Loomis and maybe one or two others — who are now dead — knew that the spheres were in the puppets."

"How?"

"Loomis was a sonopuncturist. He worked for Bookerman, trying to help him understand the full potential of the two spheres he had in his possession. He was in Bookerman's confidence but turned on him when he learned there was a third sphere. Loomis wanted the spheres for his own purposes."

"So why are Sloan, the naturopaths, and Palihnic trying to get these spheres?"

"They're valuable. They have medicinal potential, and I'm sure government scientists would be very keen to —"

"Now, when Sloan came to me, he said you guys actually had something other than battling color TV in mind. He said that you're attempting to do the same thing that the color-flash people are trying to do to the public. In reality, aren't you competing with color flash, pitting sound against visuals in a bid to brainwash America?"

"Not at all, Garth," Roger Elk chortled.

"You're sure the Russkies weren't developing this for use on their own citizens? You said they experimented on prisoners back before 1958. Color TV wasn't even on the air yet."

"But it existed in developmental prototypes, which the Russians obtained, and they made the prisoners watch color TV and monitored their brain waves after treating them to the tones." Roger stood, impatient.

"Uh-huh. But lemme ask you this: I thought nicotine and high-protein diets were the way to cleanse the color flashes from our systems. Why now the spheres?"

"HDTV. High-definition television, the 'next wave.' The color flash is more saturated, more intense, and ultimately more devastating. They're taking it to the next level. As it is now, they're making do with subliminal domination. HDTV will suppress independent thought utterly, completely. Garth, you've got to give us that puppet. We hope to test it soon on a prime-time HDTV broadcast, and we need the last sphere to effect the tone. To block the color flash."

"How? What's the delivery system?"

Roger Elk sighed, then went to the door

and knocked. "Okay, Mortimer." He turned to me and straightened his bolo tie, a grin flickering. "I could tell you, but, ah, then we'd have to kill you." Mr. Heavy opened the door and gave me a menacing squint. The growl was implied.

My lawyer waved me from the cell. "Mr. Carson here is ready to take a drive, Mortimer."

I stepped out of the room, and Mr. Heavy a.k.a. Mortimer latched on to my collar and jammed something hard into my side that felt (and hurt) like a gun. I was willing to give Mortimer the benefit of the doubt and didn't bother to confirm the weapon, verbally or visually.

As we coursed through the paneled halls and tromped down the steps to the garage, I was beyond being reasonable about all this. In short, I was fed up with getting shoved around, tired of being scared. The swell of resentment was starting a wave of hatred for these conspiracy-theory idiots for what they were putting me through. God help them if they'd put one finger on Angie.

My faith in Bookerman's good intentions was next to nil. Maybe it's just me, but any guy who can so casually order a man drowned in mud, or maintain a crew of henchmen, doesn't get the philanthropist's halo from me. Quite the contrary.

We got into the Lincoln, and Roger Elk opened the elevator. I tried to keep my nerve. The object was to get out of the building. It was the only way to escape — no way was I going to relive the disappointment I felt when I hit those glass doors. But now I had Mortimer to contend with. My odds against the Bing and Bowler duo were much better.

As before, the guy with the gun sat behind me, and after Roger Elk got us in and up the elevator, he took the passenger seat. When the garage doors opened, I saw it was night. "Is this the same day I came in here? What time is it?"

"Same day, eight o'clock. So, where will we find the squirrel?"

Although I'd considered turning Pipsqueak over and then going to the cops, there were a couple of things blocking that option. First, I didn't want to take them back to my place and risk Angie's involvement. Second, if I couldn't trust my lawyer, could I trust the police? Where did this cult/conspiracy begin and end? Third, once they obtained the spheres, they probably didn't intend to let me go. Fourth, if Elk's absurd story had any validity, I'd be handing over a weapon of potential mass social destruction. Roger had asked me before what I'd be willing to do to stop such a scheme, and now I was asking myself the same question.

I needed to find a good escape venue. I might have tried taking them to Nicholas's — he'd be just the kind who might be able to get me out of this jam. But what if he wasn't home? Besides, I needed a place with maximum options, which meant to me a place teeming with people and portals of escape, but also a place where I might have been able to send Pipsqueak for safekeeping. Maybe someplace I could have sent Otto. . . .

That little devil was being very useful of late.

"Grand Central Station."

"Where?"

"A guy who works for me runs a hot-dog stand there Tuesday afternoons. He was at the apartment this morning when Sloan came by. I wrapped the squirrel in a plastic bag and told him to take it with him for safekeeping. With any luck, we'll be able to catch him before he folds up the stand."

Roger Elk studied me a moment, then said, "Drive on." He pulled a cell phone and dialed a number. "It's me, Roger Elk.

Send some boys to Grand Central. . . . Yes, they'll do. Have them meet us at the 42nd Street entrance. We need to keep our bird from flying the cage."

Chapter 22

"Busy as Grand Central Station" is a dated simile. Since the building's restoration and 1998 rededication, you have to say, "Busy as Grand Central *Terminal*." Associated with this hackneyed expression is the Main Terminal, the kind of soaring stone room that would give Michelangelo an itchy brush finger. Below the canyonlike walls, at ground level, two sides are lined with orderly rows of old-timey ticket booths and train gates, while wide-arched passages open on all four sides. In the center of the room is a multisided information kiosk, a hefty, four-faced gilt clock on top so you can see how late you are. Commuters strut their Manhattan savvy each day through the Main Terminal, a swarm of determined, briefcased vectors who by sheer force of will and steely nerve never collide with one another or even the bumbling tourists.

Most of the station is actually composed of passages leading from the Main Terminal to subways, stores, subterminals, and the street. Overlapping matrixes of low, vaulted, and often sloping tunnels give the inside layout the look of the Paris sewers gone dry.

I could only assume that Otto's hot-dog stand was in one of the low-rent but high-traffic niches. Where, I didn't know, and as I pulled over next to the 42nd Street entrance, I explained this uncertainty to my captors.

Roger Elk's eyes narrowed as he motioned me out and into the company of a reception committee comprising four tall, lean, crew-cut gents. All wore different dinner jackets, some plaid, and I caught the view of at least one cummerbund. They smelled of bay rum. Nicholas's mummies unwrapped, no doubt.

The Four Lads ushered a kid with a spit curl and porkpie hat into the Lincoln's driver's seat. In the near distance I spied a cop marching our way, no doubt peeved by the Lincoln parked at a bus stop.

"Try the Vanderbilt entrance. We'll meet you there," Roger Elk told the kid. Porkpie roared away under the Park Avenue overpass. The cop paused and was immediately accosted by confused tourists. He hadn't come close enough for me to test my nerve. My escorts led me behind the cop's back and into the terminal.

Roger Elk led the way to the Main Terminal and up to the information kiosk. The Cummerbunds, with Mortimer as point man, led our wedge effortlessly through the throng. Rush hour was past, but the place still hummed.

Roger Elk waited twenty seconds in a short line to pose his question.

"Where do they sell a hot dog?" he enunciated into the booth.

The kiosk woman chewed her gum distractedly. A big name tag reading *Heidi Moos* hung lazily from her vest.

"Wherever there's buns, I guess, sweetie. Ha!"

Roger Elk gave her a grim look, and Heidi was suddenly miffed.

"Oh, lighten up! Jeez! There's a cart near the Vanderbilt exit." She jabbed a pencil over her shoulder.

Roger Elk waved us after him, and I fingered the Dudco™ Card in my pocket. I was running out of time and had to choose my opportunity soon or lose it entirely. Once we got to the hot-dog cart and Roger Elk asked for the squirrel, Otto would be confused or, worse yet, asinine, and I'd get hauled back to do some mud snorkeling.

We crossed the terminal, and I began

trailing to the rear of the flying wedge, glancing back at the Cummerbund I'd zap first. My plan was to take the back door out of the wedge, forcing those in front to scramble past the fallen comrade once I popped him with the Dudco™ Card.

As we moved down the passage, the Cummerbund behind nudged me onward, apparently aware of my foot-dragging. Looking ahead, over the heads of the crowds, I could see a red and white sign for *Wiener King*.

Pedestrians parted in our path, and my heart surged when I drew a bead on the lunch wagon and the striped jacket and fez of the attendant. His back was turned to us as he wiped down the frankfurter rotisserie with a rag.

Roger Elk knocked on the counter, and my ears rang with dread as I slowly drew the Dudco™ Card from my pocket.

The attendant turned, and Otto was not Otto. Otto was Nicholas, and he winked at me from under the black tassel of his red fez. You could hear my toes scrunch in my oxbloods as I tried not to register any surprise.

"Red hots, boys?" Nicholas leaned on the counter. "Let's see, six?"

"Otto?" Roger Elk asked Nicholas,

whose fading injuries *had* made him look like Uncle Fester.

"Hey . . ." a Cummerbund began.

"What the . . ." another one added.

"That's that guy . . ." a third complained.

I felt my right hand pull the Dudco™ Card between the fingers of my left. "One . . ."

Nicholas's pupils widened at the crew-cut crew, realizing he'd been made. His hand darted out at Roger Elk; I saw a flash and felt a crackle in my fillings. Nicholas had zapped him with a stun gun wrapped in his rag.

"Two . . ."

My fillings buzzed again, and to my right I heard Mortimer go "WOOF" when the wind got kicked out of him. *"Pizdyets!"* Otto said, somewhere behind me. I didn't have time to turn because I caught sight of Angie darting from the pedestrian crowd with a newspaper, which she pressed into the side of first one, then another Cummerbund. They yelped, eyes crossed, and crumpled stiffly to the floor. I heard another zap from Otto's direction.

I spun around and jabbed the card at the last standing Cummerbund, his prep-school face snarled with confusion.

"Three."

The card glowed blue. Nothing happened.

Cummerbund grabbed me by the shirtfront with one hand and fumbled for his gun with the other. I watched the card flashing blue in my hand, and I touched it to his plaid belly.

The hand on my lapel spasmed open, and the silent blue flash punched him back into the passing crowd and flat on his back.

"C'mon!" Nicholas had me by the arm, pushing me through a clot of gawkers. Angie and Otto were already running for the Vanderbilt Avenue exit ten yards away.

Freedom, and the Lincoln waiting at the curb. I flung open the passenger door.

Porkpie looked for his pals. "Say, what's the big idea? Where's —"

Nicholas jumped in the backseat and pressed his stun gun to Porkpie's neck. "Easy, hotshot, or I'll zap you like a June bug."

Angie and Otto completed the Chinese fire drill, and as the doors were still closing we made our getaway, Porkpie pouty, the rest of us panting. "Left on 42nd," I gasped.

"It's illegal," Porkpie complained.

"Do it," Nicholas prodded, and put his

fez on Angie. "Then make a right on Second."

"GA-ZAP!" Angie high-fived Otto.

"Yes, of course!" he thundered.

I cocked an alarmed eye at the rearview mirror and my backseat pals, who were sharing smiles. "What are you people doing here? How the hell did you —"

Nicholas plucked the pen from my top pocket. "Transmitter. I bugged you."

"You *bugged* me?" I felt my face heat with anger.

"Yeah, well, in truth, a little bird told me you'd been nabbed, but I used the bug to follow some of what was going on, so I could track you to wherever you were going. I had to find out what you knew. Which wasn't much, I gotta tell you. I staked out the Hanover Square place in a cab. I saw you go splat against the glass. I was in the cab across the street, reading the paper. How'd you get so muddy, Garth?"

"They've got mud baths in there, and I was about to be drowned in one if I hadn't bolted."

"I put a call in to Angie and got her to pick up the stun guns from a friend. Then we waited in the cab for an opportunity. When you rolled out of the garage, we heard you tell Roger Elk about Otto at Grand Central. Being in a cab, we made it there first, enlisted Otto. Okay, boy, pull over to the curb here." Nicholas prodded Porkpie. "That's a boy. Pull the hand brake. Good. Now get out and scat, and don't do anything cute. Your pals all got zapped, so you're the lucky one. So far."

Porkpie lit out like a bottle rocket, and I slid over into his seat and continued driving down Second Avenue.

"This rescue was a very dangerous thing to do." I gave Angie the evil eye in the rearview mirror.

Angie threw her arms around me from behind. "I love you too, sweetheart. Thank goodness you're all right!"

I was relieved *she* wasn't hurt. "When did you get home, Angie? I was worried sick they'd round you up too."

"Katie and I had lunch, then I went shopping, so I didn't get home until around four. You okay, Garth? Did they hurt you?" She ran fingers through my hair, presumably looking for bullet holes or something.

"They thought about it, but no, I'm okay. Where are the police, for Pete's sake?"

"The cops?" Nicholas sneered. "The

cops would still have us downtown trying to convince them we were for real. There was no time for them. So where is Pipsqueak?"

"Back at the apartment. Under the floorboards, under Fred. But let's talk about your little bird, your informant Vito."

Nicholas paused. "Yeah?"

"I guess your bug didn't hear my conversation with Vito?"

"Must have been too far underground. You didn't tell him where Pipsqueak is, did you?"

"No. But that's how I got it. Apparently he turned Sloan, who was trying to get Pipsqueak to you through me."

"What happened to Sloan?"

"Last I saw they had him facedown in a mud bath."

Nicholas gritted his teeth. "That's bad. If Sloan talked . . ."

"Vito!" Angie said. "They might know Vito was an informer."

"Better hurry. Those guys back there are going to drop a dime and they'll be all over your place."

We got there quick enough. Just too late.

Chapter 23

"Don't pull over! Keep driving!" Nicholas gripped my shoulder. I shrugged him off and screeched the Lincoln to a stop in front of Angie's and my apartment building. Someone was parked in my space, and then some. Two squad cars and a brown unmarked car were parked at the curb. The front shop door — the one we never open — was hanging from its hinges, smashed like so much balsa wood. I found Angie at my side as we peered in the doorway, into our living room. I looked back and saw only Otto. Nicholas had disappeared again.

It was a wreck. You'd have thought the fire department had been there with their axes and an animal rightist's bent. Small stuff like otters, pheasants, skunks, armadillos, and foxes was just tossed around. But the larger full-body floor pieces had all been chopped into pieces. Snout of a warthog. Tail of a mountain lion. Half a coyote head. Beaver feet. Bear haunches. Excelsior and sawdust from the older pieces were mixed with fluff and feathers from our overstuffed Park Avenue furniture collection. They'd slashed and thoroughly disemboweled everything from the love seat to the ottoman.

The aviary was untouched, as were some mounts out of easy reach (like the winter bobcat, thank God). I guess they didn't bring a ladder.

The police turned our way as we stepped in.

"You Carson?" one cop said to me.

"Yeah," I said, feeling slightly dizzy. Angie gasped and squeezed my arm. We stopped in front of Fred. His head was smashed, his eyes and jaw missing. The spine had been buckled, his legs ripped off, and a hatchet had diced his chest open. There was more excelsior to him now than pelt. Fred was dead, once and for all. So were the others.

The rug he'd been parked on was pulled back and the floorboards lay open, a dish towel and a gun next to the opening. Pipsqueak was gone.

"Detective?" The cop yelled to the back of the room.

Tsilzer appeared from the bedroom and eyed us speculatively a moment before entering the living room. The Embalmer appeared behind him, they whispered something to each other, and then approached. Not us, but a sheet covering something. The Embalmer knelt down and pulled the sheet back, secretly pleased.

"Recognize this person?" Tsilzer's voice was flat.

"Dammit." I turned away and gagged. It was Vito. His throat was slashed so deep it looked like he had a second mouth. Blood was everywhere.

"Vito Anthony Guido," I gulped, steadying myself on a chair.

"I have to sit down." Angie put a hand to her head and searched for somewhere to sit, unsuccessfully, so she went back out the front door and sat on the stoop. I heard her start to cry.

"You want to tell us about it?" Tsilzer sighed.

I rubbed my forehead. "I need to talk to a lawyer first."

Yeah, great, a lawyer. Hopefully the next one would be more helpful than the last. With legal representation like that, who needs a penal system?

Chapter 24

Why, oh why didn't I come from a broken home? Why couldn't I have been the one with the leather jacket, the acne, cigarette behind one ear, pack of Luckies rolled up my sleeve, and a snide disposition, the type of teen who hung around street corners planning my next drag race or rumble? No, not Garth Carson. I had to be the one the toughs laughingly referred to as Bug Boy, the one whose best friend was a fat, myopic dweeb nicknamed Mushy. The girls liked me well enough. They cooed over my wild blond hair and deep brown eyes but couldn't share in my enthusiasm for our protomechanical little friends of the order Coleoptera.

On hot summer evenings that might have been spent swilling beer behind the supermarket or "parking" with "fast" girls, I lay in wait by our back porch light, Mushy devouring Devil Dogs at my side, hoping against hope that a shadow of a giant *lucanidae* might swoop within reach.

Not that I didn't make a few attempts at delinquency. However, the local constabulary didn't give me a chance to get off the ground. Mushy and I walked down to the bowling alley one night to play the new Evel Knievel pinball machine and were summarily stopped and questioned by the cops. Our pockets were bulging with quarters, which led them to believe we were the ones who'd boosted a soda machine at the Texaco. Then there was the time we had a late-night marathon of Stratego down at the river landing. Mrs. Krugel turned her telescope our way and next thing you know the cops were storming our supposed drug den.

I've never been able to pin down the reasons, but the authorities automatically sense I'm suspect. Despite Angie's protestations to the contrary, I'm certain there's something about my demeanor that inspires passing police to give me a second, searching look. Nicholas lived up to this genetic predisposition. In an indirect and unfair way, I blamed him for my portion.

Our grandfathers were doctors, our grandmothers of sodbusting, pioneer-gal stock. Our father was the professorial type, our mother the quiet homemaker. Perhaps the bad chromosomes jumped a generation. Great-Uncle Thaddeus was spoken of in hushed tones, and out of the hearing of youngsters. In later years, I interrogated my mother at length about Thaddeus, but she pulled her "Oh, I really don't remember" bit, adding only that he was "a roustabout out west."

Had I not misspent my youth in studiousness, I might have been better prepared for the hand of jokers that life has been dealing me of late. Clearly, the fates intended that I should be a criminal; otherwise, I would not spend so much time at police precincts or need a standby attorney.

The day after the wrecking ball clobbered my collection, Dudley fixed me up with his cousin, Alex Stein, a lanky, earnest fellow with dark black-framed glasses, thick black hair, and a red sweater vest. He seemed competent, but what did I know? Except that Dudley had come through for me with the Dudco™ Card.

Darling Angie stayed home while I went to see Stein. She was dealing with the insurance, getting the door fixed, and cleaning up the apartment with Otto. The cops questioned the Russki gnome briefly but gave up any ideas about hauling him in after a protracted discourse on the KGB, hot dogs, and California nude beaches. Oh, and fast-walking women.

After going over my story with Stein, we proceeded to an interview with Tsilzer down at the precinct station. I spent the better part of an hour telling my story — the portions my counsel let me tell, that is. Like Roger Elk, he had me "massage" my telling of the events surrounding the dead woman on my stoop so that my inkling about her identity was suitably glossed over.

I filled them in on Pipsqueak, retros, Sloan, the color-flash conspiracy, Bookerman, tuning spheres, naturopaths, Roger Elk, Mortimer, the Cummerbunds, the assault on Nicholas, the Hanover Square retro digs, my kidnapping, Vito, and my rescue. Alex had me reword my telling of the rescue to omit mention of the stun guns, use of which is illegal in New York. I simply said that my friends surprised and distracted my captors — true enough — so that I could dart from their phalanx and dash from the Vanderbilt exit.

In the time it took me to tell this tale, they had a chance to look into some of the details. The Bank of Iran retro HQ was locked up, no one home. Nicholas was at large, not home either. The Church of Jive hall was also vacant. Scuppy wasn't scheduled to play at Gotham Club anymore, and the phone number the club management gave them for the Swell Swingers was a pay phone at a Bronx train station. Messages for Roger Elk with his service were as yet unanswered. And as for Bookerman, they made inquiries of his last known place of residence, a Chicago suburb.

"Lew Bookerman, formerly of *The General Buster Show*, is dead," Tsilzer intoned dubiously.

"Dead? Can't be. I mean, they all refer to Bookerman. The retros, I mean. Roger Elk."

Tsilzer checked a sheet of paper in his hand. "February twelfth, 1996. He crashed into a bay on Lake Michigan. Went through the ice, so they couldn't recover the vehicle until spring. They never found it, or the body. He was declared dead a year later by the courts. His money and assets were turned over to the corporation, Aurora, run by his nephew."

That rang a bell. Aurora . . .

"Naturally, Garth can't be sure it was Bookerman." Alex recrossed his legs. "He only saw him covered in mud and had never even seen him out of his General Buster costume, and even then that was over thirty years ago."

Tsilzer shook his head. "We're having a

hard time substantiating any of your claims, Mr. Carson." He looked me in the eye. "That's a problem."

"Wait a minute." I snapped my fingers. "Roger Elk. He had a plaque on his office wall, some honorarium from the Aurora Corporation." Tsilzer sighed, but jotted that measly morsel down anyway. Then he slid an 8x10 photo across the table. "Recognize him?"

I did. It was Sloan, who looked like he was lying in an alley somewhere. His face was dark purple, his white eyebrows and hair in stark contrast. He was still muddy from the baths. A vintage necktie was wound so tight around his neck that it had cut into his skin. At least his throat hadn't been slashed like Vito's.

He'd talked, given up Vito, and they killed him anyway.

I looked away. "That's Sloan."

"Surely you don't have any grounds to charge my client in either of these murders?" Alex snorted.

"How about obstruction of justice? Once he got wind of this whatchamacallit — 'retro' conspiracy — and its ties to the murder of Tyler Loomis, he was obligated to tell the police."

Alex threw up his hands. "Garth only

definitively knew the connection once Sloan came to his home with the puppet and admitted to the murder. Immediately afterward, two thugs kidnapped him. You know, Detective Tsilzer, you should be equally concerned with Mr. Carson's kidnapping. He's a victim, not a perpetrator."

"Carson called his lawyer, not the police."

"Garth has a right to legal counsel and every reason to suspect he'd be questioned upon matters that might be incriminating." Alex shrugged. "If you want, let's take it to a judge."

Detective Tsilzer rubbed his mustache, stared at his notepad thoughtfully. I glanced at the mirrored wall behind him, wondering how many cops and ADAs were back there scrutinizing my performance. With a heavy sigh and a screech of his chair across the floor, the detective got up and stepped out of the room. Before the door closed, I caught a glimpse of the Embalmer's waxy countenance.

Next to him, with his back toward me, was a huge man with a shaved neck. I figured that cop would sure give Mortimer a run for his money.

Stein put a hand on my shoulder. "I don't think they have anything to hold you on, Garth." He whispered, his lower lip jutted in a gesture of certainty. "I don't even think they have any idea what's going on." He fixed me with a searching look. "I mean, it's pretty far-fetched, even if it is *one hundred percent accurate*. You should be aware, however, that if for any reason your recollection of this story changes, it could make things difficult for us. That is, it could appear that you *were* obstructing justice."

I didn't say anything. He had a right to be skeptical, and I guess I appreciated what he was trying to tell me. Would that I could have obliged.

"I mean," he added, "if by the time he's returned you have any additional or revised statements or information, I don't think it would go against you. If, however, we leave here, and certain aspects . . ."

"Stein, that's the whole story, as whacked-out as it happened."

He patted my shoulder. "Just so you understand."

On cue, Tsilzer reentered the room, hands in pockets, staring at the floor. The door was open. "You can go."

Stein picked up his briefcase and put a hand on my back. We headed for the door, but Tsilzer used a finger to hold me back and said, "If any of this bullshit is true, you're in a lot of trouble with these people, my friend. Watch yourself."

As soon as we were out of the room we saw Angie in her fleece coat coming out of another room with the Embalmer.

"What is she doing here?" Stein protested to Tsilzer.

"We asked if she'd come down and answer a few questions." Tsilzer shrugged. "She said fine."

I gave Angie a reproachful glance, and she returned it with a defiant one.

"We've got nothing to hide," she pronounced, and walked out under the Exit sign. Stein and I followed, and after a few cups of coffee (Stein had a Fab Form) at a diner around the corner, we determined that her version was very close to mine. In fact, it was probably one of the reasons they let me go.

Outside the diner, Stein gave me his beeper number. "Now, Garth, you should know that you probably have not heard the end of this. In fact, you may find that the police are watching you. That's okay. In fact, it's better than okay. It's desirable. It would be a good thing for them to see you, observe you at your normal routine with no suspicious activities or visitors, including your brother. You see what I'm saying?"

I did, nodding dutifully. Bore the police to tears.

Stein hustled off to a deposition, and Angie and I started the walk home. It was overcast, and a cold gusty wind convinced me to turn up my sport-coat collar.

"I did right, didn't I?" Angie prodded.

I took her hand. "In the final result. Which is, I guess, all that matters."

"You know, if nothing else, I wanted to make sure they got the whole story, even if you did decide, for some reason, to hold something back. I'm worried, and I want the police on our side."

"So, why not take a break from all this mayhem, Angie? Take a week or so off, visit your friends in Germany. I'd go too, but I've got those snakes to —"

"Oh, no, you don't! You don't get rid of me that easy."

"Look, Angie, I don't know what's going to happen next. This could get uglier, and I don't want —"

"Well, what about what I want?" She pulled her hand from mine. "You were the one who was kidnapped! I know you're always getting all protective of me, but I worry about you too, darn it." She grabbed me by the lapels, her nose reddening and her eyes glistening. "So I'm here, by your side, got it? Thick and thin, okay? I'm not letting them get you."

I slipped my arms around her waist and smiled. "I half hoped you'd say that."

She smirked, sniffed, and kissed me. "You half *knew* I would."

We continued walking, arm and arm, down 19th Street, past the high school and the housing project, and turned down Tenth Avenue.

"Besides," Angie injected, "I couldn't go to Germany now, anyway. I just learned something exciting from Peter." She gave my arm an enthusiastic rub. "You know Princess Madeline?"

"Yeah."

"Well, the celebrity benefit she's going to? Wearing *my* earrings? The benefit is day after tomorrow, in the evening. Peter's going, and he has an extra pair of thousand-dollar tickets, but he can't find any clients that don't already have tickets." Angie's pace was getting bouncy with excitement. "So: You and I are going!"

"Great." I might even have sounded enthusiastic. Ah, the enduring allure of royalty. And to think that if I hadn't spit Scope all over the Salvation Army, I'd have nothing to wear.

Chapter 25

The next day, I dropped in on Dudley. He was tickled pink by my report on the effectiveness of the Dudco™ Card.

"Your card — or should I say you, Dudley — really saved my keister." I handed him the card.

"I hate to say I told you so, Gawth, but . . ." he chortled. "Anyways, I thank you for field-testing it. You didn't feel any electric charge yourself, am I right?"

"Not a bit. And I'd be honored to field-test it again. If you have any others around . . . What's that, Dudley? That purplish thing."

"What's what? That?" Dudley pointed his tiny scalpel at the innards of a red-breasted nuthatch he was busy eviscerating. "That's the ventriculus. That's what grinds up all the seeds."

I craned to get a better look through his giant magnifying glass. Dudley sat almost motionless, his hands resting on a block of wood. He was in full surgical garb: mask, rubber gloves, gown, headlamp, etc. All the action was taking place in a space the size of a nickel. The bird was pinned onto a paraffin block, wings spread.

"I thought the gizzard ground up the seeds," I said through my mask. He made me wear one too. I didn't rate the whole ER garb, though.

"You don't think zoologists really use the term *gizzard,* do you? *Gizzards* are something Granny cooks a mess of for Jethro. And here's another gem of knowledge. This yellowish thing is the pancreas, the reddish bit is the spleen, and the green thing is the gallbladder. And did you realize that nuthatches are the only birds that habitually climb down tree trunks headfirst? That's how you can tell a nuthatch in the wild." Dudley pinned back some flesh and picked up some snips, clipping off the nuthatch's spine just below the skull. In birds this small, the skull stays inside the mount, the contents of which must be carefully tweezered away.

"Where'd this bird come from?"

"The grille of a Pontiac."

"You must have some incredible network to find these things."

Dudley snorted. "It's called 'the Web,' ragpicker. One of these days, you're going to be doing all your business on it."

"I'm holding out as long as I can." My coral-snake hunt was going poorly, and I was afraid that the Web might prove indispensable. "Fortunately, I don't have any competition."

"You still listen to the Opry on the radio? Gawth, you have many, many customers out thay'uh you're not reaching. If you'd only let me cook you up a Web site."

"Would this site have self-defensive uses, like a Dudco™ Card?"

"Perhaps." Dudley smiled over his shoulder at me. "What would you do if you didn't have me to look after you? Me and Angie?"

"Don't forget Otto."

"Yes, and Otto." Dudley suddenly pulled back from his magnifying glass and frowned at a corner of the room. "I have to say, I'm greatly saddened by Vito's demise. Very fond of him, despite how infrequent our meetings."

"I guess he was trying to help me, that he was a naturopath. I couldn't be sure. For all I knew he was a retro."

"I should have thought of that." Dudley wagged his head in self-reproach. "I knew he was into sonopuncture. So now the retros have what they want. They have your beloved Pipsqueak and whatever is inside him. Good riddance, I say. I guess it's all over, then?"

"Hmm. What does it mean if the cops are watching me? There's been a graffitied blue van parked across the street from my apartment in an illegal spot all day without a ticket."

"They followed you?" Dudley said icily. "Here?"

"Give me some credit. No, I went out the back way, climbed the wall into my neighbor Harry's yard, and out their alley."

"By the smell, I'd say you're not out of the wallow. The deputies are probably using you as bait."

I missed that first part, but let it slide lest I get the sardonic "ignorant Yankee" translation. "Yeah, but I'll bet the retros know that. They're loopy and larcenous, but they ain't stupid. They sure fingered Angie and me at the Church of Jive, and they spotted Nicholas a mile away. Now they've vanished off the face of the earth since the cops found Cola Woman dead. Soda Boy. Whatever."

"Heard from your brother?"

"Not a peep." I crossed my fingers with one hand and knocked wood with the other. "So, level with me, Dudley. You don't have to be specific or anything, but I have to know. Is any of this web the retros are spinning possible? Or are they just seriously deluded?"

Dudley didn't say anything for a while, though by the way he twitched his lips and angled his head, I could tell he was thinking.

"Switch on the TV," he finally said.

I paused, then obeyed. It was a daytime talk show, and people were arguing.

"Turn it on up," Dudley barked over his shoulder.

Doing so, I asked, "Well?"

"Possible," he whispered.

"How possible?" I whispered in his ear, glancing back at a woman on TV throwing a chair at another woman.

Dudley's eyes pivoted away from the splayed little bird and locked onto my stare. "Possible indeed."

"And the color-flash conspiracy?"

"Part of the American Gulag scheme." His head wagged dismissively. "They'd given up on that by Sputnik. But . . ."

"But?"

"Well, in any case, HDTV, in my humble opinion, will decrease whatever flash effect there is now, beyond the optic nerve's capacity to register the variety of distinct pulses of color usually associated with complex partial seizures and resultant phe-nomena like memory distortions and déjà vu. I mean, unless they actually show flashing lights, or do flash-frame editing. In Japan, a cartoon recently —"

"I heard about that. Half the kids in Japan spazzed."

"Exaggeration. More like six hundred or so. It's probably the complex partial sei-zures that the retros would be after, though. The kind of effect they would be after to control people's perceptions and actions. So, again, in my humble opinion, the HDTV flash, while saturated, is well beyond the critical fusion frequency, and the added resolution should diminish the flicker effect, if anything. I don't see how increased resolution could abnormally stimulate the LGN cortex."

"LGN?" I had to try and keep him honest.

"Lateral genticulate nucleus. See . . ." He held up a grayish raisin in his tweezers that was the nuthatch brain. "Bird's got 'em too." He dropped it into a stainless-steel bowl with other tiny bits of guts.

"Uh-huh." Clearly, a *Popular Mad Scientist* subscriber. "And is what they're plan-ning to do with the spheres good or bad?"

"Shush!" A bead of sweat rolled down his round face. "Probably bad."

I whispered even quieter. "Didn't the NSA —"

Dudley shot me a scornful eye.

"I mean, didn't *they* give up on that idea by the Beatles?"

Dudley didn't say anything. He just tilted his head in a way that I translated as a reluctant no.

"Well, then." My lips were practically touching his moist ear. "Shouldn't somebody do something? They're going to deploy this tone in a few days."

Dudley grinned weakly. "If *they'ah* not already doing something, then it's already too late. You'd never be able to mobilize the, uh, appropriate government agency in such a short time."

"But —"

"Gawth?"

"Yeah?"

"Not a damn ol' thing you can do about it."

"But —"

"Switch off the TV, Gawth. Get yourself a cream soda. I'll take a Fab Form."

Chapter 26

Over the next twenty-four hours, life was pretty dull by comparison. Otto and I finished cleaning up the damage to the apartment. No Nicholas. No assaults, kidnappings, or gunplay. It seemed Pipsqueak and the retros had gone off to bother someone else, and we were grateful for the distraction of the imminent Princess Madeline event where Angie's jewelry was to be displayed.

The gala fete: a benefit for Princess Madeline's pet charity, the Head Trauma Foundation. Her inspiration was the death of her sister from brain injuries sustained in a car accident, a fatality that research funded by her foundation had since made preventable. She had most recently joined forces with Compton Stiles, a popular screen actor made more so by his current predicament. The handsome leading man was wheelchair-bound after a mountain bike had thrown him into a gully. Together, they blazed a crusade for the wider use of helmets. The current focus for the foundation was treating head injuries among children. Their object was to raise enough cash from a huge benefit to establish the Princess Madeline House, a rehabilitation facility for kids with damaged noggins.

Oracles of Celebville were predicting this to be the "it" New York benefit of the season.

Aside from the Princess and Stiles, the guest list included many stellar types, including possibly (perhaps, maybe) the last performance of the aging British group Speed Wobble. Rap stars, quarterbacks, fashion designers, news anchors, ex-Presidents, Special Musical Guests — like that. A big deal, and Angie had a right, I suppose, to be excited about a brush with so many famous people. All because her famous designer employer (infamous among his peers for being an insufferable boor) couldn't get anyone to go with him. Unless you count the fashion model he'd hired to showcase his gewgaws. Make no mistake: Inviting Angie served his purposes. She was to be a walking billboard for his jewelry too, much of which Angie had fabricated for him based on his designs. The way Peter had it planned, she was supposed to change earrings and necklace every hour or so to help push the range of their product line. Any indignities that one might have perceived from this scheme Angie obviously deemed worth the price of admission to the mother of all elbow rubs.

"Garth, take your tux to get Martinized. And order a limo," Angie yelled from the depths of her closet, from whence shoes ejected like balls at a batting cage.

"A limo?" I laughed, brushing off my tux. Sure, it was maybe a little wrinkled, but nothing a steaming in the bathroom wouldn't fix. Besides, I have always suspected that dry cleaners do nothing more than press and fumigate (with that noxious chemical) to make you think your suit has actually been cleaned. I can't get my brain around the idea of cleaning something without the aid of liquids, water in particular.

"A LIMO," boomed definitively from the shoe vault. "There'll be cameras, photographers out front. One doesn't pull up in a cab."

"Can't *one* ride with Peter?" I picked at a gravy scab on the jacket cuff.

"Not how it's done, Garth. Order the limo, will you please?" Her voice was getting strained.

"You think the TV cameras are going to swivel our way as we step upon the red carpet? I mean, what'll they say? 'And here comes Fine Jeweler Angie, artisan for Peter, with her companion Garth, World Famous Taxidermy Dealer'?"

"Honeybun?! I'm going to eviscerate you where you stand, with wire snips, darling, if you keep shoveling this shinola!"

I went into the bathroom, turned on the shower full-hot, hung the tux on the back of the door, and sealed the steam chamber.

When I entered the living room, I was still more than a little dismayed by all the open space and the loss of what used to be. Particularly Fred. The realization of the loss put a lump in my throat. Otto had done an admirable job making the mess go away and was currently in the process of reglazing the front shop door with new panes. He'd already replaced the hinges, reset the door, and reconstructed the broken doorjamb. New locks and knob were still in their packaging on the bar. He was a man of some handy talents, and many annoying habits, like the inane humming of tuneless Russian folk melodies.

Actually, we should have had the landlord do the work, but then we'd have waited a week with only cardboard between the mean streets of NYC and us. As is relatively common practice hereabouts with no-see-um landlords, you fix it your-self and deduct the cost of the materials from your rent. Still cheaper than if he had to pay someone to do it, not that our land-lord acknowledges that when he sees the cost, flips out, and is desperate to get in touch to discuss the particulars. That's a switcheroo I look forward to. A little pay-back for the times the boiler is on the fritz, it's subzero February, and he's in Montego Bay, outta touch. So there.

I flipped through the Yellow Pages, looking for *Limousine*. The phone rang and I picked it up reflexively, feeling a little dread as I did so. I'd promised myself to screen all calls for a while, just to steer clear of bizarre retros, Nicholas, and the like.

"Professor?! It's Stuart Sharp out in New Hope. I still got that bug. You never came up to look at the bug. And the bone, don't forget the bone."

"Sorry, Stuart, we've had a bit of trouble down here, and I couldn't get up there."

"Trouble? What kind of trouble? You mean *trouble* trouble?"

I sighed, not having the energy to give him the real scoop. "A break-in. Stuff was damaged, the front door broken, like that. I'm also under the gun to come up with some snakes for a museum."

"Wow. Price of doing business in the city, huh? Too bad. Sorry to hear it. You got insurance?"

"Not as much as I should have. Turns out between our apartment insurance and Angie's business policy, we can cover some of it and if nothing else get money for new furniture. Since we have a good source for free used furniture, I can use some of that money to buy new stock."

"Gotta get fully insured, Garth. If you had a fire, you could be ruined!"

"It's at the top of my to-do list, Stuart. So what about this bug?"

"Well, now, look, here's the thing. The reason I was calling, Carson, is that I'm going to be in your part of the woods later today on a shop run. Want I should bring the bug and bone to show you?"

My mood brightened. I was curious enough that I knew he'd get me out to New Hope eventually, while at the same time I didn't want to make the effort only to be disappointed. "By all means, Stuart, bring them by. I can show you what's left of my collection."

"Sounds good. I got your card and address. Say five o'clock?"

"Fine. But no later, okay? We're going out soon after that."

"Sure." He hung up, and I dialed a limo service.

Then another.

Then another.

The three I called were booked solid at this late date, except for town cars, which I knew wouldn't suffice. I could have gone on calling and probably found one but decided to improvise. I rescued my tux from the steam bath, took the car keys, and headed out to a costume shop and a detailer.

Chapter 27

The Savoy Revue Theater, like the Empire State Building, is a New York City art-deco landmark. It is the very antithesis of today's multiplex monastic cells. Savoy Revue seats almost six thousand. More stadium than movie theater, and more Carnegie Hall than stadium, the accouterments include plush red velvet seats, jazzy purple carpets, and gold-painted ceiling. You'd think that as a cinema, Savoy Revue would be echoey and remote, like watching a TV way down at the bottom of a well. Not so: The seating layout and acoustics are ingeniously designed. Angie and I once had orchestra seats to see a director's cut of *Blade Runner*, and the venue for that epic pic was finally simpatico with the grandness of the art.

Going north on the avenue, backups started forming in the left lanes where the detour signs were directing commoners. Actually, the traffic wasn't so bad, because all the cabs and commercial drivers knew better than to use the avenue on a Savoy Revue gala night. Straight ahead, two blocks from our target, the avenue was closed to the public. We motored toward a wall of blue police sawhorses and were eyed suspiciously by a phalanx of waiting cops, their arms folded. On the nearby sidewalk, a knot of dime-store paparazzi strained to see if we were someone recognizable. I think they were particularly excited by the lack of any barrier to their prying lenses. It had been a balmy fall day, so we decided to arrive in the Lincoln top down. Nobody popped a bulb at us.

A cop approached the driver's door, and Otto produced our ticket and proof of passage from under his chauffeur's cap. Our Russki was looking spiffy in the chauffeur's uniform I'd rented, even if it was a tad on the large side. Rubbing his mustache, the patrolman eyed the ticket, then Angie and me in the backseat. Not being recognizable celebs, the officer kindly asked to see identification. We complied, he checked our invite with the lists, and he acknowledged our passing grade with a shrug and a numbered ticket tucked under the wiper. Otto was instructed to drive into line behind the limos backed up all the way across the nearest cross street. Once he dropped us off, he'd hang a right onto a street closed for the occasion. That's where he'd wait for the end of the event, after which all the drivers would come around the block to pick up their charges in the order they had dropped them off.

As we waited in line behind the other big, black cars, I think all three of us were a little nervous.

Me? At the ramparts of Castle Who's Who, I would be attacked by a platoon of reporters and blasted by flashbulbs. Without glamour as my armor, I would surely be shot down by searching squints, derisive intermedia shrugs, and tiptoe searches for whoever was pulling up behind us. I already hated them for their disappointment. Aside from that, I was perhaps a smidgen concerned that I might pull some mortifying stunt like spill wine on Peter Jennings or elbow Dr. Ruth in the eye.

Otto? He had strict instructions not to smoke, whistle, or hum until he had dropped us off.

Angie? She was hoping that neither Garth nor Otto would bungle and embarrass her and that we wouldn't be the brunt of some mordacious Page Six gossip column for arriving in an old car. The tension didn't keep her from trying to siphon off the jitters with distracting small talk.

"Put that thing in the trunk, Garth."

I had Stuart Sharp's bug in my lap.

Several last-minute details had made our departure particularly tense. Stuart showed up just as we were leaving, and his bug turned out to be a rare bird mount that I couldn't pass up. The bone, however, turned out to be a porcelain laboratory fixture, and I declined ownership.

"Not a bad bug, huh?" I smiled at the slouching kiwi in my lap. For the uninitiated, these drab, flightless, and virtually wingless birds look like hairy gourds. If you squint, and you've been exposed to high concentrations of cleaning fluid, kiwis *might* resemble giant weevils. "A steal for fifty bucks. And with its own provenance on the bottom of the plaque detailing that it was mounted pre-'72. I have to remember to get the paperwork to Stuart. And then there's —"

"Don't touch that box," Angie growled, and my hand jumped back to my side. "Why couldn't you have left the kiwi and the box at home?"

"We were already running late. Besides, I wanted to enjoy the bird and wanted to find out what was in the box."

The box was the other last-minute detail. No sooner did we get rid of Stuart than a FedEx truck squeaked to a halt at our door. I was just holding the door for Angie to board her carriage and shouted to the FedEx guy if he had anything for me. He did, I signed, we zoomed off. Wending up the avenue, I opened the box and found that it was cold inside. Among some slivers of dry ice, wrapped in bubble plastic, I saw red, yellow, and black stripes. So I gasped and exclaimed, "Snakes!"

Angie's not squeamish as a rule, but almost everybody has an animal that makes him or her physically uncomfortable. Right: Angie doesn't exactly take to legless reptiles like they were puppies. However, I was excited. As a letter contained in the package explained, my snake woman Lorna Ellison in Phoenix had come through with a dead *Micrurus euryxanthus* — an Arizona coral snake. She'd also found a dead scarlet king snake for me. A double whammy. I just had to get them stuffed.

"Sorry." I closed the box and slid it onto the floor, away from her. My heart was still all pitty-patter over my good luck. I just worried that the ice was almost gone and that the snakes seemed in the process of defrosting.

"Aren't you worried about Nicholas?"

Such sudden changes of subject are usually the start of a tiff, this one not entirely unpredictable based on a hindsight view of the cumulative minor episodes of stress. For some reason I never see them coming.

"Not really. He knows what he's doing. Always has," I sighed.

"I wonder if he saw a doctor about his head. He should see a doctor, don't you think?"

"He doesn't go to doctors. He prefers pharmacists, nurses, and technicians."

"What? Why?"

"He sees it as cutting out the middle-man."

"That's silly. And the police are after him too. I'm worried. I hope he's okay."

"Nicholas? He's indestructible."

"I'm not so sure. You should be worried too."

"He'll save his own thieving hide."

"Garth?" I heard icicles forming. "Wasn't it your thieving brother who saved your hide from the retros? A pretty darn charitable thing for a thief to do."

I shouldn't have said anything else, but I did. "You don't know him the way I do."

"I know you, Garth, and in some ways you're more like him than I think you realize."

Now I was getting pissed off, but I clammed up as she continued.

"You're pretty cynical, you know, and it's not like you don't share his love of angles. He's got an angle on making money, figuring out how people value things, right? Selling stolen goods back to the victim is wrong? Well, if you ask me, there are shades of that in you renting out a bear for a week for what it would cost you to buy three bears. And not too different from picking up a kiwi from Stuart for fifty dollars and selling it for a thousand."

"That's just business." I was shocked at how hollow that sounded, and jumped to bulkhead the flood of feelings. "Look, I understand what you're saying, but —"

"The big difference, Garth, is that Nicholas has a shred of charity for his brother."

"Not lookink, Garv," Otto said, his eyes twinkling in the rearview mirror.

I kept my trap shut and glowered like a man. But the ice jam between Angie and me broke soon enough when we reached the head of the line and were waved on into the bowl of red light at the Savoy Revue entrance.

Much to my surprise, our arrival was a moment of glory, like so much slow-motion 16mm newsreel footage from a Grauman's

Chinese gala. The Lincoln had been spiffed up at the detailer's, and the barrage of flashbulbs lit up the deep black lacquer of her paint and glittered off the chrome bumper and trim. Even on the inside, the cracked red leather upholstery was lustrous, and a pigmented wax had made the dashboard look like new. Nobody seemed to notice the scraped taillight, the touch-up spots on the fenders, and the steering-wheel divots. Ebony, sleek, and stylish, we rolled up to the red carpet, the towering neon marquee fluorescing the red interior like black light. Media strained the velvet ropes flanking the entrance, microphones waving in the air like cattails. Heads turned, murmurs rippled, and a round of applause broke out in the crowd of haggard photogs and frazzled reporters. And it wasn't for the slinky Broadway monologist whose red-carpet chat with a *Showbiz!* interviewer was interrupted by our arrival. The applause certainly wasn't for me and Angie. I think the enthusiasm was for our retro chariot, the Lincoln.

A lobby jockey in a red tunic approached and was quickly stymied by the Lincoln's suicide doors (they swing away from each other, so the handles are side by side) until I tapped the right one. We stepped out and got one of the monologist's famous sardonic sneers, though I don't think this was part of an act.

A chuckle rippled through the crowd next as Angie took the kiwi from my hands and put it back in the rear seat of the Lincoln. Oops. She took my arm (rather abruptly, I thought) and we walked up the red carpet toward the Savoy Revue entrance. Neither *Showbiz!* nor any other TV types — though poised — made a lunge for us, for which I was grateful. I glanced back at Otto. Chin high, he motored away down the block, a cigarette already in his lips.

Angie looked smashing, she really did, and my clumsy male vocabulary can't adequately describe the ensemble. The dress was gun-metal blue, strapless, and therefore calculated to give ample canvas for Peter's art baubles, the dark metal and gems of which were more than done justice by Angie's creamy skin tone.

Of all the various used furs I've given Angie over the years, this would have been the night of nights to don one. If the year had been, say, pre-1985. Now? Nix on the critters-as-clothes. I understand some repentant rich are giving their fur coats to the homeless. So Angie had on a blue-gray mouton wrap. To be precise, that's a brushed, dyed, and satin-lined sheepskin that has both the buttery feel of a nutria fur and a uniform quality that makes it look synthetic to the untrained eye. Nobody will throw paint on you for wearing mouton, and if they do, they should pelt everybody with woolly seat covers and a hankering for lamb chops too.

Past the gauntlet of press, where ushers reached to open the theater doors for us, I imagined the worst of the self-consciousness was over.

Then the main doors opened, and camera flashes went off. Now I understand why Jack Nicholson is always photographed in shades. I guessed this was a volley of publicity photos, though among the blue blobs swimming across my retina I saw a few press tags. I further deduced that the event organizers had layered the media so that only the crème de la crème from the big magazines qualified for a spot inside.

A woman sidled up to us.

"Hi, so glad you could come. Can I check your seat numbers?" This was her polite way of saying "Who the heck are you?"

I pulled the invite from my pocket, which with nervous fumbling I'd managed to roll into a tube. I heard the woman clear her voice, caught a glimpse of a clipboard, and heard her say, "Here are your seat numbers, and you can go right down those stairs to the reception area. Okay?" I felt her hand on one elbow turn me in the right direction.

"Angie, can you see?"

"Enough." Her arm hooked in mine, she heaved a nervous sigh. "Let's go."

My vision returned enough for me to see clumps of people backslapping earnestly on either side as we made for the stairs. That and the crazy purple pattern of the carpet underfoot. The ceiling was way up there someplace.

A wide staircase spiraled us gently to the lower level, a room painted a black shade of navy with mirrored pillars. The lounge was already fairly full, and we made our way to the bar for a glass of Fumé Blanc.

"I don't see Peter. Late, like always," Angie muttered through her teeth.

"Relax, Angie, relax," I said through a clenched smile. To survive, we'd need to cooperate.

"Relax?" she said, turning to me in an artificially conversational way. "They're all looking at us."

She was right, though it wasn't like they were staring. Calculated, second-too-long glances were being shot our way from all over. But also elsewhere. Everybody was checking out everybody else, identifying, categorizing, and generally making mental bug collections of the throng.

"Not to worry. If nothing else, they must at least think we're rich. Right? So what's to be nervous about? We'll just stand here and look rich, right? Anyway, we're looking at them too."

"That's because they're famous." Angie poked at my bow tie, and I could feel her fingers trembling. "Do you know who that guy leaning on the mirror over there is? That's —"

"Yup, that's him, all right. Relax, Angie, relax. Breathe slowly, evenly." The most striking thing about celebrities is both how much they do and how much they don't resemble themselves on-screen. Surrounded by so many, I quickly discerned that while their faces are by and large recognizable, it's the rest of them that can be surprising. The proportions, or disproportions, can be quite startling. With some notable exceptions, the men are all much shorter, the women much taller. And, simply put, the bigger the star, the bigger the head. Literally. Mucho jumbo skulls. There's an osteological thesis in there for some lucky doctoral candidate with oversize calipers.

The centerpiece of the downstairs lounge area is an overproportioned aluminum deco nude, and we sidled up next to it to wait, sip, and otherwise feign small talk for a half hour. Finally, from out of the mondo craniums and Watusi females, Peter showed — a sad specimen indeed, even in a tux. He'd chosen one of those futuristic Nehru tux shirts with a black tab where the tie should be. Despite the weak chin, lanky build, beetled brow, bald pate, and long, limp curls, it was his unctuous deportment that was his endearing quality, a human skin operated from within by a bucket of live, social-climbing squid. Dismissing my outstretched hand with a squirt of smarm, he promptly set about parading us around to various designers, personalities, and silver spooners. Peter introduced Angie's jewelry to everybody. Angie and I were only introduced (by ourselves) to those well mannered enough to inquire. Facial fatigue was setting in from the amiable grin I'd plastered on my jaw, and the grind of ignominious social whoring had me praying for a time warp to the curtain call.

Praise the Lord! The lights flashed, and the horde trooped upstairs to the main lobby. A recognizable supermodel walked up the steps directly ahead of me with some swarthy, smug bastard on her arm. The libido is a lascivious janitor in a man's boiler room, and I could hear the echo of mine weeping.

Programs in hand, we wended and hobnobbed our way down the aisle. Seat-seekers squeezed by those who stopped for a brief chat. We were prime aisle plugs, not that Peter noticed or cared.

Finally, in the middle of the eighth row from the back (orchestra), we sat down, with Peter between his date and Angie (flanked by his merchandise), and me between the date and a man I thankfully did not recognize. So I was three down from Angie. I guess Peter purposely kept me sitting away from Angie either so she could schmooze someone over on that side or just to flip me the bird. This was Angie's big night, and I had already resigned myself to being highly cooperative.

The theater is oblong, and the gold ceiling is formed from overlapping arches zeroing in on the proscenium. Sort of like the bull's-eye that Porky Pig pops out of and says, "That's All, Folks!" Just on a titanic scale, like the cone of a *Saturn V* rocket booster. An orchestra pit fronted the stage, musicians' heads and instruments peeking out like prairie dogs. They were plucking, honking, and tuning up. Television cameras, technicians, and a snake orgy of cables flanked the stage. Three tiers were overhead.

Since I was out of Peter's conversation loop, I busied myself with the program. The first piece of info that riveted my attention was that this shindig was being broadcast live and digitally, though it would simultaneously be translated for analog transmission. I wondered what sinister construct the Church of Jive would build on that.

I remember looking around at that point and thinking that in this huge crowd of celebrities, with all the security in place, Angie and I couldn't have been safer from the Church of Jive. And after all we'd been through, that was a very satisfying feeling.

I turned my attention back to the program. The evening's schedule was thus: an opening Uptown Belle dance number, then an introduction by the Princess, followed by Special Musical Guest Voodoo Jive Daddy, followed by the glib and reticent magicians Glenn and Keller, then a brief slide presentation about the seriousness of head injuries by former President Gerald

Ford, then . . . blah blah blah . . . and eventually the headliner act, Speed Wobble.

But there was a slip of white paper stuck into the program. I read it, then I picked my eyeballs up off the floor and read it again, just to be sure I wasn't having a hallucination:

Due to an unavoidable last-minute cancellation, Voodoo Jive Daddy will be replaced by Scuppy Milner and the Swell Swingers.

Chapter 28

I blinked, I squinted, but the slip of paper still read *Scuppy Milner and the Swell Swingers*. I turned to show Angie, but when I waved the little piece of paper at her, she only managed to tear herself away from Peter's pontifications to give a hello wave back. I sat there, brain abuzz, staring at the slip of paper. My eyes zoomed in on the sponsors list: *Fab Form, Aurora Corp., Illinois*. Like a brick hitting my head, I remembered that plaque in Roger's office, the testimonial of some kind from the Aurora Corporation. What did that stupid drink have to do with all this? My palms went sweaty, and I took a good look around for Roger Elk.

Bookerman, or his impostor, was one of the sponsors, and there'd likely be commercial breaks with Fab Form ads. The Swell Swingers were performing. All to a huge, nationwide audience.

The glowing lightning rod in my head arced voltage into the convulsing monster of realization. This was where the retros meant to use the tone spheres.

Were this a wedding, I suppose I could have stood up just before the Swell Swingers hit the stage and said, "I object!" But if I were to make some sort of scene at Cinderella's ball, especially if no danger was readily apparent, I would likely be arrested: quickly, quietly, and uselessly.

Well, Scuppy Milner was here someplace, and my guess was many of the other culprits were as well. It wouldn't do any good for me to confront them. What, I'm going to walk into that vipers' nest and announce that they're all under arrest? The obvious move was to get Tsilzer down to the Savoy but quick.

I waved at Angie and mouthed, "I'll be right back."

A digital clock off to one side of the stage showed 8:51 p.m. Nine minutes to airtime, probably a half hour or so to the Swell Swingers.

Swimming against the current of seat-seekers, I squirmed my way into the lobby, where a distracted usher waved me to the nearest pay phones, either outside the gents' room downstairs or I could try the gents' on the second mezzanine balcony. Well, there was still a jam of people coming upstairs, and the elevators were hectic, but traffic on the up staircase was nil, probably because of the velvet rope across it. I ducked under the rope and trotted up the spiral.

At the top, I found the remains of a private reception, the demeanor of the guests on hand leaning more toward white-haired contributors than members of the Screen Actors Guild. I didn't pay them much mind, except I did a little two-step trying to maneuver around some woman in a tiara holding a script. Her bluish earrings were very familiar.

Naturally, I didn't go out that evening with any change, but I punched my calling-card numbers, spoke to the operator, got the precinct number, and dialed again. I got through and asked for Detective Tsilzer. On hold, I sat down and waited, tapping a foot and hearing the orchestra start to play, probably an overture to get the audience seated. Biting a nail, I caught sight of a familiar figure trotting up the stairs in a tuxedo. I stood up suddenly, and he turned my way.

"What are you doing here?!" he demanded.

"What am I — What are you doing here? Do you know what's going on?"

"Shhh!" Nicholas strode over, a quieting hand in the air. He had a tag on one lapel that said CATERER and on the other a stick-on name tag that said RAOUL. "Yeah, they're going to pull something off tonight. Bookerman is here."

"That's not —"

"Sir?" A voice in my ear interrupted.

"Yes?" I said.

"Detective Tsilzer is in the field. Can I take a message?"

"Yes. Tell him Garth called, from Savoy Revue, and that he better get here quick. Emergency." I hung up. That was next to useless.

"Who was that?" Nicholas prodded.

"The cops. Tsilzer. I called the detectives."

Nicholas threw up his hands. "A stroke of genius, Garth. You left a message? He'll probably get it tomorrow." Nicholas put both palms gently on my chest and showed me a Svengali eye. "Garth, no more fun and games. Fourth quarter, third and long, two-minute warning. Tell me, quickly, what you know."

Urgency had quashed any remaining qualms. "First off, the police say Bookerman is dead. So this impostor is working with Roger Elk to exploit some Russian tone spheres. They claim they can control minds with it. A lot of minds. Like, if they

295

broadcast it tonight, they'll —"

Nicholas's eyes lit up. "Of course. What's with the squirrel?"

"The final sphere, the one to complete the tone with the two others from Howlie and Possum, was in Pipsqueak's head."

"Ah! How . . . never mind, later." He patted my chest.

"How'd you get in here, anyway?" I asked.

"With the caterers. And you?"

"With Angie and her famous designer boss."

"No time for these details." His eyes pinched shut with concentration. Nicholas's head was back to normal size now, and close up I could see where he'd put makeup over the scratches. His eyes popped open. "What else?"

"Bookerman — or whoever he is — is the manufacturer of Fab Form, that awful health drink everybody loves. Made by Aurora Corporation, of Chicago. Roger Elk is Aurora's attorney." I snapped my fingers. "Hey. You know how that drink has become so popular in a short period of time? Popular starting from when Pipsqueak was stolen? They may have used the spheres to push their product. As a test. How else could something so vile —"

"Enough. They're going to use the tone during the band's number, right?"

"I dunno. Maybe. They might play it as part of a Fab Form ad."

"Got a photo ID?"

"Like . . . what? A driver's license?"

"No, no. Get your wallet."

"What the —"

"Just give me your wallet."

Amazingly, I did, and he quickly latched on to my video-rental card. "Perfect." Nicholas rolled his own peel-and-stick name tag, stuck it on the back, and pressed the ID to my lapel. "That's your stage pass."

"Say what?"

"Everywhere we go, everywhere there's somebody checking ID, gesture toward it and nod."

"You're nuts. Nobody will —"

"Just smile, nod, and wave two fingers at the ID. It'll work, believe me. C'mon."

"I've got to get back —"

"Back? What, are you kidding? We've got to get to Bookerman."

"He's not Bookerman."

"Maybe yes, maybe no. But we've got to grab those spheres. Or at least one of them. And that means we have to get backstage, or to the control booth. Let's go."

I stepped out of the phone cubby and headed for the stairs. "Sorry, Nicholas, but I'm not convinced these retros — or the naturopaths — aren't just conspiracy cultists playing games."

My burning determination to get downstairs, grab Angie, and hightail it out of the Savoy was suddenly doused. Nicholas and I stared down. At the bottom of the stairs was Roger's thug Mortimer, who was staring back up at us, his crew cut bristling like the mane on a junkyard dog. The puppy looked ready for business, not games.

"Hold it right there, Carson." He jabbed a log that was his finger at me, lumbering up the stairs.

I backpedaled to Nicholas, pointing. "Yow!" I didn't have to elaborate.

Nicholas grabbed me by the lapel, jogging me down a corridor to a door marked STAIRWELL.

"Carson!" boomed from somewhere behind us.

We took three steps at a stride up to the top landing and heard a door below fly open. Darting through the door at the next floor, we were just in time to catch the Uptown Belles in leggy, spangled regalia, filing from their rehearsal space around the corner, away from us.

"They're headed for the stage. Let's follow." Nicholas grabbed a wood doorstop idle on the floor and kicked it under the stairwell door. He tilted a nearby chair under the doorknob for good measure.

Size-fifteen shoes tromped up the stairs.

"How'll we get backstage? Who are we, what will we say?" I whispered.

Even before I finished talking, and even before the door next to us strained from the weight of Mortimer's bulk, Nicholas's eye was caught by a glass case on the wall. He pulled a gun.

Not a firearm-type gun but, as I quickly observed, a lock-pick pistol, which looks like a miniature, truncated caulking gun but tipped with a pair of metal prongs. "A little tool of the trade," Nicholas said with a wink.

As Mortimer's footsteps boomed back downstairs, Nicholas made quick work of the lock and swung open the case.

"That's . . . that's Meat Loaf's!" I gawked.

"Whatever." Nicholas lifted out the black and red electric guitar, emblazoned with the *Bat out of Hell* album cover and Meat Loaf's signature. "The band forgot their guitar player. Skippy needs his guitar man. You." Nicholas thrust the guitar into my hands and prodded me onward.

"*Scuppy,* Scuppy Milner," I corrected.

We caught up with the rear of the Uptown Belle train leaving the rehearsal space. Toting ostrich-feather fans, collectively they resembled a giant pink caterpillar trotting down the hall. The prop master was at the end of the caterpillar. He heard our approach and turned to look. This cardiganed man with orange hair, bifocals, and ashen, wrinkled face saw that we weren't one of the statuesque pinup gals and gave us a hound-dog stare.

Guitar held high, we smiled, doing our best to keep pace with the long, curvaceous legs ahead.

Mr. Prop, unfazed by us, turned his sad eyes back on the girls, uttering a mordant, unprovoked epithet: *"Musicians!"*

"Mortimer will sound the alarm! They'll be looking for us when we get down there," I rasped over my shoulder at Nicholas. I noticed that he managed to keep me ahead of him. To use me as a shield?

In a stairwell going down, the taps on the girls' shoes clacked on the concrete steps like so many billiard balls, so we couldn't hear if any footsteps were coming down behind us. But we made it down to the stage level, following the girls like part of their entourage.

For all the refinements elsewhere in Savoy Revue, backstage looked like any other backstage, except vast. That is to say, something like a well-frequented basement or garage, masonry walls hung with electrical boxes, ropes, winches, cables, and pipes. It was dark and crowded with performers and techies preparing for curtain. So many people were whispering in the gloom that the collective hiss was like a cobra convention. A stage coordinator eyed us over her clipboard, but before she got the chance to question us, Nicholas pulled me around a corner into a narrow side hall lined with cubicles and doors. Halfway down we saw the Cummerbund Squad chatting calmly in a pool of light outside a door with a star on it. They were in matching plaid tuxes and didn't seem on the alert.

"Keep moving, Garth!" Nicholas growled.

"Where are we going?"

"I dunno, but if you stop, they'll notice. It'll look suspicious. Put these on." A pair of spectacles was shoved in my free hand. Nicholas's faux ones without the glass. I slipped them on and hoped that my epoxy-strength hair gel would complete the disguise. Last time I saw the Cummerbunds, I was in retro garb with well-frazzled hair.

As we drew near, Nicholas whispered something inaudible, and there was no time to get a clear translation. So as we approached the Cummerbunds, they drew apart to let us pass. I felt Nicholas's hand on my elbow, and he yanked me to a stop in front of one of the Plaid Four.

Nicholas wheeled around. "Excushe me, but thish idiot from the orchestra needsh a guitar string." Nicholas had shoved Kleenex inside his upper lip and cheeks, and his eyes were wide as pie pans. "*Musicians!* Now he wantsh to see whether one of yoush Swingers gots one he cansh borrow? Hmm?"

They looked at Nicholas like a gang of country-club golf pros encountering the groundskeeper's assistant. My face went prickly. Nicholas's aping was way over the top, I thought, and surely we were dead meat.

Cummerbund #1 snorted at Nicholas, eyed my guitar, and gave me the once-over. I gulped.

"Nice guitar. I don't see any broken strings."

"Almost broken," I blurted. "Up here. You can't see. It's, uh, wound around the peg. It'll break soon as I start to strum." I was nodding furiously.

"Musiciansh!" Nicholas threw up his hands, nodding at the other Cummerbunds in nonexistent commiseration.

Cummerbund #1 rolled his eyes, letting them come to rest on Nicholas. He leaned on the door and turned the knob. "This guy needs a guitar string. Got any?"

The Swell Swingers were decked out in baggy blue sharkskin suits, black shirts, and purple ties. Some sat at lighted mirrors, primping. Others sat backward on folding chairs in the middle of the room, smoking and chatting. The walls were yellow, the furnishings Spartan and strewn with instrument cases. Scuppy was not there.

A Swinger with a small beard, flat-crowned fedora (brim up), and sharp blue eyes stood up from the center of the room. He started backing toward an open guitar case. "Which string?"

"Oh. Well, it's the, uh . . . G-string, of course."

A locker-room laugh bounced around the Swingers, and a rivulet of sweat slalomed down my back. Comments like "Sure," "I *like* that string," and "Hubba-hubba" erupted from the other musicians.

"One G-string coming up." Sharp Eyes approached me with a smile and a coil of wire that was the string. "Whoa, wouldja look at this guitar!"

"What guitar?" The bandleader, Rob Getty, came in the room smelling faintly of booze. "What's going on? We've got a gig in thirty minutes, fellas. Look sharp."

"Who's the squares?" Scuppy strolled in and stood next to me, holding a small suitcase and a music stand. I noted that the stand was fitted with three hemispherical cups of different sizes.

"Broken string. Just came in for a G-string . . ." I muttered, and turned to go.

"Wait, wait, wait." Scuppy pulled me back by my biceps. "You don't get away that easy. Let's see that banjo. Baby! Signed by Meat?"

"Musiciansh!" Nicholas blurted, and got a withering round of furrowed brows from the gang.

"You know Meat?" Getty pointed.

"Wait, I know this guy," Sharp Eyes said. "You're . . . whatsisname . . . that guy. You know, he played with Meat. He had that crazy mustache or something."

"Right," Getty snapped his fingers, turning to me for an answer.

Perspiration cascaded down my shoulder blades as I once again considered my wasted youth. Beetles, not Beatles. I had no idea how to answer.

"That's right," I said, nodding, smiling as best I could, backing to the door. "Gotta go. Thanks for the string. Catch you after the show, okay?"

I got to the door and saw that Nicholas and the Cummerbunds had abandoned me. Traffic was heavy in the narrow hall, opposing streams of talent and crew headed for their battle stations, and my retreat was blocked by another band moving toward the stage. Their wardrobe was variously of leather, T-shirts, headbands, hairy chests, buckskins, granny shades, and long, teased hair.

"Comin' through," one of them groaned.

"What's this!" one leather-faced, toad-mouthed British rocker exclaimed, hand extended at my guitar. "Derrick, 'ave a look!"

"'Scuse us," I heard Rob Getty announce, closing the dressing-room door.

"My, my, my!" Derrick backtracked, looked at the guitar, then at me over his granny glasses. "Meat give you that, did he? You should keep that in a glass case."

I was confronted, of course, with Bart Derrick and Liam Madden, lead singer and drummer respectively of Speed

Wobble. Via the miracle of hi-fi, they played my first slow dance in the junior-high gym, as well as my first run at the bases, a hot box where — as I wistfully recall — I was tagged out rounding second.

"Derrick, m'boy, you know who this is? It's that fella. You know the one. He played with Meat."

"Aw, yeah, right you are." They nodded at me, waiting for my response. "He 'ad that mustache thingy —"

"That's me," I chirped.

"Di'n't you used to play wid Stevie Winwood?" Bart stroked his chin.

"Don't be silly," Liam scoffed. "That was Pat Thrall."

"No, it was Kasim that played wid Winwood," Bart countered. "But you are right, this 'ere's the other bloke."

Liam gave Bart a derisive shove. "Kasim played bass for Cheap Trick, y'fool."

"Gotta go, boys." I started to drift down the hall. "We'll, you know, rap after the show." As I approached escape velocity, I ran smack into Roger Elk.

The sweat on my back breached the belt line.

Roger Elk looked me square in the face, turned, and continued on his way to the dressing room, into which he vanished.

I couldn't believe it: He didn't recognize me. I was beginning to feel somewhat Teflon holding Meat's guitar, and I made for the stage area. As I approached, the stage coordinator leapt up from her stool, waving her clipboard at me. I hesitated.

"C'mon, this way! Take your place. Let's go!" She held back a black curtain in the rear stage wall, and as I drew near I saw a door there.

"Right in there. Curtain in sixty seconds! Let's go!"

Without any other direction, I did as I was told, and when the door closed behind me, I heard the bolt flip. Pausing, I tried the knob. Locked.

Before me was a steel spiral staircase down a brick shaft to a landing and cat-walk that went right. The only available light was coming from below. Clutching Meat's guitar, I slowly descended until I could peak into the lighted room.

Imagine the propeller room in a battle-ship. Or a mite's-eye view inside a pocket watch. The room was a three-story brick vault, shiny steel shafts extending the width and height of the room, the ends fixed with giant pistons, pinions, gears, and chains.

"Come on down, Junior, an' join the

campfire," Bing's voice called up to me. I couldn't see him at first, but he and Bowler stepped out from under the catwalk, lazy pistols in their hands. Nicholas was with them, wrists shackled by cuffs in front of him.

"The Four Lads only look dumb," Nicholas called out. "They ID'd us. Might as well come down, Garth."

Chapter 29

Bing held a pistol to Nicholas's head. Bowler, still in that same Lucky's Speed Shop shirt with the two red dice, twirled a set of handcuffs. "You two pixies have been a genuine nuisance," he sneered. "For the last time."

I started down the gantry, then down the metal steps to the machine-room floor. Overhead, I heard what sounded like goose-stepping Nazis. I looked up at the wooden, joisted ceiling and saw that the verticals of the steel shafts ran up to platforms connected to the ceiling. The stage was overhead, and the shafts, cables, pulleys, and chains operated a complicated system of stage elevators. Gantry catwalks overhead served as access for the troupe to various elevators. The Nazis, I assumed, were the Uptown Belles opening the show with their high-kick signature fan dance. From below stage, *Lord of the Dance* would sound like a die-stamp factory.

The subbasement level where we stood was strictly for the mechanics and maintenance people. Hither and yon were yellow signs warning of imminent mechanical peril.

"Now what?" Nicholas shrugged at our captors.

They didn't have to answer. A latch clicked, and down the spiral staircase behind me came Roger Elk and Scuppy, the former in a tight little tuxedo, the other in a cream dinner jacket with shoulder pads built like Jane Russell. Sporting smug grins, they rested their forearms on the railing and admired their captives. I stopped at the top of the short stairs separating me from the clutches of Bing and Bowler. I lifted the guitar sling from over my head.

"They may think they've been a big nuisance," Roger Elk began, "but like raccoons, they are too easily caught."

"I'm curious, Roger." Scuppy folded his arms, projecting his voice like there was a stage audience to please. "I'm curious about what keeps our two chums going. What did they want?"

"Well, Scuppy, the one — Garth, the one with the guitar — wanted the squirrel puppet. Can you imagine?"

"The puppet?! Is it valuable?"

"Not particularly. Obviously, it is to him."

"That's going to cost him dearly, wouldn't you say? And how about the other one? The one with the swelled head?"

"I'm not sure what he wanted. I'm not sure it matters."

"I dunno. Mind if I ask him?"

"Go right ahead."

Nicholas answered before he could ask. "Cards on the table. I'm looking for Bookerman."

"You told me you were looking for Pip-squeak," I grumbled.

"It amounts to the same thing."

Roger Elk and Scuppy seemed highly amused.

"Looking for Bookerman? Why?"

"Insurance fraud. Chicago Mutual, like most insurers, doesn't like paying out a lot of money on big double-indemnity life-insurance claims. They also don't like accidents where the body is never recovered. Lost control, broke through a guardrail, spun out onto the ice, dropped through the ice into Lake Michigan. They paid it to Scuppy Milner Bookerman, his nephew and executor of his estate, and he used it to bankroll the launch of Fab Form. But they don't pay out that kind of money without following up. They keep tabs on the benefactor for years, see what he does, try to figure if there's been a scam. Lotta times, they manage to get their money back, people go to jail. They had a big, thick file on Bookerman and knew all about his efforts to regain his puppets. When one of their legions of researchers saw that one of the puppets was stolen in New Jersey, and someone was murdered in the exchange, and that you were in New York . . . well, let's just say insurance companies don't believe in coincidences. They hired me to check it out for a percentage, which amounts to a nice piece of change. That's why I'm here."

Roger Elk's smile was gone.

A vein in Scuppy's sizable forehead threatened to burst like a fire hose. Scuppy looked at his watch. "I'd better get upstairs."

"Tell me one thing," I said, looking up at Roger. "Why tonight? Why here?"

He grinned. "We've got a huge live-TV audience at rapt attention, and some of the most influential people in the nation are here. We influence them, they help influence the rest of America. Do you really think we wouldn't be better off without video games, Web surfing, and reality TV?" Roger's grin faded.

"So, Scuppy and his boys twenty-four/seven on the boob tube?" Nicholas asked. "Or is that why Aurora Corporation has been buying up all those forgotten, bargain-basement AM radio stations all across the country? Going to one-better all those conservative talk-show hosts?"

I gave Nicholas a cross look. "You didn't tell me that part."

"Yeah, well, you weren't exactly a well-spring of information either."

Roger Elk waved a hand at Bing and Bowler. "When you're through, drop them in the counterweight shafts. Nobody will find them there for a while." He trotted up the spiral stairs after Scuppy.

"Hey, don't I even get to know about Bookerman?" Nicholas complained loudly. "C'mon!"

"Shaddup." Bowler gave Nicholas a lazy slap across the face and turned to me, waving a set of handcuffs. "You. Get down here."

I methodically plunked down the steps, holding the *Bat out of Hell* guitar across my belly. I had been expecting the immobilizing fear, the twist in your gut that keeps you from doing anything counter to your best self-preservationist instincts. But the fear wasn't there — yet.

"C'mon, buster, we don't got all night, you know."

Ultimately, it was the wisecrack that stung my fear into a savage anger. I got to the bottom step.

Gun at his side, Bowler said, "Gimme that guitar."

So I gave it to him. With a sweeping diagonal uppercut to the jaw.

A few teeth and a cloud of blood vapor replaced Bowler's grin. Meat's guitar resonated with a beautifully discordant chime.

That one was for Fred.

Bing swiveled his gun from Nicholas's head and aimed it at me. I was still a step away with the guitar, and he fired at the same time Nicholas shoulder-slammed him. The ricochet pinged through the room. They both went down, the pistol clattering off to one side.

I stepped over to where Bing was just grabbing his pistol, wound up, and delivered a golf swing to his head. The gun went off again as he crumpled back to the concrete floor, sparks bursting across the room where a circuit box got punctured. Lights flickered.

That one was for . . . well, it was for Fred too, dammit.

"Garth!" Nicholas hobbled to his feet,

kicking the guns to the far end of the room, under some machinery. "Brilliant! Brilliant!"

Bing's cardigan covered his head, but there was a growing red stain on it. I turned back to where Bowler was sprawled, to make sure he was still down. Blood gurgled from his empty mandible, and one of his sleeves was torn. Time for a new bowling shirt.

The Uptown Belles ceased their Nazi tromp, and our ears were filled with the machine-room hum. Nobody upstairs would have heard the shots over that racket.

I propped Meat's guitar against a shaft. That's when I noticed the bullet hole through the soundboard. I eased down onto the ground to keep from falling.

"Okay, Garth, take it easy." I felt Nicholas's hands massaging my shoulders. "Breathe into your sleeve. You're hyperventilating. Attaboy, easy, now."

I'm not sure how much time passed, but it was only a minute before Nicholas broke the calm.

"Okay, now. Stand up, Garth. We still got work to do."

I looked over at the two sprawled retros. "They dying?" The question was completely academic. It's not like I spent any time thinking about how many people they may have killed or which one killed Vito or Marti. I really didn't care.

"Probably not." I saw that Nicholas had one of his hands free and that the handcuffs still dangled from one wrist. "There's nothing we can do about that now. Look, Garth, if they're trying to kill us, don't you think that this thing with the spheres needs stopping? They wouldn't be going to all this effort if the spheres didn't have some effect."

"Listen!" I held up a finger at the ceiling. Ever so faintly, and echoey, I could make out a drumbeat and Scuppy's wailing voice. "They're playing."

"Shit!" Nicholas ran for the stairs.

"Wait. The elevators." I pointed to a panel on the wall, from which conduits piped throughout the room to hydraulic pumps and motors. At the panel, there was a diagram, and it quickly became evident that a series of three-position (UP–STOP–DOWN) lever switches were manual overrides to the elevators. Not only were they unnumbered, but they were locked with small padlocks.

Nicholas patted his pockets and shrugged. "They took my lock pick."

I grabbed a fire extinguisher from the

wall, one of those big, old silver jobs.

"What are you doing?"

"This is the first switch. It should be the first elevator, right?"

Nicholas looked overhead and then back at me. He smiled. "Sure."

Raising the extinguisher over my head, I brought the bottom edge down on the pad-locked switch. I hit it again, and then again. The third time was a charm.

Chapter 30

Angie told me later about the series of events that unfolded onstage.

The lights came down, the Uptown Belles did their fanfare and left the stage. Princess Madeline and her pal Compton Stiles followed, making a brief introductory welcome, assisted by a nonmusical and teleprompted appearance by Speed Wobble, who for the moment were there just to hype their music segment later in the show. "So without further ado . . ."

Then the curtains at the back of the stage parted to the tippity-tap of a snare drum, followed by some tinkling ivories, full lights, and blaring horns. The Swell Swingers were building up a head of steam. As the lights came up on the band, fulgent Scuppy was shimmying center stage. Applause swelled from the audience, and Scuppy rewarded them with a Hollywood wink. Angie noticed a music stand not far behind him. On it was a row of three dull, black spheres, sized from navel orange to small lime. A wee redheaded mallet was in the top pocket of Scuppy's cream dinner jacket.

The dancers reemerged from the wings in sequined zoot suits, and a dance routine started to take shape at the band's feet.

As the band wound up its intro, Scuppy danced over to the spheres, and with an impish grin he gave each a tap.

My Angie was no fool. As soon as Scuppy appeared onstage, she registered that I hadn't returned to my seat and knew something was up. Angie stuck her fingers in her ears but noticed a ripple effect across the heads in the audience. She described it as a mass twitch that nobody but her seemed to notice.

That's when Scuppy started to sing "Blinking Light," the retro anthem we'd heard at the Gotham Club.

He'd gotten to the first refrain when there was some commotion in the orchestra pit, but Angie couldn't make out what it was.

From over the whir and peal of the motors, rotors, cables, and shafts in motion, Nicholas and I heard an excited murmur behind us.

"Maybe we should try the next switch," Nicholas said as we looked over our shoulders. The entire orchestra pit, replete with excited musicians, was sinking into the far end of the room. Our abductees hungrily scanned the unfamiliar surroundings for any sign of either culprits or escape.

"Wrong elevator." I threw the first switch past the STOP position into the UP position, the resultant jolt tossing musicians from their seats and toppling more than a few music stands. Horns collided with clarinets, and a pair of cymbals slid into the kettledrum.

"Allow me?" Nicholas brandished the fire hydrant.

Angie later recalled that no sooner did the orchestra pit go quiet than it suddenly got louder again, and heads of musicians with tousled hair and fists of sheet music appeared over the rim of the pit.

The Swell Swingers saw something was amiss but played on.

The Uptown Belles were all on their backs on the floor, fans high and waving, when they suddenly submerged like so many synchronous swimmers. A flash of confusion — a shade of red — swept over Scuppy's face as he watched the Uptown Belles disappear below the boards in an unscripted stage direction.

Peter put a hand on Angie's forearm. "What's going on down there?" he growled.

According to Angie, that was the moment she knew for certain that I was okay.

"Oops," Nicholas and I said collectively, putting the platform of sprawled, feather-floundering Belles into reverse.

It was at this point that anybody paying attention got the idea that something was wrong. With ample hand gestures, camera operators spoke rapidly into their microphones. Electricians and gaffers jogged down the side aisles toward the back of the arena.

Heads among the audience swiveled, interchanging quizzical glances.

The Swell Swingers' tempo began to falter, but Scuppy urged Rob Getty and the band back into rhythm, belting out the refrain as he danced over to the three spheres, his red mallet poised.

Angie put her fingers in her ears again.

Scuppy no sooner hit the first sphere than he and his ensemble began to sink below stage. He stumbled, grabbed the music stand, and all three spheres tumbled to the floor. The Uptown Belles reappeared on all fours.

★ ★ ★

"Got 'em!" Nicholas shouted as the platform overhead lowered, a dropped drumstick clattering down and landing at our feet.

Off to the side, on the gantry leading from the stage door, footsteps clanked into view in the person of Mortimer, followed by Detective Tsilzer, two electricians, several uniform cops, and a gang of men in dark suits, earmuffs, and radios.

"Now what?" I nudged Nicholas.

Before Nicholas could reply, we were distracted by something else falling from the platform, an outstretched hand clutching air in its wake.

It was a small, opaque sphere, a little bigger than a Ping-Pong ball. Charcoal gray and spinning, it fell very slowly at first, like a feather that might just float away.

"Nicholas!" I pointed at the sphere. "Your ears!" I shouted at him, plugging my own with my fingertips.

The new arrivals on the gantry saw me pointing and froze when they saw the falling sphere. Everybody knew it for what it was.

I held my breath as I watched the sphere pick up speed. But it was still falling no faster than a hanky when it struck a pulley.

The feather turned into a bullet. When it hit the pulley, it suddenly ricocheted like a gunshot. You couldn't see it, only hear it as it twanged off a vertical shaft, chinked off the floor, pinged off the wall, clanked off the gantry, twanged off another shaft, and suddenly slowed in an arc toward the ceiling. It was like one of those hard rubber Super Balls, seemingly defiant of gravity. I could feel the vibration from the sphere in my joints and solar plexus. The descending squad on the gantry was doubled over, clutching their heads. Except Mortimer, who had his fingers in his ears and an evil eye on me.

Completing a wide, lazy arc through the air, the sphere hit the concrete floor next to the metal stairs. There was a flash of blue light and a concussive force that hit me like a bucket of warm water. In fact, for a few moments afterward, it felt exactly as if I were soaking wet. I didn't actually hear anything, because my hands were clamped over my ears. But a haze of smoke hung in the air, and as it lifted, the point of impact was a lattice of fine cracks in the concrete. Next to that, the metal stairs were warped like they'd been subjected to extreme heat. No debris.

The platform overhead jolted with a clatter to a stop, and the musicians started to stumble off, some bleeding from their ears. Scuppy pushed past them to the police and wheeled a finger down at Nicholas and me. If looks could kill.

"Them! They ruined the show — arrest them!" he shouted, the vein on his forehead wriggling like a night crawler. The uniform cops were still recovering from the sound of the bouncing sphere and couldn't hear him. The dark suits seemed only concerned with pushing past the musicians and onto the platform. Mortimer rushed forward, and Scuppy Milner grabbed him by the lapel. "Get them!"

Angie reports that the sudden disappearance of the Swell Swingers, the jumble of Uptown Belles, and the dismay of technicians had the audience at the verge of some mass reaction. What hung in the air was a sense of imminent danger, as though anyone or anything might suddenly fall through the floor, victim of the Great New York Collapse. Some of the men in the audience stood, searching the perimeter for an escape route, and ushers standing by the exits pulled at their bow ties uncertainly.

Women collected their purses, bracing for what might happen next.

Then came the sound of the sphere exploding below stage. A deep thud shook the whole building. A fading dissonance followed, a cross between a distant bell tower and resonating stemware. Five thousand people jumped to their feet and turned. A rush for the doors was on.

Many would argue — or agree — that success in the entertainment realm is not so much the result of an excess of talent as it is a keen sense of timing, of recognizing opportunities for what they are and capitalizing upon them. Celebs during interviews sometimes betray modesty and refer to this aptitude as luck.

Many would also argue that riots are ephemeral phenomena. As easily as they can be triggered, they can just as easily be thwarted. The catalyst to either is often something simple: a shout, a car honk, a flashing light. The stage was set for stampede and tragedy at the crowded Savoy Revue.

A pair of spotlights targeted the air over the stage. Sharp white beams shot from the back of the auditorium to the stage, and at the pivotal, decisive moment, all eyes turned away from the doors. Lowering slowly on invisible wires, dressed in butterfly outfits, were masters of the stage and sleight of hand: Glenn and Keller.

"And for our next trick . . ." Keller's oaken voice boomed.

Mortimer reached into his coat.

Nicholas and I, staring up at the troops on the catwalk, started to back into the corner, looking for a place to run that wasn't there.

A flash of silver was in Mortimer's hand, and the next thing I knew that silver came down on Scuppy's wrists.

Handcuffs.

Milner's surprise resonated through the room like the ping of the sphere, his jaw unhinged like adjustable pliers. "No, Mortimer. Them, not me!"

Mortimer pulled something else from his pocket, but it was gold, and it was a badge, which he put into display from the top pocket of his jacket.

"But . . ." Milner looked to Tsilzer and the uniform cops for help. All he got in return was the half-lidded stare of men already doing the paperwork in their heads.

"Sorry, Scuppy. Party is over," Mortimer grunted. He waved the electricians toward the stairs, and in a moment they and their dirty looks were down with us at the switches putting the stage back into one piece. The roar of laughter and applause from the audience was snuffed out as the platforms whirred into place.

The detachment of dark suits filed off the elevator platform with the spheres wrapped in big white pillows and duct tape. Mortimer pointed at us.

"You two. Get up here." He then turned to Detective Tsilzer and exchanged words. The uniform cops were cuffing the rest of the band.

"He's a cop." Nicholas, walking to the steps, shook his head at the ground.

"Can't be," I said, picking up my guitar by the neck. "Brute like that? He doesn't seem the type."

Nicholas waved a finger at me. "What you know about *types*, Garth, wouldn't fill a gnat's bladder." Or that of a nuthatch, even.

We ascended the steps and stood before the expanse of Mortimer's back, which blocked our passage. He was talking in a rumbling tone to Tsilzer. When he finally turned around, his moon face puckered into a frown, the short hairs on his neck and that white forehead scar flaring. I realized now that it must have been

327

Mortimer's back I'd glimpsed at the police precinct when I gave my statement to Tsilzer. He eyed us like a couple of pesky flies mired in his banana split.

"You two monkeys just about screwed the pooch." He glanced over to where some of the dark suits were seating two spheres carefully into a foam-filled brief-case. "And we lost the Pipsqueak sphere."

I looked up at his badge. A banner across the bottom read FEDERAL AGENT. Across the top it read NSA, which either meant Numismatic Society of America or National Security Agency. I didn't notice any of the telltale stamp fatigue on his tongue, so I assumed the latter.

"What's this all about?" Scuppy trumpeted.

"Conspiracy, terrorism," Mortimer barked. "And I'm obliged to suggest you shut your trap until you get a lawyer, Milner."

Like kids with a truant officer, Nicholas and I looked at our feet and dug our hands into our pockets.

"I was just looking for Bookerman," Nicholas complained. "If those jokers in cummerbunds hadn't —"

"Shut up," Mortimer boomed. "Listen, Palihnic: Bookerman *is* dead. Yeah, Roger Elk and Milner probably killed him, see, once they got wind of the spheres and what they could do. Don't think you'll be able to prove it, much less get the insurance money back."

"Yes, but I saw him in the mud bath," I ventured. "He was bald, and —"

Mortimer swung his large arm over to Scuppy and grabbed his scalp. There was a tearing sound and a yelp as Mortimer plucked Milner's hairpiece — a vertically impressive rug — and threw it at my feet like so much barber's-floor flotsam. No explanation offered, and genius that I am, I didn't need any. Well, perhaps a slight clarification.

"Bookerman's nephew, right?" I snapped my fingers.

Mortimer wagged his head, impatient and mocking. "He and Roger Elk were on the Aurora board of directors, cashed out Dad, and bankrolled a push to go national with Fab Form, using the spheres in the ads to get people to buy it. It was so successful that they decided to go a step further. To start a cult to use as a captive consumer base."

"I still don't understand. Why start a cult?"

"You haven't been paying attention, have you?" he sneered, which I gathered meant if I hadn't figured it out, he sure as hell wasn't going to tell me.

"What about Elk?" I persisted. "You got him?"

Mortimer looked even more annoyed. "We'll get him."

Nicholas cleared his throat. "Hey, I'll need paperwork from you boys, you know, for my insurance-fraud investigation."

Mortimer leaned in close to Nicholas, and I'll be damned if my steely brother managed not to shrink from that imposing mug. In a soft, ominous voice, Mortimer mapped his position in no uncertain terms.

"NSA don't give out papers on nothin'. Listen up, Slick. I ain't seen you. You ain't seen me. If you walk real slow and steady and don't look back, maybe, just maybe, we won't reach out an' squash you two. This is a matter of national security, which gives me a shitload of discretion and authority when it comes to due process. Maybe the murder cases of Tyler Loomis, Sloan, and Marti Folsom will just shrivel up and disappear, and you two won't get charged with obstruction of justice, go to jail, and mysteriously find the parole board keeps you in the jug twenty years past your parole eligibility." His face lightened, the spittle at the corners of his lips ebbing back into his mouth. "That's not advice, boys." A friendly, hideous glow shimmered on his face. "That's a warning."

Mortimer stepped aside, daring us not to take the long, slow, and ultimately wise walks of witness denial that are at the core of all cover-ups.

A uniform cop led us out of the theater basement, and in the gloom we found a line of police leading to an open back door. Outside the line, the production staff scurried about their business as though the police weren't arresting the Special Musical Guests. Someone was talking earnestly onstage, and we walked through a narrow space behind a giant screen. Pictures of kids with bandages on their heads were being projected onto the screen, and the unfortunates loomed over us. Must be President Ford talking. As we reached the other side of the screen, the audience broke into applause. And just before we reached the exit, Speed Wobble came around the corner, presumably headed for the stage for their farewell performance. Bart and Liam stopped and stared as we were led out.

"Aw, that's a drag, man," Bart hailed, looking over his granny glasses at me. "Narcs!"

Liam put up a peace sign. "Keep the faith, Todd baby! Our best to Meat, awright?"

I got outside and realized I was still carrying the *Bat out of Hell* guitar.

Chapter 31

"Don't take this off until you get home." Our escort slapped a red sticker to our lapels. "Shows you're clear to leave the perimeter."

"Wait!" In her high heels, Angie ran on her toes and would have fallen flat on her face if I hadn't caught her. "Garth, what's happened? Are you okay?"

"Don't worry about me, I'm fine." Nicholas grinned and sauntered out of earshot.

"The short answer? The retros are finished. The long, incredible answer will have to wait until I've had a beer. No, five or six beers. Won't Peter be missing you?"

"Oh, no. I need at least one juicy detail to hold me. Did they get General Buster? Did you see him, even?"

"Not yet."

"You know" — Angie's brow was knit, the puzzle machine at work — "I find it very interesting that through all this, Bookerman hasn't shown himself."

"Look, go in and finish the gala."

"Not after what just happened in there. Besides, I want to make sure you're okay.

Peter can stuff it." She made an annoyed face and waved the subject of Peter away. "Come on, let's go home."

"What, and miss the Princess wearing your jewelry?" I took her by the shoulders and smiled. "Not on your life. I'm fine, just exhausted. Look, Otto and I will come pick you up when you're done. I just need some air."

"No, Garth —"

"I insist. Really. I'll see you in an hour or so. And I'll tell you about the whole thing."

She was pouting.

"And be careful in those shoes. You don't want me to worry."

"Promise me." Angie squinted and held up an admonishing finger. "Promise me you'll just go sit with Otto."

"I promise, I promise."

She turned and went back down the hall.

When I was ushered clear of the perimeter, past the paddy wagon full of musicians, and sent on my way, I found Nicholas headed back toward the front of the theater.

"See you later, Garth. A little unfinished business, you know how it is."

"Nicholas, I wouldn't do anything to piss off Mortimer. Besides, it's over. Bookerman is dead."

"Yeah, well . . ." He grinned. "I'll catch up."

I gave a lazy salute and watched him turn the corner. The maniac was going to get in more trouble, I just knew it. I was done, no more trouble.

No need to go back and return the guitar, either. I could return it another day, anonymously. The Savoy Revue probably wouldn't be too happy about the bullet through the soundboard.

No, I made up my mind to do what I wanted to do in the first place that evening. Go sit with Otto in the Lincoln and have a cigarette. Pulling my bow tie loose, I tromped across a plaza toward the cross street. Sure enough, the joint was wall-to-wall limos, each end of the block stoppered with uniform cops and plainclothesmen. The way they dashed to and fro, touching antennae, checking people's IDs, double-checking that shop doors were locked, they were like ants who'd just had a twig stuffed down their hill. Some of the men-in-black types started to fan out among the closer limos, checking underneath, talking to the drivers. Looking for an escaped retro, I thought.

I found Otto sitting on the hood of the Lincoln, smoking. He was parked under a faulty street lamp, the luminaire flickering orange light and buzzing overhead. In front of him were several other chauffeurs, chewing the fat and smoking. I heard the distinctive purr of muttered Russian. It seemed Otto had found pals among the other émigrés.

"Garv, vhat you do, my friend!" Otto clapped his hands together, then showed me his palms as if showing me his disappointment. "Vhy you not show do sit at watch? Vhere Yan-gie?"

"She's okay. Angie is still inside. I've had all the excitement I can take for one evening." I handed him the guitar, climbed into the front passenger seat, and melted into the upholstery, my eyes half closed, the Russians in front of the car a blur of silhouettes.

"Ah, very nice." Otto stroked the guitar. "Gatar, it is belong to Meat, yes?"

My eyebrows went up. "You know Meat?"

"Yes, of course, I to know Meat. In Russia, very many peoples know to Meat. Eh? *Yob tvoyu mat!*" He explored the bullet hole with a fingertip. "Garv not vorry. Otto to fix hole."

My eyes drifted to the front again, just as a chauffeur was extending his lighter toward another driver's unlit smoke.

Otto began singing "Paradise by the Dashboard Light" to himself:

"Bey-be, beybe let me slip on eet, bey-be, beybe let me slip on eet. Let me slip on eet, I tell you I lose you in mornink!"

In the Zippo light, I caught a glimpse of a face, a face that pulled back from the chauffeurs and vanished among the flickering orange shadows between the limos. Perhaps I was seeing things. But I didn't think so, and Angie's words echoed in my head.

I find it very interesting that through all this, Bookerman hasn't shown himself.

"I must know — right now!" Otto falsettoed. What next? Phil Rizzuto?

I snapped my fingers. "Otto!"

"Eh?" He leaned down to where I was slumped, the waft of his nicotine washing over me.

"You know these guys? The ones here you were talking to?" I whispered.

"Know? I know all Russians," he whispered back, singing: "Bey-be, beybe let me slip on eet —"

"I mean, have you met them before?"

"No, I not to meet."

"Were they all Russian?"

"Yes, all Russian, Garv. Beybe, beybe let

337

me —" Now he was doing air guitar.

"No . . . foreigners?"

"Eh?"

"Like dark skin."

"No. Like Yakut, meybe."

I grabbed his forearm to halt his swaying and hopefully the singing. "Yakut?"

"Yes, Yakut."

"What's a Yakut look like?"

"Siberia, many Yakut."

"They look like you?"

"No, Garv, they to look like round face."

"Hair?"

"All time blek."

"Skin?"

"Brown skeen."

"Eyes?"

"China, eh?" He tweaked the corner of his eyes.

I sat up, then stood up, holding on to the windshield as I scouted the crowd of drivers in the flickering light.

A whistle blew down the block, and drivers started to clamber for their cars. The police were starting the post-event car queue, and I could see a search gauntlet forming at the head of the line. Police cars blocked the back way out of the street.

"Garv, vhat you do?"

"Get in," I waved, climbing out of the

car. From the backseat I grabbed the FedEx box. "I'll catch up to you."

It took me about fifteen limos before I opened the correct driver's door and found him behind the wheel. I got in and closed the door. Roger sighed, with what sounded like relief.

"Thank goodness you aren't hurt, Garth." He adjusted his grip on the steering wheel and checked his mirrors. "You know, Scuppy was intent on killing both you and Palihnic."

Roger was in an ill-fitting black suit, white shirt, and black tie. His gray ponytail was tucked up under his chauffeur's cap. He was a natural for the part.

"I could have sworn it was you, Roger, who told the boys to throw us in the shaft when they were through."

"You didn't think, Garth, that I meant them to harm you? I'm as much a victim in this as you. Scuppy is a desperate character. I was in fear for my life. I only hope you and I, working together, can get out of this traffic jam and escape him." He gave me a fatherly pat on the knee. "The shocking truth is, Garth, that Scuppy has my daughter hostage. If we hurry, we can get to the girl and free her before Scuppy catches up to us. Will you help me?"

"Your daughter?" I gasped. "Shouldn't we get these policemen to help us, then? I mean, isn't this a matter for the police?" I noted that the limo line was creeping forward steadily. The front of the line was only five cars ahead.

"I wish we could, Garth, by God I wish we could." He thought for a moment. "But it's too risky. You must know by now that Milner's plot involves all kinds of people."

"The police too?"

"Yes, even police. If they . . ." He paused, carefully checking his side mirror.

I ducked to check the passenger-side mirror. A group of plainclothes cops were advancing through the limos, looking under cars, talking to drivers.

"Who do you think they're looking for?" I wondered aloud.

"They must be onto the retros. We may be in luck, Garth."

"Then —"

"But we couldn't risk it. What if they're looking for us?" He hastened to add, "Poor Brenda. I hope these scoundrels haven't hurt her."

"Well, we're almost to the front of the line. But won't they want to know who I am?"

"Just say you're a bodyguard. I'll cover for you."

Roger buzzed his window down and rolled up to the head of the line. "Yes, Officer?" He blinked into the cop's flashlight, a toothy smile on his face.

The policemen bent down and flashed a light on me, the luminous circle of which came to rest on the tag I'd been issued at the backstage door. They checked their clipboards and exchanged glances. "You can go," one of them waved.

We lurched forward, Roger sitting higher in his seat. I put a hand on the steering wheel. "Stay with the others."

"But . . . Brenda," he intoned.

"You don't want to tip your mitt, do you?" I peered into my mirror. "Look, they're still watching."

He leaned down, scrutinizing his mirror closely.

I reached over and pressed my thumb — hard — into the side of his neck. Under my thumb was the open mouth of the dead coral snake.

Crotalids, such as rattlesnakes, have folding fangs. Elapids, such as death adders and — you got it — coral snakes, have fangs fixed in grooves where their teeth would be. Fresh dead or thawed, they're still poisonous.

Roger struggled, but I must have ground the snake's open mouth into his neck for a full three seconds. Long enough, I hoped, for the small fangs to deliver the poison.

I let the snake fall out of my sleeve to the floor as I reached for the ignition, killed the engine, and palmed the keys. Roger was too surprised and too busy groping at the painful abrasion on his neck to stop me.

"*Yob tvoyu mat!*" he wheezed, then screamed, "Shit!" The veneer gone, his angry face was brick-red ruddy.

Then his eyes latched on to the striped snake draped over the transmission hump. His voice squirmed with revulsion. "A goddamn snake!"

His next move was to reach under the seat, but I grabbed him by the collar and pulled him toward me, away from what I imagined was a gun. He fought, but he was, what, seventy-something? He did look sixty-something, but that was probably thanks to an overabundance of bean curd and carrot juice. I mean, I'm mid-forties, so he had to be pushing eighty to have worked *The General Buster Show.*

"The more you struggle," I warned,

prying away the hands reaching for my neck, "the faster the neurotoxins go to your brain."

I felt him shudder. He began coughing. "Why, Garth?" he rasped, trying to lapse back into his Father Duffy act. "You're hurting me, Garth. Brenda, we —"

I could feel his hand making a cagey reach toward his side of the car.

"Cut the crap, Bookerman."

He paused in his struggles and looked up at me, his right eyelid drooping slightly. Maybe he meant to say something, but he didn't. He was obviously struggling with the muscle-relaxing effects of the venom. I hoped that the venom might also loosen his tongue. It was now or never to get to the bottom of all this.

"That's right, I figured you out. You are *the* one, *the* only, General Buster. And you may look like an American Indian, with the hair, the boots, the turquoise belt buckle — but you're a Yakut. You and Milner faked your death, and you either took Elk's identity or you just made him up, I dunno which. What I don't understand is how you got here, running a cult, from doing an afternoon kids' show."

His face started twitching. "What do you know about it — about anything?" he spat.

Disdain, tinged with apathy, swept over him, the kind drunk elders reserve for youngsters. "The world's going to hell and we were going to do something about it."

"Turn the world's clock back? But c'mon. You were a cartoon-show host. Then you go into health food, get hold of the spheres, and make a big success of Fab Form, a nasty-tasting health drink. Was it really always your intention to go from General Buster to a jive führer? To abolish TV entirely?"

Bookerman tried to glare at me but didn't seem able to focus. His gaze softened, drifting toward the floor. "You wouldn't understand. I've been places, seen things, horrible things."

I thought of Otto and his memories of the gulag.

He tried to clear his throat. ". . . crazy things . . . you need to possess. Minds. People. Souls. Power. The power to change the very fabric of . . . We were so close."

Was that much different from my own yen for Pipsqueak? Actually, it was very different but struck me as eerily parallel, and I shuddered. Bookerman's big, lovable, button-eyed face was twisted in bitter, am-biguous regret. That and growing numbness. I thought he was done. Not quite.

"You wanna know how something like this happens?" he slurred. "You wanna know? What really started all this?

"The bastards . . ." he hissed, "canceled my program for *Banana Splits* reruns. Took my puppets. With the spheres, I knew, I could ruin them."

"You don't seriously mean . . . all this . . . because of *The Banana Splits*?"

He forced a scowl. "Fleegle, Snorky, Drooper, and, uh . . ."

I snapped my fingers. "And Bingo. *Oh-oh! 'Danger Island' is next!*"

"I mean, gimme a break." He groaned. "They forced my hand. Don't you see? The choices we make," he whispered, eyes closed, ". . . aren't always our own."

His admonition was ominously close to home, close to how Nicholas viewed life. I've since marveled at how revelations aren't found ablaze in neon but printed on the backs of ticket stubs you find in your pocket the next day. I couldn't spell out the words to the tune being plucked on my heartstrings, not then. Something about how people change, about how they're the same, about how the two are integral to finding forgiveness.

A cop started tapping on the driver's

window with the butt of a flashlight, doubtless wondering why we were blocking egress to the front of the theater. As I let go of Bookerman's coat collar, his head, sweaty and panting, settled onto the seat next to me. The puppeteer was down for the count. The silhouette of another cop appeared at my window, and I buzzed down the glass.

"Hey, what . . ." The faceless cop's voice tightened as he tried to make sense of the front-seat tableau. His flashlight beam did a double take on the snake. "Sir, I'm going to ask you to —"

"This man needs a hospital." I blinked up into the flashlight, a smile on my face.

Chapter 32

No, I didn't end up at the police station.

Nicholas burst through the doors of the emergency room, a pillow sack over his shoulder, Angie and Otto in tow. But as soon as Angie saw me, she dropped it into overdrive and got to me first with a flying love-tackle that knocked me back onto the sofa.

"Whoa!" I protested.

"What happened?" She started looking me all over for wounds, again turning my hair into a Buckwheat Special. "Are you all right? What —"

"Jeez, Garth!" Nicholas — the quick study — could see I was fine. "When you said you were at the hospital, I flipped out! I ran into Angie in the lobby, and Otto broke every Russian *and* American traffic law getting us here."

"If you had let me explain," I moaned, "but you hung up."

He waved his tiny cell phone at me. "It's called *disconnected,* a lost signal. Well, so what's the deal?"

"Vhat you doink?" Otto's two cents.

I stood up and smiled sheepishly at Angie. "I've got a little something for you, Nicholas."

"You've got something for me?" His eyes and smile lit up like he'd just touched the third rail. "I've got something for you!" The power to his face experienced a brownout of confusion, perhaps suspicion. "You have something for me? Here?" Absently, he handed me the pillowcase. "Not a CAT scan?"

"Come here. . . ." We went to the door of the emergency ward, and through the window we could see doctors hovering over the snakebite victim. "See that guy?"

"Which one? The one —"

"Old guy, gray ponytail?"

"Yeah?"

"Bookerman." I put my arm around Angie.

"Hmm?"

"That is Bookerman. He was posing as a lawyer."

"Oh, my goodness!" Angie jabbed me in the ribs. "Roger Elk! He was Bookerman! All this time . . . He was there in New Jersey, and everything. He was right there, all the time!" I could see she was kicking herself for not figuring it out.

"Roger Elk?" Nicholas rolled his eyes and laughed. "Elk? *Losc* was Bookerman's Russian name."

"*Losc?* Eh? How you say . . ." Otto put pointed fingers to his head.

Nicholas patted Otto on the cheek. "Translated into English, it's *elk*. How'd he end up here? How'd you —"

"That's more than you need to know. Besides, it would give Angie the creeps. Anyway, I got him here, a little worse for wear, but he'll be okay." Like any good hospital, they had a little *Micrurus fulvius* antivenom on hand. Snakebites are rarely lethal in any case. "Point is, I knew if he fell into Mortimer's hands right away, you'd never see your fee from the insurer. I figured this would give you a few hours to get the paperwork you need, some photos maybe."

Nicholas stared blankly at me. Pins dropped. Utterly expressionless, he turned and walked quickly out of the hospital.

I started to follow, but Angie grabbed me by the belt.

"Let him go," she said.

Otto took off his hat, nodding gravely. "I thinkink meybe, Nicholas, he feelinx too big."

I was at a total loss and plopped down

on a sofa module. Was he upset? Angry? Moved? Now *I* felt snakebit.

Angie sank down next to me.

Otto moved toward the front door, cigarette in his lips, singing Meat Loaf's poetry softly: "But tune out of tree is not bad. . . ."

Angie slipped an arm around me. "What's in the bag?" I could tell she already knew.

"Huh? Oh . . ." I'd forgotten I was still holding it. Together we peeked in and then dumped the contents on the floor.

Out tumbled Pipsqueak, Howlie, and Possum, seams on the backs of their heads split open and some stuffing gone, but none too worse for wear. The goofy threesome stared gleefully at the dimpled acoustic ceiling.

Angie squeezed my arm. "He went back into the Savoy, and somehow, despite all the police, he got them," she marveled.

I could feel the roof of my mouth stiffening, and my eyes felt hot and blurry. "Damn" was all I could think to say, if thinking was what I was doing.

The front doors to the emergency room flew open and Nicholas raced back through the waiting room, a disposable camera in one hand, a newspaper in the other. Without a second look at us, he marched into the emergency ward, an argument with a nurse erupting from within.

My arm around Angie, I sniffed and then laughed. "My brother — the criminal type."

About the Author

Brian M. Wiprud

Home: New York City
Age: Still chews bubble gum
Physical Description: Sinister & Dangerous
Profession: Mystery Author, Outdoor Writer, and Photographer
Hobby: Exotic travel and fly fishing
Favorite Books: *Necronomicon*, Abdul Alhazred; *That Darn Cat*, M. Gordon
Favorite Films: *Dr. Goldfoot and the Bikini Machine*, *That Darn Cat from Outer Space*
Favorite CD: *Theremin! Theremin! Theremin!* Theremania
Favorite Kitchen Device: Ronco's Smokeless Cobb Knobs
Favorite Lines: "I like to keep a bottle of stimulant handy in case I see a snake — which I also keep handy." — W. C. Fields
Favorite Scotch: Bourbon